Soul Bound

The Moonstone Saga

By Courtney Cole

Soul Bound

Lakehouse Press, 2012

Copyright © 2012 by Courtney Cole
Cover design by Tammy Luke

Library of Congress Cataloging-in-Publication Data

Cole, Courtney.
        Soul Bound/Courtney Cole --- Lakehouse Press trade pbk.ed.
        ISBN: 978-0615627403

Printed in the United States of America

Dedication

To Douglas,
Our own personal Ares.
As fiercely loyal as you are strong,
you are one of my best friends in the world.
Thank you for inspiring my god of war.

Courtney Cole

"The moon's an arrant thief, and her pale fire she snatches from the sun."
-William Shakespeare
The Life of Timon of Athens

Other titles by Courtney Cole:

The Bloodstone Saga:
Every Last Kiss
Fated
With My Last Breath
My Tattered Bonds

The Moonstone Saga:
Soul Kissed
Soul Bound
Princess of the Night (Coming soon)

The American Princess:
Princess
Glass Castles (Coming soon)

Guardian

Prologue

Brennan

The circle of hooded women regarded me silently as they waited for a reaction. Their breaths panted into the frigid night in quick puffs and each head turned toward me, illuminating a row of solemn profiles draped in fluttering capes.

The moon hung heavily in the sky above us, a beautiful and fitting symbol of the woman that I loved. The pale yellowed light glinted onto the polished stone that I laid upon, casting shadows that stretched far into the circular clearing.

I flexed my fingers, itching to throw off my restraints. I had learned to harness my demi-god strength so I knew I could easily break the chains that held my wrists. But just as I knew that, I knew that if I did such a thing I would seal Empusa's fate. That mere thought refueled my determination to silently face my own.

Empusa. Her beautiful, ethereal face suddenly filled my mind. Her bright smile, her magnificent gray eyes, her pale skin. I would give anything to see her just one more time.

How did we get here? What had brought us to this?

No sooner did the question cross my mind and I knew the answer. Love itself had brought us to this. The love that was destructive and dangerous even while it was amazing and exhilarating. She was the moon and I was the sun. How could something like that ever end well? I would give my life to keep from burning her. But would my life be enough? I closed my eyes and braced myself to find out.

Chapter One

Empusa

Reality exploded around me in various earth-toned hues as we burst into a wet, green meadow filled with fluttering grass.

Honeysuckle.

The smell of honeysuckle filled my nose and I looked around before I realized that the smell wasn't coming from around me. It was coming *from* me. Since I had drunk from Harmonia's blood and it still pulsed through my veins, her scent lingered on me. I shook my head, trying to regain my grasp on reality. Traveling through time was disorienting at times.

"Where are we?" my boyfriend asked curiously as we stood on the swell of a slippery, rolling hill. He held my hand with strong fingers and I appraised our surroundings.

Wet earthy smells filled my nose...moss, wood, rain. My thoughts were returning to me by the second and I was able to think more clearly, remembering where we had just come from and where we were now.

Rays from the sun shone weakly through the low-hanging clouds above us, but the filtered light was enough to make Brennan seem radiant. The golden light outlined his blonde hair and tanned, muscled frame. He looked enough like Apollo to be his father's twin brother. Both of them were beautiful. I took a slow breath and exhaled.

"We're far from home," I stated the obvious calmly as if that fact wasn't apparent already.

As I spoke, a group of women emerged from a clump of trees across the clearing. Moving in a quick blur, I yanked Brennan down until we were concealed from view as we knelt behind the waving wildflowers. Flopping onto our bellies, we observed the strangers in the hollow below us. They wore muted ankle-length tunics and their long hair was pulled back into neat braids which were held away from their faces by woven leather bands.

"Well, that much is apparent," Brennan muttered as he took in their ancient dress. "Could you possibly be a little more specific?"

I smiled. One of the things I loved about Brennan Delacorte was his sense of humor. And I cherished it even more now.

Five minutes ago, he had broken up with me. But in the space of those minutes, in between running from my father who was trying to kill us both and landing here in an ancient Celtic land, Brennan had decided that as my soul mate, he couldn't live without me regardless of the risks that our relationship posed for the world. And that left me almost giddy with relief.

"We're in ancient Britain," I answered by way of explanation, as though time traveling was common. And when you were the daughter of the goddess of witchcraft like I was, then it wasn't really out of the ordinary. But when you were new to the whole world of gods and immortals like Brennan was, I had to admit that it must be a bit of a shock. As a new demi-god though, he was definitely handling it well.

He arched a golden eyebrow. "And I thought you were going to say someplace interesting. Or remote."

I smiled again. We had been able to catch our breaths now since fleeing Death Valley a few minutes ago after Brennan had pulled me out of a burning crevice of lava and carried me away from the danger.

We had left my parents dueling there in hand-to-hand combat. My mother was fighting to save my life and my father was fighting to take it. It was enough to make a girl crazy.

But I had a lot to fight for now. Brennan, for starters. And my freedom from the wretched curse that my father had inflicted upon me, the curse that caused me to suck away mortal souls in order to remain immortal and to drink mortal blood to stay young. I absently twisted the moonstone bracelet that circled my wrist.

My mother had given it to me long ago in an effort to protect me from my father. She had enchanted it to alert me whenever he was near. But in the process, my soul had become tied to it. If something happened to the moonstone, I would die. As in, dead-as-a-doornail forever—even Zeus' sword wouldn't be able to save me. And that was a daunting thought.

"Why are we here?" Brennan asked curiously, still watching the strange women in front of us. It appeared that they were spreading wet clothing out to dry on large rocks, an archaic but effective laundry system.

"It's hard to say," I answered, fingering the small bag of runes in my pocket. My mother had given them to Brennan in Death Valley, telling him that they would instruct us where to go. But she didn't tell him why. And that was a very good question.

"Well, what do we do now that we're here?" Brennan asked, finally turning to face me. "Do we wait for your mom? Do we need to hide from these people?"

I honestly didn't know. The runes had told me where to go. They certainly hadn't explained why or what we should do once we arrived. I stared helplessly at Brennan, but his question was answered by someone other than me.

The woman in front, a tall statuesque woman, turned as though she could see us. Her flame red hair hung to the small of her back and her eyes, as gray as mine, swung around the meadow as though searching for something. I gasped. There was no way she could have heard us, yet her eyes zeroed in on our location with laser precision.

"What the hell?" Brennan muttered. "She can't see us, can she?"

But she could. I could sense it. The woman was mortal, but she something was very *immortal* about her. She had supernatural senses somehow.

At my thought, she smiled slightly as though she could hear my thoughts. But that was impossible. I knew that much, at least. No mortal could read the thoughts of the gods. It had never happened. With that, she threw her head back and laughed, causing the other women to look at her curiously before going about their business of doing laundry.

What the hell?

I raised my head slightly and her gaze caught mine. She took one step and then another, then she was walking confidently towards us from across the meadow. The hem of her saffron shift was wet from the dew on the grass and her feet were bare.

There was no point in hiding, so I unfolded myself from the grass as gracefully as I could. Brennan and I stood still as we waited for the woman to reach us. The other females had stopped doing their laundry, but they remained across the meadow. They didn't look bothered by our appearance.

I could hear Brennan's unspoken question since I could read his mind. *Who is she?*

"I don't know," I answered out loud. Taking a step forward, I asked the woman that very thing.

"Who are you?" I asked. She was no more than six feet away from us. "Do you know us?"

She didn't answer my question. Instead, she drew to a stop in front of us and knelt at my feet.

"Princess, I've been expecting you."

I fought the urge to roll my eyes. As the daughter of the goddess of witchcraft, who also happened to be the goddess of the moon, I was deemed the princess of the moon. It was, at times, an honor I didn't appreciate. I could feel Brennan's eyes on me now. He wasn't accustomed to this side of my life. He had only seen me act fairly mortal. Being goddess royalty was a new facet of my personality for him.

Gritting my teeth, I reached my hand down. "Please, get up. How do you know me?"

She looked up at me doubtfully as she remained in her submissive position. I felt certain that this strong woman was not submissive often.

"Truly?" She raised one red eyebrow. "How could I not know you? Our father has spoken of you often."

"Our father..." The words died in my throat as realization set in. Her eyes were identical to mine, a unique gray. I stepped away from her.

"Don't be alarmed," she reassured me quickly. "I mean you no harm."

"How can you say that?" I hissed, stepping further away. Brennan poised himself as if to provide protection for me. I put my hand on his arm. "This can't be right, Bren. My mother surely didn't intend for us to come here."

The woman got to her feet and stared me in the eye. Like my own, the sunlight made her gray eyes seem incandescent.

"I recognize the danger Mormo poses to you," she told me quietly as she remained motionlessly in place. I could see that she wanted to seem nonthreatening. "Like you, he poses a danger to me as well. Unlike you, his threats to me could be quite permanent."

"You're mortal," I said bluntly. She nodded.

"Yes. I am. But we share the same immortal father. It is true."

"Why did my mother send me here?" I asked her brusquely.

"Because she thinks I can help," the woman answered simply.

"Help me?" I asked.

"Of course. Who else?" She stared into my eyes again and I felt as though she was looking directly into my soul. It was disconcerting.

"Your name." I didn't ask, I stated. I was simply too tired for pleasantries at this point.

"Branwyn. You and the son of Apollo should rest. Allow me to show you to a safe place, princess."

"My name is Brennan," Brennan interjected. "It's not 'son of Apollo.'"

"Whether it is your name or not your name, it is still who you are," Branwyn replied. "I cannot help that and neither can you. There are worse things."

I had to admit that I liked Branwyn's matter-of-fact manner. Her attitude was simple and definitely not flowery. I had the distinct impression that I would always know where I stood with this woman. My sister. The thought almost floored me. I had no idea that I even had one.

"Come," Branwyn urged. "We have much to discuss, but I believe you should rest first and we can speak after your minds and bodies have rested."

Brennan looked at me, his amber eyes concerned. "You really should rest," he said quietly. "You've been through a lot today. You're strong, but even the strong have the need to rest."

I nodded curtly, just once. I hated to admit it, but he was right. My legs were quite literally shaking from weariness. Hanging over a ledge, dangling over bubbling lava would do that to a person.

"Good," Branwyn smiled. "You must believe me, princess. I wish you no ill. I only want to help. Your mother is very strong and very respected here. We would do anything to keep her daughter safe."

She smiled again and I studied her for a moment. She was sincere, I could tell that much. I glanced around again. The druids sought wisdom. I quickly flipped through my memories regarding this ancient people.

Druids had priests, priestesses and seers. They sought higher powers in many forms, including gods and goddesses. They worshipped my mother, for one, although they didn't typically use her true name. They thought she was the mother of everything that ever was.

Priestesses and Seers lived simple lives. They were self-sacrificing and loyal. It didn't surprise me that Branwyn was opening her home to me. It was very possible, probably even likely, that she had seen me in a vision. They worshipped nature, they opened their minds to powers that they didn't understand. And sometimes, they channeled visions. It wouldn't surprise me a bit if she had seen me in one.

"Did you see my coming in a vision?" I asked curiously as we walked together over the meadow toward the small gathering of huts.

"No," she glanced at me. "Your mother told me."

"My mother literally came to you and told you that I was coming. She appeared to you?"

"I am your mother's faithful servant," Branwyn said quietly. "Your mother knows this. She trusts me. I have proven my loyalty to her in every way. I only hope to prove it to you, as well, princess."

"You don't need to call me princess," I told her wryly. "Empusa will do."

She met my gaze. "Wonderful. Empusa, it is."

My feet fell on the wet velvet of the wild grass and I realized with a start that I had lost my shoes along the way. Probably while I was dangling over the hot lava. Perfect.

Brennan read my thoughts and smiled at me. "It's alright, Emmie. I'll carry you wherever you need to go." I rolled my eyes and laughed.

"I'm good," I assured him. "I can conjure shoes."

He nodded thoughtfully. "That you can. I had forgotten."

We approached the other women who stilled their movements in order to watch our approach. They were all calm and interested. I could see that they had been expecting me, as well. As I stepped inside the perimeter of their camp, they each dropped to their knees, their heads bowed.

My breath caught in my throat at the show of reverence.

"I told you that you and your mother are respected here," Branwyn murmured. "They won't get up until you give them permission."

"Please, get up," I stammered quickly. "There is no need to kneel to me. My mother is a powerful goddess of the moon. I am just her daughter, no more and no less. Only that. There is no reason to revere me."

"You are too modest, princess," Branwyn observed. "Surely you are aware of your own value. But you heard her, ladies," she turned to the others. "The moon princess has said to rise. You can resume your duties. We'll meet in the Meadow of Peace later this afternoon to meditate."

The women resumed their laundry duties while Branwyn continued leading us away from the common area to a small but well-built hut.

It was made from wood and rock and was solid and strong. It stood in the middle of the others, larger and away from the perimeter. The perimeter was clearly marked with a boundary of stones. I recalled that the druids believed that there was protective magic within circles. And I was not one to determine who had more valid or powerful magic. Magic, as a whole, was a very fluid thing. Even mortals could channel it if they concentrated enough.

"While you are here, you will occupy my home," she told us as she ducked her head slightly to enter the doorway. We followed and once inside, we could easily stand to our full heights.

The hut was simple, but clean. There was a largish bed in the center of the room covered in animal pelts. A fireplace adorned the back wall, simple and stone, with a roaring blaze inside. Cookware hung on hooks beside it.

"We cannot take your home from you," I told her quietly. "There must be somewhere else we can sleep."

"We have no extra homes," Branwyn said in amusement. "We are a simple people. We only take what we need and we only use what we must. We do not waste. I am honored for you to use my home. I will share with someone else."

She showed us a few things inside of the hut and pulled a buckskin over the single window before turning back to us.

Pulling a silver ring off of her finger, she handed it to me. The silver knotted ring glistened mutely in the dark.

"Promise me, Empusa, that you will wear this. It's enchanted with protection. Never walk outside of our circle without it. Do I have your word?"

Her face was serious, her voice solemn. It would not hurt me to wear it, so I opened my fingers and allowed it to fall into my palm.

"Of course. Thank you."

She nodded and turned to leave. "I'll send someone for you when it is time to eat. You should rest."

With that, she was gone.

Brennan and I were left staring at each other in the dim light of the hut. He reached out to me and almost without thinking, I collapsed against his chest. His heart thudded against my ear, its strength a throbbing cadence. I memorized the rhythm, tracing the outline of his collarbone with my fingers.

"We should rest," he reminded me gently, staring down with his amazing golden eyes. His father, Apollo, was known throughout the world as being beautiful and charming. Brennan had inherited the best of those traits, which was a little funny since he had never actually met his father. He had been raised by mortals.

My fingers made their way to the cleft in his chin and I rose on my tiptoes to kiss his lips.

"I didn't get the chance to thank you for saving me from the lava," I told him, my gaze frozen on his. He smiled, his perfect lips stretching over a white smile.

"Anytime," he answered confidently. "Anytime, anyplace, moon princess."

"Ugh," I rolled my eyes. "Don't you start." Twisting out of his arms, I padded across the dirt floor to the bed. Brennan followed closely on my heels.

"What?" he raised a golden eyebrow. "You don't enjoy adulation?"

I cringed even at the word. "I don't deserve adulation," I replied quietly. "Nothing about me is deserving of that kind of respect. My mother, yes. Me? I've never been given the chance to earn it. I've spent my entire life, my entire existence, running from my own curse."

Brennan inhaled sharply, pulling my chin up with his index finger. "I don't ever want to hear that you are not worthy or undeserving of something again," he cautioned me. "Your curse is what it is.

You didn't ask for it and it isn't your fault. We will search the earth from top to bottom to find a way to reverse it. If we can't find an answer on the earth, we'll search elsewhere. I promise you, by all that is holy, we'll figure it out."

I nodded tiredly. I knew he wanted to believe that.

"I believe that because it is true," he told me firmly. "Now, hop into that bed. We're going to rest."

"Yes, sir," I answered with a weak smile. Pulling the skins back, I did as he said. He climbed in beside me, pulling me into his arms. It was my favorite place to be.

"And when we wake, you will need to feed," he told me. "I know that you're weakened now from everything that happened in Death Valley."

My heart raced at the thought. "I can't feed from you," I stammered. "We haven't mastered our powers yet and your strength has grown. I don't know if I could control it." The thought, the simple thought, of drinking Brennan's blood now terrified me enough that I started to see his aura. The colors blinded me and I closed my eyes against the light.

"Don't worry," he whispered softly into my hair. Cupping my face, he ran his thumb lightly along my cheekbone.

"You don't need to drink from me. We'll think of something else."

I squeezed my eyes tightly closed. This part of my curse was truly a curse. But it was something I'd think about after I'd rested. Brennan was right. I was in a weakened state. A little rest would go a long way.

Chapter Two

When I awoke, Brennan was gone. Sniffing the air, the acrid scent of a dying fire filled my nose. Glancing sideways at the fireplace, I saw that its red embers were the only remainder of its once roaring flame. Sighing, I propped myself up on one elbow.

The crack of light that peeked from the buckskin covering the window was dim. It was late in the day. I glanced at the skin of my arm. Even here in the dark of this closed hut, I could see that I was deathly pale. Brennan had been correct. The scene in Death Valley had taken my energy and I desperately needed to eat. With a sigh, I swung my legs over the side of the heavy bed and sat up.

A wave of dizziness passed over me and I steadied myself with my hands before I stood. I really was weak. It was never good to allow my strength to become this replete. I couldn't remember the last time it had been this bad.

"Son of a –"

"You're up." Brennan interrupted my curse as he ducked into the hut. He was followed closely by Branwyn and another girl. The girl trailing Branwyn had wide frightened eyes and milky white skin. My stomach dropped into my toes at the look on their faces.

"What's going on?" I asked uncertainly, taking a step backward.

"You need to eat," Brennan said firmly, crossing the room in three strides.

"And?" I raised an eyebrow. My gaze flew to the girl behind Branwyn. "No."

"Why?" Brennan asked. "What difference is it from when you peruse high school parties on the beach? You'll feed and then take her memories. No harm, no foul. If you don't eat, you're going to suffer. I can't watch you suffer, Em."

"Shayla is happy to help you," Branwyn told me quietly. "She understands the situation. And like Brennan has pointed out, you will simply take her memories. She'll never remember anyway. But know that you have her full permission. It is an honor to serve you."

She ducked her head slightly and the girl, Shayla, dropped to her knees and extended her arm to me.

"It's an honor, princess," she repeated after Branwyn, her eyes averted from mine.

"Are there no men?" I asked Branwyn with a sigh. I already knew the answer. Many pagan priestesses secluded themselves from the rest of society- away from men. They felt it purified their magic. They only mingled with the other sex during times of ritual and sacrifice. I sighed again when she shook her head.

"Crap," I muttered.

When I drank from a mortal's blood, it was sexually pleasurable for them. I had long since learned that, and learned that it simplified things to simply drink from men. This girl would have erotic dreams about me for weeks to come after this.

"Very well," I muttered. "Shayla, you may rise. And you might as well get comfortable." Without meeting her gaze, I motioned to the bed. She leaped to her feet and practically bounded to the bed, eager to please me. I hated this.

Brennan laid a hand on my arm reassuringly. "You don't have a choice, Emmie. You won't drink from me and there are only these priestesses here. What other choice do you have?"

As much as I hated it, he was right. I climbed back onto the bed and sat next to the girl. She was shaking.

"Calm yourself," I told her quietly. "It won't hurt and I promise you that you won't remember it."

She nodded, the freckles standing out on her nose as the blood drained away from her face. I swallowed hard. I hated being the thing that invoked such fear. It made me feel like a monster.

"You're not a monster," Brennan replied to my unspoken thought as he moved around the bed to hold the girl's arms. He looked uncertain, like he wanted to help but didn't know what to do.

"You don't need to restrain her," I told him wearily. "She won't try to get away. Trust me."

Hovering above her quaking body, I looked into her blue eyes.

"Do you trust me?" I asked quietly.

It was a brazen question, I knew, because she had only just met me. But part of my curse was an ability to draw people to me. Men and women alike wanted to be near me. And it was no different with this girl. She nodded, her confidence in me absolute.

"Yes," she whispered.

I paused for just one beat and then picked up her wrist. Without hesitation, I sank my teeth into it. She gasped once, quickly and loud. But then she relaxed as pheromones exploded within her veins. I could taste them as I drew her blood into my mouth and allowed it to slide down my throat. Female blood was sweet, sweeter than a man's. I sucked it in, allowing it to run down my chin.

Shayla was moaning by this point, thrashing beneath me in pleasure. I knew she would be mortified if she was truly conscious, which by this point she was not. I knew her mind was fuzzy, clouded by my curse. She arched up against me, trying to draw nearer to me, trying to run her lips along my neck.

Brennan watched in amusement. He had never seen this before. I had drunk from him, but he had never watched as a by-stander. He lifted his hands helplessly. He didn't know what to do.

"You can restrain her now," I said quickly as I drew in a breath. "She wouldn't want to behave in such a way. She doesn't mean it."

"She won't remember it," Branwyn reminded me firmly. "Go ahead and finish, Empusa."

Nodding, I drank for a few minutes more, then wiped my mouth. My fingers and toes had regained their warmth and I could feel color returning to my face. As much as I hated feeding, I loved feeling strong again.

I glanced at Shayla. The girl laid against the bed skins, her cheeks flushed with pleasure, her eyes glazed.

"Shayla," I said quietly. "You will not remember this. If you remember anything at all, you will think it was a dream. Do you understand?"

She looked up at me, her eyes still unfocused. But she nodded.

"Good." I looked to Branwyn. "Thank you. I'm quite finished here."

She nodded and motioned to Shayla. "Come with me, child."

Shayla got to her feet and trailed behind Branwyn as the exited the hut. Branwyn turned. "Dinner for the rest of us will be soon. Feel free to join us."

She left and Brennan stared at me, an unreadable expression on his handsome face.

"That was... intense," he said quietly. "I wasn't sure what I'd think. But it was impressive. You were very gentle with her. You didn't have to be. She never would've known the difference."

"But I would know," I replied. "Brennan, you have no idea what it has been like for me. For a thousand years- and think hard about how long that actually is- I have had to do this. I have had to drink from mortals. I literally steal their blood. That's the very essence of who a person is. I have to look into their eyes and watch as their body reacts to my curse. It makes me...dislike myself. It's something I struggle with every day of my life."

His face clouded, the light that normally shone in his eyes dimmed. Turning, his voice cracked.

"Empusa," he said softly, opening his arms. I shook my head.

"I'm fine," I replied, stiffening my shoulders. I didn't want pity. I didn't want reassurance or comfort. I didn't deserve it. Every word I said was true. I was, in essence, a thief of the worst kind.

"Empusa," he repeated, this time more firmly. "Do not think like that. You are forced to do these things because your father is a pathetic creature. You are beautiful and kind and you do your very best to avoid hurting people. We will figure out a way to return your life to normal and you'll never have to do these things again."

"I do my very best to avoid hurting people," I repeated, completely disregarding his last sentence. "Really? How did we meet, Brennan?"

His face clouded over again. I had struck a nerve. He and I had met in the hospital, right after I had taken his uncle Daniel's soul which had killed him. Granted, Daniel had terminal cancer and he was going to die very soon anyway, but regardless, I had shortened his life. It was something I knew Brennan struggled with.

He clenched his jaw. "I've dealt with that," he said firmly. "You couldn't help it. Daniel was going to die anyway."

"Yes, he was. But he wasn't going to die *that day*," I answered wearily. "I kill people Brennan. It is what it is. Whether they are sick and dying or not, it makes no difference. I'm a killer."

At his impassive expression, I continued. "And what do you think is going to happen here? I don't see a cancer ward here. I haven't seen one sick person in this village. What will happen when it comes time for me to take a soul? Let me tell you what will happen. I will either have to kill a healthy, happy priestess or I will die myself. That is what it will come to. Do you still think I'm not accountable… that it's not my fault?"

His face remained expressionless when he replied with slow concise words.

"Yes, I still think it isn't your fault. We'll figure something out. Perhaps, just maybe, we can get this issue fixed by then."

I had to laugh. "Brennan, one of the things I love the most about you is your optimism. I probably have a couple weeks *at most* before I will be forced to make a decision. My life... or one of theirs."

Turning my back and gulping down the lump that had formed in my throat, I pushed my way out of the hut into the dim evening light.

Women were standing around chatting outside of various huts and in the middle of common areas. Worn dirt paths criss-crossed throughout the little civilization, giving unspoken directions to the most traveled destinations in the village. I turned and headed down one path as I blinked back tears.

"Not that way," one woman told me kindly. "Are you searching for the eating area?"

I nodded, unable to trust my voice.

"I'll show you," she said quietly, taking my elbow. I shrugged away from her touch. The last thing I needed was for her to become enamored with me, too. She looked at me in puzzlement, but didn't say anything. I realized that I seemed rude.

"I'm sorry," I offered.

She shook her head. "Think nothing of it. My name is Elin. I'm happy to assist you with anything that you require, princess."

"Does everyone know who I am?" I asked.

She nodded. "Yes."

"Great," I sighed. Elin's lips curved into a smile.

"Embrace it, princess," she answered. "Each woman here would give you her home or her life if you asked it."

"But why?" I asked in bewilderment. "I've never met a one of you. I never even knew that Branwyn was my sister until today. Why is there such deference to me? Trust me, you don't know what I am or it wouldn't be so."

"We know who you are," Elin said firmly. "And that is enough. You are important. Your role in this life is important both to you and to many people around you. The sooner you realize it and embrace it, the better off you'll be."

I practically snorted. "My role in this life? Elin, now I know you don't understand. I've lived for a very, very long time. My role has been played out time and time again in the form of a horrible curse. Trust me, it hasn't been helpful for people around me."

"Empusa," Elin leveled a gaze at me. "Your role in this life is only just now beginning. You and your soul mate have found each other and now your true purpose will begin."

I sucked in my breath. "How did you know that?" I asked in amazement. "Do you prophesize? You couldn't possibly have known that."

"Yet it is true, is it not?" Elin raised an eyebrow.

"It is true that Brennan and I only recently found each other. But we have been warned. If we cannot control our powers around each other, we could literally end the world as we know it. We could cause an apocalypse. That is a great burden to bear. Is that what you speak of when you say that we have a purpose?"

Elin looked at me, her eyes solemn. "Princess, when you have a purpose, no matter what it is, there is no escaping it. Your purpose, whatever it is, will come to pass. You need to embrace that, as well."

"Do you know my purpose?" I whispered. "Have you seen it?"

She stared at me for a moment longer, before shaking her head. "I have not personally seen it, no. But Branwyn has."

"Can I just tell you how tiring it is when people see me in visions and I have not one inkling of what is going to happen in my own life?"

I sighed, allowing the air to expel slowly and loudly from my lips. "I'm sorry. It's not your fault and I didn't mean to snap at you."

"No offense taken, princess," Elin nodded. "And here we are."

I looked up to find that we had made our way to the area that the priestesses used for eating. There were women congregated into small groups, eating some sort of thick porridge from wooden bowls. It didn't smell good and I tried not to wrinkle my nose.

"Elin!" one of the women called and Elin turned to me. "Will you be alright now?"

I nodded. "Of course. Thank you so much for showing me the way."

She left to find her friend and I made my way to an empty wooden table. It was made from thick-hewn logs sawed in half and I had to make sure I didn't get a splinter. Before I could sit or even blink, Brennan sidled up to me.

"Thought you could lose me, did you?" he asked with a grin.

"Of course not," I assured him. "Nor would I want to. I just needed some air. My burden is sometimes difficult to bear."

"So allow me to carry it for you," he suggested.

My breath froze in my throat and I stood still. "What?"

"I thought of a way," he explained quietly. "I can take your curse for you, Empusa. In the same way that your father passed it to you, you can pass it to me."

Everything around me blurred together as my emotions exploded in a way that was too much to bear, too much to remain conscious for. I fainted, but before I hit the ground, I was pretty sure that I heard myself scream.

Chapter Three

I woke with ice cold water being poured on my face. I sputtered and sat up, fighting against the strong arms that held me down. Coughing, I twisted to find that Brennan was the one restraining me as we sat next to a rushing river.

"Don't ever do that to me again!" Brennan said as he released his hold. I slid from his grasp and crouched next to the water. My throat burned from water running down the wrong pipe.

"Why were you trying to drown me?" I rasped as I continued to cough. "And do what to you?"

"Don't ever scare me like that again," he clarified firmly. "I mean it. Don't."

"I wasn't trying to scare you," I answered, looking around. I was surrounded by priestesses. Branwyn hovered nearby, along with Shayla, who was still staring adoringly at me. "Your offer caught me off guard. And it's pure craziness," I added. "You are not taking my curse from me. Absolutely not."

Brennan started to protest, but I cut him off.

"No arguments," I snapped. "I can't believe you would even suggest it. We'd be in the same exact boat- one of us being cursed. It doesn't really matter which one of us carries it. We just need to find a way to get it removed... not transfer it back and forth. You have no idea what it entails, trust me. I don't want to talk of this anymore."

He gazed at me, his eyes golden in the light before he stood and extended his hand to me. "Alright," he agreed. "For now. We can speak more of it later."

"No," I said firmly. "There will be no more talk of it ever."

I grasped his hand and allowed him to pull me to my feet. His touch still sent jolts of electricity shooting through my arm, reminding me of what we were. Soul mates. Once upon a time, Zeus had split our soul in half, creating two separate souls. He had a theory that if people spent their lives searching for their other half, their true mate, then they would not be focused on over-throwing his crown.

I had not searched for my soul mate, however. I had happened upon him entirely by chance after I had just killed his uncle. In most cases, that might put a damper on the relationship. But soul mates had a connection; an unmistakable, undeniable connection. It both reassured and terrified me at once.

The women surrounding us moved back so that I could walk through them. The funny thing was that I didn't know where to go. What was my purpose here? I stopped moving.

"Follow me," Branwyn told me quietly as she moved forward. "I have answers that you seek."

My eyes shot to meet hers and found her gaze to be sincere and knowing.

She nodded.

"Yes, you can trust me. I am here to help you."

Brennan put his large hand on the small of my back, a weighty presence that comforted me. His intense warmth, which stemmed from being the son of the god of the sun, radiated through my back.

"I trust her," he murmured into my hair from behind. "I don't know why but I do."

I twisted just slightly to answer him.

"She can hear you, you know."

He smiled slightly and I turned back to Branwyn.

"How do you know so much about me? I need to know."

She nodded. "Come, then. I will explain."

We wound our way out of the small village, past the stares of the other women, until we stood on the edge of a nearby forest. The grasses were tall, almost up to our knees, and we stood quietly for a moment before entering.

"This is a sacred place," Branwyn told us. "We come here to worship, to sacrifice, to pray. You must be respectful of it while you are here."

"Of course," Brennan agreed. "We would never be anything else."

Branwyn nodded, satisfied. "We channel the spirit of the earth here. The water, the trees, the sky and the earth meet in our meadow here. They pull from the four corners and meet as one. We draw strength from that. You are fortunate. You will be here for Samhain. The barrier between our world and the Otherworld will be at its thinnest. This will assist you in your purpose."

Without explaining, she stopped speaking and began walking into the darkened trees, her feet peeking out of her long shift with every step she took.

Brennan and I glanced at each other and then quickly followed.

Enormous oak trees closed around us, creating an atmosphere of mystery and solitude. The massive trunks of the trees were cloaked in green velvet moss which also grew across the worn paths beneath our feet. It smelled earthy here, damp and rich, and I inhaled deeply as we walked. The air here did actually feel sacred. It had a certain reverent feel that made me want to fall silent so that I didn't disturb anything around me with noise.

We made our way to a circular clearing and the feeling of reverence intensified. It was clear that the circular meadow in front of us had been developed by the priestesses. It was encircled with trees, then a ring of stones. In the center of the circle, a glossy black stone shimmered in the light.

I sucked in my breath as I stared at it. Round, heavy and flat, it sat in the exact center of the meadow. Shadows from the rustling tree branches overhead swayed against the stone. Dried flowers were scattered upon it, their petals fluttering in the wind. This was an altar. That much as apparent.

As we approached, it almost seemed as though the grasses beneath our feet stopped moving and the breeze itself died.

"What is this place?" I whispered, running my fingers along the cool length of the stone.

"I told you," Branwyn said, turning to me with a puzzled expression. "It is sacred ground. "

"But why?" I asked. "What makes it sacred?"

Branwyn shrugged. "You do. Or we do. Or combined, we both do. I know not. You and your kind have powers that I do not, but I know enough to channel them. That majestic presence is felt here, in this place where everything comes together, the earth, the water, the sky and the sun. It is sacred here. That is all I know."

"My kind?" I raised an eyebrow.

She smiled pleasantly back at me.

"I know you are different from me. I know you are even different from our father. Yours is a power truly to behold and revere, a power born from the goddess herself."

The goddess herself.

My mind started spinning backward, sifting through memories of mortal history. The ancient Celtic Druids were known to have believed in an earth goddess, although mortals didn't document which gods and goddesses Druid priestesses truly worshipped. They were known to worship natural elements, such as the earth, the sun, the moon... but other than that, their religion was not a written one. So, modern mortals truly didn't know what had gone on here.

My mother was the goddess of witchcraft. So any magic that was channeled here must be from my mother.

My mother was who they referred to as *the goddess herself.*

Suddenly, I felt closer to my mother than I had in awhile, as though her very presence was here. The wind picked up and lifted the hair from my face and it felt as though my mother was actually speaking to me, letting me know of her unseen presence. I knew it was silly, if she was here she would simply materialize and show herself to me. But it still felt true.

"It's not silly," Branwyn murmured as she stretched her arms out wide and lifted her face to the muted evening sunlight that filtered through the trees. "Your mother is here. I can feel her."

A thought occurred to me and I turned to her. "Have you ever actually seen my mother? In person?"

Her eyes popped open and she stared at me in surprise.

"Of course not. I have not acquired that much value to the goddess yet. But she speaks to me here. I channel her strength. It is through her that I am able to sift through the thoughts of others."

"My mother grants you the power to read minds?" I raised an eyebrow.

"I do not do it alone," she answered in wry amusement. "I am but a mere mortal."

"Somehow, I doubt you are a *mere* mortal," I told her. "Especially since I know that you have seen my future somehow. Can you tell me now? What is my purpose? What have you seen?"

"Come," she nodded and gestured toward stone altar. "Both of you are part of this, both of you are more important than you know. Lie down here."

I glanced up at her sharply and she smiled. "You'll have to trust me, Empusa. I mean you no harm."

"You'll have to excuse me," I answered slowly. "It is hard for me to trust."

"I know," she answered solemnly. "Please, lie down. I give you my word that I will not harm you. Join hands."

"You couldn't harm me," I shook my head as I did what she asked. Climbing onto the stone, it was cool and smooth beneath my hands. Brennan leaped up next to me and we both settled onto our backs, staring up at the sky above us as our fingers joined together.

Tingling electricity fingers caressed my arm as our palms drew together. Brennan turned to me and smiled.

"I doubt I'll ever get used to that," he admitted softly, leaning in quickly to brush his lips against mine. The electricity spread to my lips.

"Me either," I told him.

"Focus," Branwayn admonished us as she stood on the edge of the stone. "I need you to clear your thoughts. The images that come into your mind here today will be your answers. You will trust what you see far more than you would trust what I say."

She began murmuring an incoherent chant in the same tone I'd heard my mother use a thousand times over. I watched her lips move, forming the soft words, before I shifted my gaze to the sky above me. The trees practically met in a canopy above us, their long boughs stretching and reaching as the wind moved them.

The warmth of Brennan's body next to me lulled and comforted me as the clouds above swirled and melted into the treetops. I became aware of a crackling, heavy presence in the meadow, something that lifted above us and hovered. Yet when I opened my eyes, there was nothing there. Branwyn's eyes were squeezed tightly closed as she chanted and Brennan was staring at the sky.

The heaviness clung to my arms and legs, creeping upward over my body until it felt as though it was holding me down, tying me to the altar. It should have been unnerving or terrifying, but it wasn't. I felt a sense of calm transcend over me and I closed my eyes once more.

When I did, the visions started. There was blood.

So much blood.

Harmonia, Cadmus, Ares, Hecate and Aphrodite stood with weapons in their hands. A smear of blood was on Harmonia's cheek, her green eyes glassy in her anger. Cadmus and Ares were covered in blood from head to toe. A vein stood out in the side of Ares' neck as his chest heaved from heavy-breathing.

They were clearly battling something.

My vision expanded and I could suddenly see my father facing them. Of course. I should have known he was involved. My pulse picked up at just the sight of his pale, emotionless face. And then my heart practically stopped when I saw that he stood with Brennan's father, Apollo. If I could have taken a breath, I would have gasped. Why were our fathers together? Apollo was beautiful and golden, but he was covered in blood as well.

Horrible, wretched screaming filled the stadium that they were in. And that's when I saw them.

A cage of mortals hovered above the arena, thick gilded bars imprisoning the frightened people. Fear was thick there, so overwhelming that I could taste it in my mouth. Something horrible was about to happen. I tried to open my eyes, to end the visions, but I couldn't. I could not physically move.

One of the mortals unexpectedly dropped from the bottom of their cage. He tumbled through the air and landed on his feet on a long platform filled with moving objects. Swinging pendulums covered in large razor points, spike-tipped columns rammed up and down from the platform itself, massive swinging maces and sweeping logs covered in glistening knives. The points of each of the weapons glinted in the light, each one of them clearly deadly. This was a sick, twisted gauntlet.

The mortal was frozen in terror, but he was forced to move because one of the deadly pendulums was swinging toward him. He leaped forward and somehow, over the course of the next several minutes, he managed to twist and leap through the rest of the challenges. Fear for his life made him fearless and desperate.

He emerged triumphantly on the other side of the deadly game. But his relief was very short-lived. It seemed that his challenge was far from over. He was dropped from the platform onto the dirt of the arena, amid the dust and circling gods and goddesses. What was this?

The mortal tried to run toward my mother, but was thwarted by Apollo, his beautiful face set in determination. Cadmus, handsome and also deadly, lunged forward and swung a sword at Apollo's torso. Both Brennan and I flinched as the sharp blade connected, carving a deep crevice on Apollo's flawless body. He growled and retaliated, kicking at Cadmus' legs.

While they were occupied, Harmonia pivoted and rushed around, grabbing the mortal and attempting to drag him with her back to her side of the stadium. Mormo leaped forward and ran the mortal through with a lance. I gasped, aware that hot tears were sliding down my cheeks as the mortal slid from the lance lifelessly to the ground. Brennan gripped my hand hard.

"What is this?" I whispered, finally able to move enough to speak. The visions melted away and the beautiful meadow once again surrounded us. I fought to remain calm.

"What is this?" I shrieked at Branwyn. "Why were they fighting? Why were they using mortals?"

Branwyn was calm and placid, standing ever so still at our feet. Her face was pale, however, an outward sign of her distress. Yet when she spoke, her voice was slow and expressionless and it wasn't her own. It was my mother's.

"It is a game, Empusa, between the gods. I appealed to Zeus for your life...to get your curse removed. Zeus was at first happy to oblige, but Apollo interfered. It seems that he didn't realize he had a son. Now that he knows and he also knows that Brennan is tied to you, he wishes for that tie to be broken. He had no wish for your curse to be lifted. He does not want his son endangered- he hopes for a strong alliance between himself and Brennan. He used the argument that if you cannot control your combined powers, it would trigger an apocalypse in the mortal world. It was a strong argument and Zeus could not decide who should prevail, so it will be settled with a game.

"You and Brennan will be faced with tasks that you must face together, which means you must control your magic. These tasks will not only test your magic, but your mettle. You must prove that you are worthy to be a god. If you succeed, Zeus will grant Brennan immortality, per Apollo's request. Per mine, your soul will be separated from your moonstone and your curse will be lifted. Each time you fail, a mortal will be dropped into the arena. If the mortal lives, each side will fight to claim him. At the end of the game, whoever retains the most live mortals will win. If Apollo wins, he wants your death as his prize.

"I am sending Circes to you with a package and instructions written by Zeus himself. You and Brennan must endeavor to complete the challenges. For each challenge you complete, a mortal will be released unharmed. If you complete every challenge, Zeus will handle the situation however you wish. If you fail some, but we still retain the majority of the mortals, he will defer to your wishes. But if you lose, Apollo and Mormo will have their way and all will be lost."

Branwyn opened her eyes and for a moment, I stared into my mother's ice blue gaze.

"Why would Zeus do this?" I whispered to her.

Branwyn shrugged and spoke again in my mother's voice.. "The gods grow bored. They feel invincible. Whether an apocalypse occurs or no, it makes no difference to them. They will be entertained either way. Empusa, do your best. Focus as you have never focused before, my child."

At that moment, a shadow as large as the meadow descended upon us in the shape of a raven. It quickly grew smaller and dwarfed into the shape of a stooped woman. And then Circes materialized in front of us, her black cloak swirling.

"The gods play games, princess," the old witch told me, her faded eyes cloudy. "It is up to you to win."

Chapter Four

O ver a flickering bonfire, Circes shared with us the rules of the twisted game. Amid the cracks and pops of the fire and the moving shadows from the trees, the old witch was an unnerving presence.

"Once the gods have entered the arena," she said, her voice creaking eerily in the dark. "Their powers are rendered impotent and they cannot die from any wound they receive. It is a game and the mortals are mere balls in their court. Zeus and the other Olympians will watch from the stands above, but they will not interfere."

The old woman was perched on a gnarled wooden chair, her shoulders stooped and her voluminous cloak gathered around her legs. Her ancient face was creased and pale and for the first time in my life, I saw a concerned expression on it.

"Circes, I don't understand this," I said in frustration. "Why does Apollo even care? I thought he was a decent god. My mother told me that he was."

She studied me for a moment, appraising me with her spooky, sightless eyes. She could not see, but she turned her face toward you in a way that indicated that she could. It was unsettling at best.

"All of the gods have the ability to be decent," she acknowledged with a slight nod. Her white hair rustled in the breeze around her like stringy cotton. "But all of them have the ability to be ruthless, as well. And every one of them grows bored from time to time. Immorality wears on a person, even a god."

"But Apollo didn't even know I was his son," Brennan protested, his forehead wrinkled in agitation. Even in his anger, he was beautiful. Just like his father. I gulped.

"True," Circes agreed. "But this is another trait of the gods. They can be selfish, as well. Since you are his son, he doesn't want your power to go to someone else. He wants you with him, your power available for his use. In addition to that, everyone knows what might happen if you and Empusa cannot control your power when you are together. It is intriguing to them. What would happen to the gods if the mortal world ceased to exist? It is an interesting thought."

"What do you think would happen to the gods, Circes?" I asked her. She had been around for a very, very long time. She had to have a good idea.

She shrugged, her bony shoulders frail. "I know not," she admitted. "Nor do I truly care."

"Why does my father think that I would align myself with him?" Brennan asked. "He does not even know me. I won't do it. I'll never be an ally of someone who would harm Empusa."

Circes threw her head back and laughed, a thin sound in the night.

"Ah, dear boy. You have entered an entirely new realm here in the world of the gods. Things are never what they seem, including your own free will. Can Apollo force you to comply? Perhaps. But most likely, he will bend the situation to his will and make you think that you *want* to comply. Apollo is very, very good at that."

"You mean trick me?" Brennan asked, his face incredulous. "That will not be an easy task- not where Empusa is concerned. She is everything- my world, the air that I breathe. Since she is at the forefront of my mind with every thought that I have, it will be impossible for him to confuse any issue where she is involved."

Circes gazed at him, still amused. "You will learn, boy," she creaked. "You will learn. The gods are not to be trifled with. Apollo could consume you with breakfast and go on to have a long and fruitful day afterward. You will learn."

Branwyn finally spoke up. She was seated at the campfire with us, but had yet said a word. Channeling my mother earlier had worn her out and she was still pale from the experience.

"Why was Empusa sent here?" she asked curiously. "How can I help the goddess?"

The goddess. My mother. The woman who was fighting for me even as we spoke.

"I must be safe here," I murmured. "That is why she would send me away. There is something here that keeps me safe. Am I correct, Circes?"

Circes nodded once again. "You are safe here in the circle. It is a haven for you. Neither Mormo nor Apollo can breach the circle. Although they will be distracted with the game, anyway."

The game. The heinous, terrible game that will take the lives of mortals if I fail. I swallowed hard and then swallowed again. Why were the lives of mortals too often in my hands?

"Our tasks," I whispered. "My mother said you would bring us a list of tasks that Brennan and I must complete. What are they?"

Circes dug around in the inner lining of her cloak and finally came up with a rolled parchment. It was tied with a lavish purple velvet cord. It was sealed with Zeus' own crimson seal. It might as well have been blood.

I took it with shaking hands and held it for a moment before I opened it. I was scared to see the words, afraid that we would fail. Taking a deep breath, I studied the scrawling handwriting that sloped across the page.

After I had read each startling word, I looked back to Circes. "There is only one challenge listed here, yet it says there will be ten. Where are the rest?"

She shook her head. "They will be revealed to you one at a time. That is all I know, princess."

"What is the first challenge?" Brennan asked grimly. He looked as apprehensive as I felt, but he was facing it bravely. Warmth flooded through me. He had no idea what we were truly facing, but he was willing to do it anyway. With me.

"Hubris," I answered slowly. Brennan looked at me in confusion.

"Hubris? What is that?"

"Have you ever heard the story of Athena and Arachne?"I asked him. "It is in the history books of mortals."

He shook his head. "If I read it, I have forgotten it. Back when I thought mythological stories were simply myths, they didn't interest me. They take on an entirely new light now."

"True. It's amazing how perspectives change when something affects you personally," I agreed. "Athena and Arachne is an interesting story…a story of divine justice and one that perfectly illustrates how petty the gods can be."

He lifted an eyebrow. "Go on."

"One time, long ago, a mortal named Arachne found her skills at weaving to be the best in the land. She boasted about them to those around her and even went so far as to say that she could outweave the gods themselves. Athena caught wind of this boast. This is the dreaded hubris, an affront that rarely goes unnoticed by the gods. It is when a mortal challenges or boasts about a god. It has never gone unpunished.

"In this case, Athena then challenged Arachne to a weaving contest. They both worked throughout the night on beautiful tapestries. But in the morning, it was clear that Arachne was the winner. Her tapestry was perfect. But Athena's pride could not allow her to admit it, so in her rage, she turned Arachne into a spider, doomed to weave for all of eternity."

"That seems a little harsh," Brennan answered slowly. "And that's how spiders came to be?"

I nodded. "Never underestimate the gods, Brennan. Not ever."

"Point taken," he answered. "So how does this hubris affect us in this challenge?"

I turned back to Circes and Branwyn. "Branwyn, apparently someone in your village has boasted about her magic, declaring it to be superior to even my mother's. It did not go unheard. Zeus himself heard the words. Brennan and I are tasked with testing this girl's magic and then meting out the appropriate punishment for her boasts."

"Hubris," Brennan said slowly.

"Hubris," I confirmed with a solemn nod.

I could tell I wasn't going to like this game in the slightest. For as long as I could remember, I had tried to live my life as though I wasn't a goddess. And now, unless I could prove to the Olympians that I had the skill required to be one, I would die.

The 'handling my abilities' portion wouldn't be so difficult. It would be the 'acting like a goddess' parts. They were at times cold-hearted and ruthless, two things I tried hard not to be. Sighing, I turned back to Branwyn.

"Who would it have been?"

Branwyn looked stricken.

"I'm not certain, princess. I don't know for sure who would have made such a wild, unfounded boast."

But I could see on her face that she had a good idea.

"You have a good feeling who it is," I said firmly. "I need a name."

Branwyn stared at her hands. "Kenna."

"Thank you. Can you retrieve Kenna from her bed and bring her to me?"

"Now, princess?" Branwyn's gaze shot upward and met mine.

"Now."

Without a backward glance, Branwyn turned and left the bonfire. An owl hooted softly in the near distance and the night breeze rustled the grass around them. Moisture hung in the air, heavy and chilly, causing me to shiver slightly.

"Are you cold?" Brennan asked, moving to me instantly and wrapping his arm around my shoulders. His warmth was truly like the sun and I melted into his warm body as we waited for Branwyn to return. Circes stared sightlessly into the fire, not saying a word.

"What do you think?" Brennan asked softly, his lips very close to my ear.

"I don't know," I answered honestly. "I don't see that we can win."

"Why would you say that?" he asked in surprise. "We have as much a chance as our fathers do, don't we?"

"We're the ones being tested," I reminded him wearily. "Not them."

"True," he agreed. "But we have the most to lose. That makes us hungrier."

"True," I answered with a smile. Brennan was such an optimist. He saw the good in every situation. Sometimes, it was refreshing. Sometimes, it was annoying. Tonight, it was comforting.

Movement caught my eye and I looked up to find Branwyn entering the circle with a young woman. Kenna had a thick brown braid hanging down her back and was dressed in a white nightdress. The look on her face was set and mulish. I could see that Branwyn had explained the situation.

"We're up," I said to Brennan. He released me, his warm arms sliding from my shoulders. I instantly missed his warmth, but turned my attention to the two women approaching us.

"Kenna?" I asked, keeping my voice as even as I could.

This girl had not personally affronted me. The Olympians were the ones who had paper-thin skin when it came to these things. Not me. But here I was, doling out an "appropriate" punishment. And what in the world would an appropriate punishment for a ridiculous offense be?

They stopped directly in front of me and I watched the girl. She wasn't sorry for what she'd said. I could see that.

"Do you admit that you boasted of your magic, that you said yours was better than even that of the gods?"

Kenna stuck out her chin, her voice ringing through the night as her gaze met mine unflinchingly.

"Yes."

"You have no remorse?" I raised an eyebrow.

"No, princess. I would feel sorry for it if I had lied. But I did not. It is the truth."

"While I personally admire your spirit, most of the gods would not. It is never wise to threaten them in any way," I told her. "And to make sure your punishment fits the crime, we must first decide if your magic is in fact as good as you say. My mother is currently occupied and unable to be here. But you can match your magic against mine."

Kenna's gaze flew to my face, startled. It was clear she hadn't expected to be tested and truly, it was a spur of the moment decision. It suddenly seemed the appropriate move to make. I wasn't really sure what difference the outcome would make. And there was no way that a mortal would have stronger magic that me. It just wasn't possible.

"Yes, princess," she bowed her head slightly, still unafraid.

I felt the slightest stirrings of resentment in my belly. This mortal truly believed she was better than I was? Besides having the blood of gods coursing through my veins, I had been alive for a thousand years.

"Careful, Emmie," Brennan cautioned, reading my thoughts. "You're sounding a little like them." He was right and I quickly tried to shake such thoughts from my head. The last thing I wanted to do was become like the Olympians. They were arrogant and shallow, for the most part. I didn't want that for myself.

"Come with me," I told Kenna. I turned and I felt her following closely on my heels. I leaped onto the stone of the altar and stood squarely in the middle, my bare feet cooled by the stone. Kenna walked quietly to my side.

"What would you like for me to do?" she asked. She was no longer arrogant or brash, she was simply matter-of-fact.

"Do you realize that your magic comes from my mother herself?" I asked her. "As a mortal, all you can do is channel the magic of the gods. You do not have such magic of your own. And do you believe that my mother would allow more magic to flow through you than me in this situation?"

For the first time, Kenna looked unsure of herself.

"I doubt it, princess," she finally answered. "When I made those boasts, I was not thinking that I would ever be facing you in a challenge. Certainly in this situation, the outcome will be different."

"Certainly," I answered, smiling slightly at the girl. A little of her arrogance had seeped away and I felt a surprising amount of satisfaction from that.

"Empusa," Brennan cautioned again.

But this time, I didn't check my thoughts. In this situation, I was right to feel the way I did. This girl had been arrogant.

"You must learn that you can never foresee situations that you might find yourself in," I told Kenna. "This situation will serve as a lesson for you."

Pointing my finger at her, I summoned goddess strength from deep within and channeled it out of me. It erupted in a rush, directed at Kenna.

Kenna flew from the altar and crashed into the side of a nearby tree. She slid to the ground, but she was unharmed and quickly got to her feet. Her face was red and a vein thrummed in the side of her temple. She was embarrassed and angry.

Pointing back at me, a thin stream of light shot from her fingers and shattered the stillness of the night. But the light itself served as a warning. I saw it coming and deflected it back to her- forming a shield in my mind and hurling it at her. My magic smashed into hers, blocking it and reflecting it back to her. It collided into her and once again, she was thrown into the trees, this time by her own magic.

"Your magic is good," I called to her. "I've never seen a mortal channel such power. But you will not beat me. Do you wish to continue?"

I was confident and slightly annoyed that this girl still had the arrogant spirit that she had when she started. Her eyes spit fire as she once again climbed from the ground. Her braid was coming apart now, her clothing torn and dirty, her hands smudged. Meeting my gaze determinedly, she raised her hand once more.

And then quickly turned it toward Brennan. Her power coursed from her fingers into Brennan, ripping a hole in his chest. He flung backward and fell, his arms and legs splayed unnaturally around him, his eyes widened in surprise.

I gasped and before I could stop myself, I killed the girl with one blow.

One single thick thread of energy left my fingers in an instant and sliced cleanly through Kenna, ripping her apart. I heard a sickening, loud pop as her rib-cage cracked. She slid to the ground, her eyes staring sightlessly at me. I had done it without thinking, in a quick reaction to her attack on Brennan. She had attacked the man I loved and I had killed her for it.

Divine justice had been served.

As I rushed to Brennan, I glanced at Circes and she nodded, releasing an inky black raven from her hands. It flew screaming into the trees and into the night beyond. She nodded once more to me and I knew.

I had passed this first test.

Chapter Five

rennan quickly got to his feet and I stared in surprise before I remembered. One of his gifts was healing more quickly than normal. It was a gift he had inherited from Apollo. Even now, the gaping hole in his chest was closing up as though the wound had never happened at all. I expelled a long breath of relief as I rushed into his arms.

"I'm sorry," I hurried to tell him. "I wasn't expecting that. I had no idea she would turn on you like that. I was focused on what she would try to do to me. I didn't know she would be ruthless."

"You must think more like a god," Circes interjected firmly. "A god wouldn't have hesitated to use any advantage, something that Kenna was inclined to do as well. Never let your guard down, princess."

I nodded. "It has been hard-learned, but I will remember that."

Branwyn was kneeling at Kenna's lifeless body and I rushed to her, laying my hand on her shoulder.

"I'm so sorry, Branwyn. I didn't mean to hurt her. I truly did not."

Branwyn turned to look at me, her eyes filled with pain.

"What do you mean, Empusa? Of course you had no choice. She attacked Brennan. I still weep for her, however. Aside from her arrogance, she was a good girl."

I nodded, a lump forming in my throat as I watched her fold Kenna's arms over her torso. She stepped back as Brennan bent and picked the girl up.

"Tell me where to take her," he instructed Branwyn.

If Branwyn looked surprised that Brennan would carry the girl who had just tried to kill him, she didn't show it. She simply led the way out of the clearing and back toward the village. Brennan strode behind her, his shoulders wide and strong. I stayed with Circes.

"Circes," I began uncertainly. "Can we win this?"

Circes looked at me with her unnerving eyes.

"I know not," she said quietly. "Your mother also does not know. But you must try, princess."

"Have you not seen the outcome?" I asked in disbelief. "Nor my mother?"

Circes shook her head slowly.

"No. The outcome is darkened to us. We cannot see it. We have seen many different outcomes, but we cannot tell which is the true ending to this story. Perhaps because it has not yet been written. It is entirely dependent on you."

"And Brennan," I added. "He plays a role as well."

"Yes, he certainly does," Circes acknowledged. "And never forget what I saw awhile ago, princess."

"You saw that Brennan would be a threat to me-that his very existence would threaten me and that I would risk everything for him."

"Yes," she answered simply. "Remember that."

"How could I forget it?" I asked painfully.

"If you are wise, you will not," Circes said before closing her eyes and warming her hands by the fire. "My old bones are weary. I'd like to rest."

"Of course. We'll find Branwyn and get you settled into a hut for the night."

Circes didn't answer, instead she remained still by the roaring flames.

"I worry about you, Empusa," she said softly, her eyes still closed. "Medea and I have watched you grow, watched you change into the woman that you have become. I worry that you are making rash decisions now, that you aren't considering your own well-being. Instead, you are placing your concern within someone else. The sun god's son will likely be the death of you. Can you not see that?"

I swallowed hard, the taste of Kenna's death still in my mouth and lingering on my heart.

"Of course I can see it, Circes. Of course I know that it isn't the safest thing for me and perhaps not even the smartest. I just killed someone to protect him. And I would do it again. Feeling so strongly for someone makes me vulnerable. I know that. But what else can I do? It is what I feel and there is no changing that. He and I are soul mates. We're connected in ways that we don't even fully understand. All I know is that I will stand behind him until the end of time or the end of our lives, whichever comes first. It's the only thing I can do."

"That is exactly what I thought you would say," she said slowly as she rose from her seat and turned to me, taking my arm. "I would expect nothing less from you. Take me to a bed, child."

She shuffled toward the village and I held her frail arm. Peeking backward over my shoulder, I glanced toward the treetops. The raven that she had released was nowhere in sight.

"When will we find out what our next challenge is?" I asked the old woman anxiously.

"When Zeus feels like revealing it," she shrugged. "All in good time, child. All in good time."

* * *

Brennan lay facing me in the dark, his expression serious. He was oh-so-handsome. Reaching out, I traced the contours of his face with my fingers and he leaned into my hand. I could feel his stubble on my fingers. He needed to shave.

"Are you alright?" he murmured into the darkness. "I'm sorry that happened, Empusa. Really."

"Surprisingly, I'm fine," I answered. "Is that bad? I don't feel remorse at all. She tried to kill you so I killed her first. I didn't even think about it. It had to be done."

"It's a normal instinct to protect those that you love," Brennan replied. "It doesn't make you bad. It makes you normal. I would've done the same thing for you, trust me."

I nodded and nestled into his strong chest. He wrapped his arms around me and I felt safe for the first time today. I breathed slowly and deeply, inhaling his masculine scent and enjoying the solitude. We were alone for the first time all day.

"Do you find it strange that my father is competing to keep my abilities 'safe' and to keep us apart when he hasn't even met me?" Brennan asked thoughtfully. "You told me that he was a decent person and that he was a lot like me. It sure doesn't seem like it at this point."

"I know," I sighed. "I can't tell you what his true motives are right now. That's one thing about the Olympians. They are always driven by ulterior motives. It is best to always be on your guard."

"I'm gathering that," he answered. "What do you think is truly going to happen, Em? Do you think we will fail?"

"That is not an option," I told him firmly. "If we fail, all is lost. We'll be separated forever. That isn't something that I want to think about."

"Me either," he replied. "I'll do anything to prevent that."

"Agreed," I answered. "We should sleep. It's hard to say what we will face tomorrow. We'll need to be prepared."

Brennan tightened his arms around me as I rested my face against his bare chest. Our little hut was quiet and dark, the only light coming from the fireplace in the corner. The soothing crackle sounds coming from it combined with Brennan's warmth, quickly soothed me into sleep.

But my sleep wasn't soothing.

The second I drifted off, my mother filled my thoughts, standing in the middle of my dream. She was as beautiful as always, her long blonde hair pale and soft, her lips full and red. But she was smeared in blood.

"Why are you bloody?" I asked her in surprise. "The game only just begun and we achieved our first challenge."

She nodded grimly, her lips pressed together in a firm line. "Yes, you did. However, Zeus wanted a practice run… mainly for their amusement. We fought over a mortal."

"Did you win?" I was almost afraid to ask.

"Yes," she sighed. "And Zeus set him free. He won't contribute to our tally for the end score."

"It's alright," I reassured her. "That's better than Mormo receiving a point."

"I suppose," she acknowledged. "Empusa, this is very, very serious. I want you to realize that. Zeus realizes that he already committed to reversing your curse. But Apollo made such good points that he couldn't ignore them."

"Can we win the rest of the challenges?" I asked.

She studied me, her ice blue eyes solemn. "You are my daughter," she said proudly. "You can do anything you set your mind to. You are brilliant and strong. But I do not know what the challenges will be. You'll need all of your wits to overcome them, I'm sure."

"Well, I will be ever on my toes," I answered wryly.

"I'm serious, daughter," she snapped. I took another look at her. She looked bone-weary and she was covered in the dirt of the arena.

"I'm sorry, mother," I said quietly. "I know this is hard on you. And I take this very seriously. I do. When was the last time you slept?"

"I'll sleep when this is over," she answered tiredly, pushing her hair from her eyes. I had to admit, it was the first time in a very, very long time that she didn't look absolutely perfect. "You are what is important to me now, Em. I wish I could help you more, but my hands are tied. It is not something I'm accustomed to. Zeus is going to give you challenges and you will have to overcome them yourself- without my help. It's maddening."

I wrapped my arms around her slender shoulders and laid my head against her arm.

"Mother, you will help me. Everything you've ever taught me will be of help. And you've taught me so much. Please don't worry. I will keep your wisdom close to my heart and I will come through this. I promise that."

A single tear slipped from my mother's eye and down her smooth cheek, causing a rivulet in the dirt that smudged her skin. "You do have my strength," she admitted, brushing impatiently at her tears. "I have faith that you will win. I just don't want you to lose focus, daughter. Think of your own well-being first, please. I beg of you. Think of anyone else second."

I drew in a sharp breath.

"You mean Brennan," I said slowly. "You want me to think of myself before Brennan."

She nodded. "You have to, Empusa. The only person that one can ever truly count on is their self. You must have learned that by now."

I backed away from her slightly.

"Mother, what you haven't learned yet is that I can count on Brennan. He's a part of me. Just as Mormo is of you. Surely you understand."

"What I understand is that Mormo would kill me in a moment if he had to," she answered. Before she could continue, I cut her off.

"Brennan is not Mormo," I said firmly. "That is something that should be apparent to everyone. He is kind and good and he loves me like no other."

"I know," my mother answered softly. "But he has no experience with the gods, with his father. It is something that takes practice to withstand unscathed. He doesn't have that practice yet."

"It doesn't matter," I dismissed her concern. "I will always be the most important thing to him. And he is the same to me."

"Very well," mother answered. "I can see that I will not change your mind on this. Just assure me that you will pay attention. I am not certain, but Zeus may very well send you surprise challenges. He may not announce them ahead of time. Be on your guard."

"I'm always on my guard," I murmured. "My father taught me that lesson long ago."

She nodded. "I know," she answered softly. Leaning forward, she kissed me lightly on the cheek and hugged me hard. She smelled like lavender and dust. "I love you, Empusa. Remember that."

"I love you, too," I told her. And she was gone. I stood alone in my dream and the dark shadows swirled from the edges of my consciousness and I drifted back into sleep.

Chapter Six

I woke to someone staring at me.

Brennan was propped up on one elbow, running one finger slowly along my exposed thigh. Glancing around, I found that it was still dark outside and the fire in our hut had died down into embers. There was a chilly feel of dew forming in the air. It must be near dawn.

"I couldn't sleep," Brennan answered my unspoken question. "I'm sorry that I disturbed you, though."

"You touching me is never a disturbance," I assured him. Grasping his moving hand, I clutched it to my heart. His fingers were warm and strong. "You can touch me whenever you'd like."

"Is that an open invitation?" he asked, one golden eyebrow raised. I gulped at his suggestive tone.

"Perhaps," I whispered, snuggling closer. Brennan's body was warm and hard, his muscles perfectly formed, his jaw chiseled, his eyes a liquid topaz. I had never in my life seen a more breathtaking man, mortal or god.

"Thank you," he murmured into my ear. I had forgotten he could read my thoughts and I felt my cheeks get hot as I blushed.

"It's true. You're beautiful," I whispered, swallowing my embarrassment.

I felt him grin against my neck. "And so are you," he said as he ran his nose along my skin, inhaling. "And you smell nice."

"Thank you," I answered, taking a sharp breath as he ran his palms along my hips, pulling me even closer. His body was so hard next to mine that I gasped. He covered my mouth with his and kissed me in a way I'd never been kissed before.

My heart raced and I clutched at his back, feeling the strong muscles beneath my fingers contract as he moved. I slipped my foot along his calf as I returned his kiss, licking his lower lip lightly. He groaned and plunged his tongue into my mouth and I arched against him.

"Sweet heavens," I gasped, trying to breathe. Electricity sparked in the air, crackling around us. It caused my hair to stand on end.

"I want you," Brennan said softly, nipping at my lip lightly. "You're all I think about, Em. Every minute, every day."

"I know," I answered. "We're going to have to focus, though, Brennan. We have to concentrate on the matters at hand."

"This *is* the matter at hand," he growled lightly against my mouth. "You're in my hands right now, Em. We'll think about the rest later."

"Alright," I panted, trying to catch my breath as Brennan ran his hands everywhere on my body. Everywhere he touched felt like it ignited into flames and it was growing more and more difficult to catch my breath and focus.

Colors from around the room swirled together in the corners of my eyes and Brennan's aura appeared to me, bright golds and yellows outlining his body as bright as the sun. I blinked hard and struggled to focus.

I could feel the essence of his soul pulsing in his chest along with his heart. It was pounding hard and I could hear each individual beat. I unconsciously moved toward him, an automatic response to his aura. I struggled to move backward but the urge to be near him, to inhale him, was very, very strong.

"I can't do this," I gasped, pushing at him. "I can't. I'm going to kill you by accident."

He grasped my face in his hands and pulled me back to him.

"Yes, you can, Em. We have to master this. You can do it. You won't hurt me."

His breath was on my lips, a mere inches from mine. I felt an obscene amount of desire to simply take a breath and inhale his soul... the soul of the man that I love. It was an unconscious need. I fought hard against it, but it was still there, loud and clear.

"Easy for you to say," I muttered as I swept my hands against his flat abdomen and sucked in my breath again. "You don't have to try not to kill *me*."

Brennan rolled me over abruptly, pinning me to the bed beneath us and hovering above me. The dim light from the dawn outside gave him an ethereal feel, as though he was an angel...or a god.

"True," he acknowledged. "But I have to try and not be killed. I think that's equally as daunting."

He lowered his head and kissed the side of my neck, his lips feather soft. I shivered as a chill ran up my back from the light touch. He smiled in response.

"I don't think that's a great plan, as far as staying alive," I mentioned as I leaned up to meet his kiss. "You should be moving away from me."

"Yet I'm not," he pointed out.

"I know," I groaned and sucked on his bottom lip. He moaned in response, triggering a surge of need in me that I didn't expect and couldn't control. I arched up to meet him and a sudden flash of light caught my attention. I froze and an acrid scent swept into my nose. And then a crackling sound filled my ears.

"Fire!" I gasped, pushing out from under Brennan.

We both lunged to our feet and found that the roof to our hut was smoldering and then before we could even move, it burst into a roaring flame. I couldn't help but screech and point as Brennan threw open the door and raced outside. I could hear screaming from outdoors, but didn't know who it was coming from.

Smoke was quickly filling the small hut, so I joined Brennan outside, coughing as I stumbled out the door.

Brennan was staring at the fire, an expression of extreme concentration on his face. Within a few seconds, the fire fizzled and died. He turned to look at me triumphantly.

"I did it!" he crowed. "I channeled enough power to put the fire out."

I couldn't help but smile at his proud expression. It was a big step for him. He was learning to harness his power.

"Good job," I commended him weakly. "You're doing great."

He took in my expression and crossed to me immediately, grasping my elbow.

"Em, this wasn't your fault. We'll figure it out, I promise," he said solemnly. "We just need practice. We'll get the hang of it."

Behind him, Circes emerged from her hut, her cloudy eyes knowing. She sniffed the air, sightlessly glanced in our direction and then shook her head. Without a word, she retreated back into her hut with her long black cloak trailing on the dirt behind her.

I glanced at Brennan. "Ignore her. You're right. We just need practice. We'll get it."

He nodded wordlessly.

"We should get ready for breakfast," he said softly, leading me back into our smoldering hut. I ignored the gazes of the women watching from their doorways and closed the door behind us. Leaning against the door, I slid to the ground, exhaling heavily.

"What if she's right, though?" I asked softly, staring up at Brennan. I could feel wetness forming in my eyes at the mere thought. "What if we can never learn to harness our power when we're together? We'll destroy everything- including each other."

Brennan knelt in front of me, staring directly into my eyes. I concentrated on the amber flecks hidden in his as he spoke.

"Don't ever think like that, Emmie," he said slowly. "We can do anything we decide to do. And we've already decided that this is worth it. We'll fight this battle, we'll win it, and then we'll live happily ever after."

I stared at him. "That only happens in fairy tales."

He shook his head. "No, it doesn't. It happens all of the time in real life. It will happen to us. I promise you that."

I sighed. "You shouldn't make promises that you might not be able to keep."

He sighed back. "Haven't you learned by now… I always keep my promises."

His confident tone made me grin and I leaned forward to kiss him.

"I love you, you know."

"I know," he answered happily. "And I love you back."

We rose from the floor and cleaned up for breakfast and I couldn't keep the deliriously happy thoughts from my mind. Maybe he was right. Maybe all it truly took was the will to triumph. And certainly no two people had ever wanted something so badly. I had to admit that.

Brennan was dressed and ready before I was and he turned to me.

"Do you mind if I get some fresh air? I'll meet you for breakfast?"

I shook my head. "Of course not. Go ahead. I'll be along shortly."

He kissed my forehead and ducked out of the hut.

I finished straightening my shift, belting it loosely at the waist. Branwyn had provided us with period-appropriate clothing so that we didn't stand out quite so much. Jeans and t-shirts weren't the thing here. Pulling a comb through my long hair, I twisted it into a knot at my neck and stuck a couple of chopsticks through it. The chopsticks definitely weren't period-appropriate, but I didn't care. I had never been one to completely conform.

There was no mirror here and I didn't want to conjure one, so I could only guess that I looked passable. Pivoting, I turned to head out of the hut, but stopped short. With a gasp, I realized that I wasn't alone.

A beautiful woman was standing directly behind me, perfectly still and quiet. Deep red hair flowed in waves to the middle of her slender back. She was wearing a slinky beige gown that puddled around her feet like a mermaid's tail. The plunging neckline exposed creamy white skin and she had deep emerald eyes that were gazing directly into my own.

"Hello, Empusa," she breathed softly. Her voice was feminine and sexy, slightly throaty.

"Do I know you?" I asked cautiously, keeping an eye on her.

She laughed, a tinkling, light sound. "No," she shook her head. As she did, her fragrant perfume drifted toward me. And I closed my eyes, inhaling her scent. Everything about her was appealing, and drew me to her.

My eyes snapped open with a realization.

"You're a siren," I gasped.

She laughed. "Something that you're not unfamiliar with," she nodded. "And Empusa...I'm sorry."

"For what?" I looked at her curiously because she hadn't moved.

"For this."

She waved her hand and two men in black cloaks and hoods appeared next to me, grabbing my arms. They held me with vise-grips, impervious to my goddess strength as I kicked and thrashed.

Before I knew it, they were spinning me around and around and I realized that they were wrapping a mesh-sort of cloth around me, restraining my arms and legs. I started to scream and realized that I couldn't open my mouth. Somehow, they had rendered me mute.

Aghast, I stared at the woman helplessly.

She looked at me sympathetically.

"Relax, Empusa. This won't take long and you will be released again."

She looked at the men. "Zeus said to conceal her somewhere where she could watch. She needs to bear witness to this." She looked around the room. "It's too small in here, though. He'll see her." She snapped her fingers. "I know. Invisibility."

With a few murmured words, I felt a familiar lightening of limb as I faded from sight. I could still see everything in the room, but I knew that anyone who entered would not be able to see me. The two men on each side of me had faded with me and they pulled me into the back corner of the hut, directly in front of the bed.

A bad feeling formed in the fit of my stomach as the woman arranged herself on the bed. *My* bed.

She pulled her gown until the straps were hanging alluringly off of her shoulders and she positioned herself just-so, posing herself so that she looked beautiful. As she did, I realized something.

This was another challenge. My mother had been correct- we were going to have unexpected challenges. I felt panicky. Brennan wouldn't be prepared for this. It was almost impossible to stave off a siren. I should know.

The siren finally finished preening and turned to gaze into my eyes. I stared defiantly back, unable to move. She smiled just slightly.

"Don't worry, Empusa," she said softly, her eyes glued to mine. "I won't hurt him."

I squeezed my eyes shut. For some reason, I believed her. Killing Brennan now would spoil the game for the Olympians so that wasn't what I was worried about. Seeing Brennan in the arms of another beautiful woman... that was an entirely different story.

Chapter Seven

It didn't take long for Brennan to wonder what was taking me so long and come to find me. The wooden door creaked open causing me to open my eyes. The two men on either side of me gripped my elbows hard, although I don't know why. The strange gauze wrapped around me held me surprisingly tightly. I couldn't move at all.

Brennan stopped short when he saw the siren on our bed. I gulped hard and tried not to close my eyes. I wanted to, but I had to see what happened here. It was an undeniable and unpleasant need.

"Who are you?" Brennan demanded. To his credit, he kept his eyes on her face, not on her half-naked body.

"Helen," the Siren murmured in answer. "Come sit with me, Brennan."

Her voice was like a song, soft and beautiful. The serene sound made me feel relaxed and tranquil, as though I could float away on the sound without a care in the world. No wonder sirens were so successful at luring men to their deaths in the ocean.

"Okay, Helen," Brennan replied politely. "It's very nice to meet you. Now tell me...why are you here? And half-dressed? Where is Empusa?"

I again had to give him credit. He still had me on his mind even faced with the siren's blatant attributes. It was impressive.

Helen smiled again, lifting one elegant hand. "She's nearby. But you need to focus on me now. I'm your challenge, Brennan. Do you think you can win?"

Brennan looked confused.

"*You're* my challenge? How so?"

I wanted to throttle him. When a siren tells you that she is your challenge, you don't stand there and question her. You turn around and walk away. But then, to be fair, I guess he couldn't do that. We had to win our challenges or the game would be lost. Struggling to swallow, I kept my eyes frozen on the pair in front of me.

I could hear Brennan breathe as he tried to wrap his mind around his current situation. I skimmed through his thoughts quickly and I knew the second that he figured it out.

"No," he stammered. "That's an unfair challenge."

"No one ever said the game would be fair," Helen answered simply.

She patted the bed beside her, her hand slender.

"Come, Brennan. Let's get this started. You must withstand me- every temptation that I might offer you. If you do not, you fail. And you know what will happen if you fail."

Brennan nodded. "Yes."

Helen giggled, seemingly unaffected. "So come. This will be fun. Let us begin."

Brennan sighed a heavy sigh that seemed to shake the room, but that might have been my own breath quivering in my chest. He slowly approached the bed and stiffly sat next to the beautiful siren.

"What do I need to do?" he asked.

Helen moved so quickly that I didn't even see the movement. She was just suddenly behind Brennan on the bed, her mouth directly behind his ear.

"Nothing," she breathed into his neck. "You don't have to do a thing."

"But withstand temptation," Brennan added.

Helen only laughed. "Good luck."

I gulped.

Helen slid around Brennan smoothly, like a beautiful snake sliding along a branch. She wrapped herself around Brennan and kissed him lightly on the mouth. The room was so sexually charged that I could practically taste the energy and it was all I could do not to vomit. My stomach was clenched into an iron ball.

Brennan didn't respond. He sat motionlessly on the bed. Helen pulled back a little bit and stared into Brennan's amber eyes.

"Is that all?" he asked coolly. Sweet heavens. She would take that as a challenge. I wanted to slap him.

"Oh, dear boy," she cooed. "I'm only just beginning."

She snapped her fingers and he was instantly lying on his back, each wrist and ankle bound to a corner of the bed. I gulped again. This couldn't be good. I wriggled within the confining gauze but there was no way I was getting loose. It was so tight that I could barely breathe.

Hovering above Brennan, her hair dangling along his body, Helen licked him. She traced little trails along his skin; up his legs, over his hips, across his chest. She paused at the most sensitive areas, causing me to close my eyes and Brennan to shudder in pleasure even though he kept his lips pressed tightly together.

Against his wishes, he was enjoying it. I could hear him pleading with me in his thoughts.

Empusa, I don't know where you are, but I am not enjoying this.

Where are you?

I don't want to like this. I don't. What the hell is this woman?

I tried to answer, but found that my thoughts had been blocked, as well as my movement and my voice. I couldn't communicate with him at all. I was utterly helpless.

Helen turned to glance at me, her eyes knowing. She was reading my thoughts, she could hear my frustration. Her lips curved upward in a slight smile. I gritted my teeth. Brennan moaned and then clamped his lips tightly together again.

He really was trying. His knuckles were turning white as he gripped the skins covering the bed. He was doing everything he possibly could to avoid being affected. But he was a man. He couldn't help having a physical reaction.

"Do you want to make love to me?" Helen purred into his ear as her hand stroked his body. He shook his head and I knew it was because he didn't trust his voice to speak.

She licked the skin on his neck, blew on it and then whispered again in his ear, ever-so-softly.

"Are you sure?"

Brennan gritted his teeth and once again nodded. He was literally pale with his efforts to remain unfazed by her. I had never been so proud of him. He was certainly tapping into his demi-god abilities. A regular mortal would have been butter in Helen's hands by now.

Helen sighed.

"Why must you be so difficult?" she asked softly, breathing into his ear. Her breasts were pushed into his face and the seductive scent of her perfume filled the small hut. I honestly didn't know how Brennan was restraining himself. It was taking a Herculean effort.

"I don't want you," Brennan said firmly, even as a thin bead of sweat broke out on his forehead. "Not truly. You are simply making me feel like I do."

"But aren't feelings the most important things of all?" Helen asked innocently, weaving her fingers through his.

"Lust is not a true feeling," Brennan told her, his voice stronger now. "It is a fleeting sensation. It isn't important. The moment this challenge is over, I won't ever think of you again. Caving into you now would not be worth it."

Helen laughed again. "Oh, trust me. I'll make it worth it."

But Brennan shook his head, his jaw set stubbornly.

"Fine," she sighed, rolling her beautiful green eyes. "We'll have to do it this way."

I could taste the alarm in my mouth, the metallic taste lingering on my tongue. But before I could even think one more thought, Helen started singing.

In a wordless melody, she hummed and sang a song that was absolutely breathtaking. The beautiful notes hit high and low, weaving a tapestry of music that I'd never before experienced. Along with the music, she was somehow releasing pheromones into the air. I could taste them as they wrapped around me and I breathed them in. It compelled me to move toward her, so much so that if I wasn't restrained, I would have walked straight to her and offered myself to her in whatever way she deemed fit. Her song was that profound.

I realized in that moment that her song was her deadliest weapon. When her physical charms failed to work, she simply opened her mouth and sang her siren's song. And it was powerful. My heart pounded in my chest as I waited for Brennan's reaction.

His face drained of color, his knuckles turned purple from the strength that he was clenching them with. He even stopped breathing. He was literally holding his breath in his effort to restrain himself. I ached for him, because I knew the tremendous effort it must be taking.

Helen ceased her singing just long enough to stare down at him, perched as she was atop his chest.

"I know you want me," she murmured.

She started singing again as she bent and draped herself on his body. She trailed her fingers lightly along Brennan's arms and I could see him begin to shake as he fought hard to resist her.

"Just say the words," she suggested to him. "Tell me you want me. Tell me to make love to you. And this torment will be over."

Brennan gritted his teeth as sweat poured down his temples.

"No." One word. He rasped it and the effort that it took for him to speak was unmistakable. And one word was all that he could muster.

But one word was enough.

Helen stopped moving and stared at him, shock apparent on her face.

"What?"

"I said no," Brennan repeated, this time sounding stronger. "I do not want you."

"Yes, you do," Helen said uncertainly, leaning forward and brushing her lips across his. "I know you do."

"My body wants you. But I do not. Please get off of me. We can sit here and do this all day, but I won't cave in to you. I won't. So you won't like the outcome."

He was abrupt because he had to be. He needed to focus his energy on keeping his body in check and resisting her. But his tone was firm. He meant what he said. And Helen knew it.

She sighed in defeat and instantly the mood in the room changed.

The smell of sex and pheromones disappeared as Helen climbed off of Brennan and stood on the floor next to the bed adjusting her clothing. She snapped her fingers in my direction and the men holding me shoved me in front of them. I felt to the floor and I knew my invisibility was lifted.

Brennan stared at me in shock as I writhed helplessly on the floor in the impossibly strong gauze.

Within a second, he broke the bonds that held him to the bed and leaped to my side. He was able to untangle me from the gauze in just a few seconds and helped me to my feet.

"Empusa, are you alright?" he asked quickly, staring into my eyes.

As I looked into his, I was so overcome with his dedication to me that I wanted to cry. In fact, my eyes did tear up. He was instantly concerned, followed by fury at Helen. Turning to her, he started to grab her arm, but I held him back.

"It's not her fault, Bren," I insisted. "She was sent here by Zeus as part of the game. And you won this challenge. It's fine. It's wonderful, in fact. I can't believe you did so well."

"I can't either," Helen sniffed. "No one can withstand me."

"Brennan just did," I told her with a cocky smile. "Now go home and lick your wounded pride. And on your way, you can tell Zeus that we have another point."

Glaring at me, Helen snapped her fingers once again and she disappeared along with the two hooded men.

Alone, I stared at Brennan. "You do love me, don't you?" I asked softly. He looked surprised at my question.

"You doubted me?" he asked, one eyebrow raised. "You should never bet against me, Emmie. Especially not when it is something concerning you."

I nodded slowly.

"Alright. I'll have to remember that. I love you, Brennan."

"And I love you."

He opened up his strong arms and I flew into them. Cradling me softly to his chest, he kissed my forehead.

"And I just forfeited some pretty hot-and-heavy moments for you. Are you going to compensate me for that at all?"

I yanked away from him and looked up to find him laughing. I swatted at his arm. He was so large that I seemed about as effective as a gnat, but still.

"You're impossible."

"I know." He smirked and I had to laugh before I once again straightened my clothing and hair for breakfast.

Chapter Eight

Y2ou've done well," Circes creaked from across the breakfast table. She paused with her soup spoon midway to her mouth, the steaming porridge dripping back into the wooden bowl. "I'm impressed, son of Apollo. Mortal men can never resist a siren."

"I'm not a normal mortal, Circes," Brennan pointed out calmly as he took a bite of his own breakfast. "Although, some advance notice would have been helpful."

"I did not know in advance," she replied. "Zeus alone knows his plans."

"Circes," I interrupted. "When do you think we'll hear of our next challenge? It's maddening to not know."

She shrugged, dipping her spoon once again into her soup. "I know not, Empusa. Be patient, young one."

Young one. I had to smile. Only the very ancient could call someone who was a thousand years old *young*. I heard Brennan chuckle, as well.

"I don't know what you're laughing about, young pup," I told him, jabbing him in the ribs. He laughed even harder until Circes silenced him with an icy, sightless stare.

"There is nothing to laugh about," she told us. "There is much that still lies ahead. You will need to focus more now than ever before."

"We know, Circes," I assured her, quickly finishing up my soup so that I could step away from the depressing conversation. "Trust me, we know."

She nodded, placated. I grabbed my trencher and left to scrape my dishes off with Brennan on my heels.

"She's pleasant," he remarked as we took care of our dishes. Handing my bowl to a young girl, I nodded at her and then replied to Brennan.

"Circes means well. She's so old that I think she's lost her tact."

"You think?" He laughed at my obvious statement. "If she were any less tactful, she would be a Mack truck."

The village still sparkled with dew and we strolled through it, enjoying the morning sun. The grass was thick and wet and the air smelled fresh and new. I breathed it in and tilted my face to the sun. As the warmth bathed me in its glow, I found myself comparing Brennan to it. It was impossible not to draw the comparisons. He was a child of the sun, after all.

"I wonder what other powers you hold," I mused, grasping his thick arm tightly as we walked. "What powers you might have that we aren't aware of yet."

Brennan didn't seem concerned. "It's hard to say," he answered. "But I'm sure we'll find out soon enough."

"I'm sure," I answered absently.

I stared at the beauty surrounding us. The magnificence of nature was impossible to ignore here in this serene place. The air was always hushed, as though it was waiting for something. I almost felt as though I should whisper. The sunlight filtered through the limbs of the trees, creating a beautiful glow. It seemed to illuminate everything around us. I turned to Brennan.

"Have you ever actually thought about how different you and I are? You are born from the sun. You are glowingly beautiful. The sun's power is bright and warm, illuminating everything that it touches. I am from the moon. I dwell in the shadows, the darkness. Moonlight provides a buffer for the night, hiding things that are frightening...things like me. We're so different, you and I."

Brennan stopped in his tracks, his eyes pensive and thoughtful as he appraised me.

"Are you serious right now?" he asked. "Truly serious? Because that is the most ridiculous thing I've ever heard." He reached over and grabbed my hand, his voice earnest.

"Empusa, you are the most beautiful creature, inside and out, that I have ever laid eyes on. You *do* glow. Your glow is ethereal because it comes from the moon. So many beautiful things come out at night. There are actually night-blooming flowers that solely bloom in the moonlight. You remind me of those, actually. Do you truly feel that you belong in the night because you should hide?"

I swallowed, trying to swallow the foolish tears that threatened to form at his sweet words. I finally settled for nodding. I just couldn't trust my voice.

He took a long breath and grabbed me, clutching me to his chest. I could hear his heart beat against my ear as he spoke again.

"Emmie, you're the most delicate and beautiful thing in the world. Your soul is pure and sweet. You are not frightening, not in the least. I want you to put that thought out of your mind right now. I love you. I wouldn't love you if you were a monster."

That thought was meant to be comforting, but it wasn't.

"Brennan, you would love me no matter what-because we're connected. My mother still loves my father, who is the most heinous monster in the world. She cannot help it because they are soul mates, like we are. So, you'll have to forgive me if I discount your opinion based on bias. You would love me even if I was just like my father."

One tear broke rank and streamed down my cheek. Brennan wiped it away and kissed the spot where it had been.

"I can tell you with no bias whatsoever, that you are not like your father at all. You are the opposite of your father. You have taken a horrible curse, one that put you in the worst position thinkable, and have managed it in the most humane possible way. He would never have done that. Mormo doesn't care who he harms. I have read that he used to drink the blood of children because it tasted the sweetest. That is a monster, something that you are *not*."

His words buoyed me, lifted me out of my dark thoughts. He was right. I would never kill a child simply because their blood tasted sweet. It was true. My father did indeed do horrific things like that just because he wanted to.

"Thank you," I whispered to him, kissing him lightly on the cheek. "You always know just what to say to me."

"That's my job," he shrugged. "It's in the soul mate handbook."

"Really?" I raised an eyebrow. "I haven't seen that part. In fact, I haven't seen the book at all. Do you have a copy?"

He grinned. "Well, it's not so much a printed book as it is a book that I have stored in my head. But don't worry. I'll fill you in on the wifely duties that will be expected from you after we get married."

My heart immediately began racing and I tried not to allow the idea of marriage terrify me. Because it wasn't marriage that I was afraid of. It was the thought that we might not survive this game so that we could in fact get married. In spite of that, I smiled anyway and tried to keep my thoughts light.

"Really? Such as... I'll have to give you a foot rub every night?"

"Well, that certainly wouldn't hurt," he answered with a laugh. "And a back massage too. But I was thinking of your other wifely duties." He waggled his eyebrows suggestively and my cheeks burst into flame.

"Oh. *Those* duties. Care to elaborate?"

He shook his head. "Nope. I'll fill you in when the time comes."

"Great," I answered wryly and he laughed.

"Don't worry," he told me. "You'll like it."

"I'm sure," I replied dryly.

"I hate to interrupt," Branwyn called from behind us. "But I thought perhaps Empusa would like to come down to the hot springs to bathe with me?"

"Hot springs?" I almost broke my neck, whipping around to look at her. "A bath sounds heavenly."

"I thought you might think that way," she replied with a smile. "Come with me, princess."

I glanced at Brennan. "I hate to abandon you, but I'd really like a hot bath."

He nodded, giving an exaggerated sigh.

"Women," he huffed. I rolled my eyes and kissed him on the cheek before I joined Branwyn. She had her arms full of bathing towels and a small wooden bowl that I assumed held soap. I took some of the things from her and we strolled towards the woods.

"I had no idea there was a hot springs here," I told her conversationally.

"Oh, yes," she nodded. "It does wonders for our skin."

We fell into silence as we walked, but our journey wasn't far. A few minutes later we found ourselves next to a babbling brook, which curved into an inlet encased in rock. Water bubbled up in the inlet from the earth itself, from hot springs below the earth's crust.

I knelt and dipped my fingers in the water. It was the perfect temperature, hot enough to steam. I closed my eyes in pleasure.

"Brennan was right," I told Branwyn. "I don't think there is a woman alive who doesn't enjoy a hot bath."

I glanced up and found Branwyn disrobing on the edge of the water. She stepped out of her saffron shift and it puddled around her feet. My gaze flew to her face in surprise as she turned to me, laughing.

"What? You seem shocked, princess. There are no men here, but for your sun god. I feel certain that he won't venture out here on his own...so we're safe to bathe in peace."

I was still shocked. I couldn't help it. I wasn't a prude, but watching Branwyn step into the water buck-naked without a care in the world was startling, to say the least. Her milky white skin seemed even paler in the bright sunlight and she laughed at my expression.

"Still mortified, princess? Come. Bathe. You'll feel better." Laughing, she splashed onto her back and lifted her face to the sun.

I shrugged. What the hell? It didn't matter much in the large scheme of things.

So, casting off my clothing as well, I stepped into the inlet. The hot water swirled luxuriously around my ankles and I sank into it, relishing the relaxing warmth. Seating myself against a rock wall on the side, I immersed myself up to my chin and leaned my head back, closing my eyes.

I had so missed baths. The bubbling sounds immediately soothed me and I tuned out any other noise... the birds chirping, the wind, the trees. I concentrated solely on the water sounds and it wasn't long before the tension had left my shoulders and my spirits were lifted.

"I have dreamed of you since I was a child, Empusa. It's so strange to have you here now in person."

My eyes popped back open.

"You've dreamed of me?" I asked with interest. "What were the dreams?"

Branwyn paused, washing her arms in the pleasant water, staring thoughtfully at nothing.

"There were all kinds," she said. "Beginning when I was just a child. The strange thing was that I always knew that you were my sister. Your mother was sometimes in my dreams, her presence, her voice. She would tell me how I was so important because someday I would give my life for you."

I sucked in my breath and froze.

"What?"

Branwyn ignored my question, instead choosing to continue bathing her body and telling her story. "Sometimes I almost feel as though my very life is because your mother willed it so, so that I would be here for when you needed me. When I saw you from across the meadow, I knew the time had arrived. I knew that very shortly, I would be given the highest honor...I would die for the goddess. Thank you for giving me the opportunity, moon princess."

I completely froze now, staring at her in horror. "You can't mean that," I said slowly. "Branwyn, you're not going to die for me."

"I'm quite certain that I am," she replied calmly. "And I've had years to come to peace with it. I am honored, princess, truly. When I was a child, it scared me, I will admit. I used to lay awake at night and wonder when it would happen and how. All night long I feared that it would happen on the morrow. But time went by and I emerged each day unscathed. And then when I grew old enough, I came to realize the great honor that had been bestowed upon me. Your mother told me how my life would save yours, how she would forever be in my debt. It is the highest honor."

"How is it the highest honor when you will be dead? I mean, if this is true," I hastened to add. "Because I don't believe it."

She looked at me solemnly. "Why would it not be true, Empusa? I have dreamed of it my entire life. I saw your face years ago when I was but a child. You looked just as you do now. That is no coincidence and it isn't something that I could have conjured out of my imagination. Your mother sent me the visions to prepare me. Serving the goddess is a great honor, Empusa. Giving my life for her... that's the highest honor."

"I can't speak of this any more," I murmured. "I do not wish to think of it. I can't believe it is true. Let us just enjoy our baths."

"Very well, princess. I do not wish to trouble you with unpleasant thoughts. I apologize."

"It's not a trouble, Branwyn," I assured her. "I just don't like to think that your words are true. I don't want you to sacrifice your life for mine. I am no more important than you are."

"That is where you are wrong, princess," she said quietly. "You have a purpose in life that is vastly important. My purpose in life is to help make sure that you attain it."

I fell silent. The air around us was pregnant with meaning, unspoken thoughts, emotions and even my confusion. There was a lot swirling through my head and I wanted time to process it. So instead of speaking further, I simply allowed myself to enjoy the hot water, the breeze brushing the hair off of my face and the birds chirping in the background. After a good twenty minutes, I spoke in a murmur to Branwyn.

"This was a good idea, Branwyn, thank you for bringing me here."

No answer.

"Branwyn?"

I opened my eyes to find her staring at me with wide eyes, her mouth clamped tightly closed.

"Branwyn? What's wrong?" I asked in confusion. Her eyes darted to a spot above my head and I twisted around in my seat to look, the rocks beneath me grinding into my bare legs.

"Hello, Empusa."

Apollo, the god of the sun and Brennan's father, perched on the banks behind me. Blood was smeared on his arms and legs and his face was dirty, but even in spite of that, he was breathtakingly beautiful.

Honey-blonde hair that reflected glints of light, warm hazel eyes, perfectly proportioned features, well-muscled limbs. He was staring at me now and he wasn't smiling. In fact, as that realization dawned on me, a few other things occurred to me as well.

The sun had stopped shining.

I was sitting naked in front of Brennan's father.

Apollo was holding a golden, sharpened dagger in his hands.

This couldn't be good.

Chapter Nine

id you truly wish to become part of my family?" Apollo asked slowly, unfolding himself from his crouch and standing to his full height. "Did you truly think that would happen?"

He twisted the dagger in his hands, turning it over and over as he spoke. The hilt was jeweled, each gem catching the light as it moved. I shifted my gaze to Apollo and stood from the water.

I forced my mind away from the fact that I was as naked as the day I was born and that the water streaming down my body was catching the breeze and causing me to chill. Neither thing was important.

I focused on the dagger in Apollo's hand because *that* was important.

"You know you can't kill me," I pointed out slowly. "That would take Zeus' sword. Your little knife is most certainly *not* Zeus' sword."

Apollo's lips stretched into a beatific smile. The beauty of his face, even though he was threatening me, was literally breathtaking.

"Little Empusa," he said condescendingly. "Of course I know that. But, this little knife will prove to be quite deadly to your friend."

He motioned with the dagger toward Branwyn, who was still completely overwhelmed from being in the presence of a god. She literally shook her head back and forth silently, unable to give voice to words. I struggled to remain calm.

"What purpose would you have in harming Branwyn? She's nothing to me." I fought to keep a poker face, trying to remain impassive as I hoped that my words didn't hurt her. I needed Apollo to believe me.

He smiled again.

"I know that you've tried for many, many years to avoid harming mortals," he smiled encouragingly. "And that is commendable. Because of that, I know that you will choose to do the right thing now."

At just that moment, Branwyn managed to shake off her fear enough to move. She lunged from the water, trying to scramble over the slippery banks of the brook. Before she had managed, it, Apollo smiled in her direction and lifted his free hand. In response, Branwyn flew into the trunk of a nearby weeping willow tree, crashing hard.

The long, spindly limbs of the tree immediately wrapped around her, holding her fast. The vine-like branches quickly covered her entire body so that only her frightened eyes and part of her mouth were showing. Apollo returned his gaze to me.

"And what do you consider the right thing to be?" I asked him calmly.

Goosebumps were starting to form on my naked flesh. I knew that I could conjure clothing in a mere second, but I didn't want to give him the satisfaction of thinking that he affected me or made me self-conscious. For good measure, I jutted my chin out arrogantly as I stood naked before him.

He threw his head back and laughed.

"You're a feisty one," he observed. "No wonder Brennan is taken with you. I can see the attraction."

In a flash, before I could even blink, he was standing behind me. Leaning in, he nuzzled the side of my neck. I held completely still, not breathing, not moving, not even thinking.

"I can certainly see the attraction," he repeated. He smelled like the sun, like Brennan did. He looked enough like Brennan to be his twin brother. But that's where the similarities ended.

Brennan still saw the world through young, fresh eyes. Brennan was able to see the good in everyone. His father looked at life through the jaded eyes of an Olympian who had lived for eons. He was studying me now as though I was something that he could dissect, something without thoughts or feelings. He was completely detached from emotion. It was terrifying.

Apollo cocked his head.

"So you just figured me out, then?"

I met his gaze. "What do you mean?"

"You just came to the conclusion that my emotions left me long ago. I am hardened to the world. It's quite alright, moon princess. I know that. And I prefer it this way. Emotions can sometimes cloud your vision while mine is crystal clear."

He stepped away from me and I took a deep breath.

"And what do you see?" I asked him.

"I see a girl who is letting her emotions run away with her. They are forcing her to make poor choices. She could easily have it all, if she simply makes the right decision."

"And what is that?" I asked. Although, I already had a good idea what he was going to say.

"Leave Brennan to me. Give me your word, sworn in blood, that you will never reunite with him and I will give up my arguments to Zeus that you should be sent to the Underworld or killed. I will stand firmly in your corner which means that nothing will stand in the way of having your curse lifted. All you have to do is leave Brennan alone. Forever."

My heart constricted at the mere words.

"I can't," I breathed. Physical pain assailed me at the very thought. "We can't be apart now. Not now that we've found each other. You don't understand."

"Don't I?" Apollo cocked one perfectly sculpted golden eyebrow. "This was the very reason that Zeus created soul mates. We are distracted in trying to find them and once we do, they are all we think about. We bear no threat to him when we are distracted. You are playing right into his hands, princess."

"I don't care," I told him in agitation. "I don't wish to usurp his throne. That is not a concern that I have. I only wish to have my curse lifted. I want to live in peace with Brennan. That is all I want."

"How sweet," Apollo remarked drily. "I appreciate your loyalty to my son and I'm sure he does as well. But it isn't necessary any longer. I'm here now. I'll take it from here."

"No," I said firmly. "Brennan loves me as much as I love him. Why do you want him so much? You only just found out that he was yours."

"So, you admit that he's mine?" Apollo asked smoothly.

"I admit that he's your son. Clearly there is no denying that. As far as now, no. He is not yours to keep. He is mine and I will fight until my dying breath for him."

Determination filled me up and I stuck my chin out again. Apollo laughed.

"You're like a small wet kitten with your dander up, princess. You are no match for me. Surely you realize that. Just concede now and you'll still get what you want the most: your curse lifted."

I leveled my gaze at him. "You still don't understand. That's not what I want the most anymore. I want to be with Brennan. That will always trump everything."

"And you would sacrifice everything for that?" Apollo was incredulous and then shrugged his shoulders. "That just illustrates my point, my dear, of how emotions cloud judgment."

"My emotions enhance my judgment at times," I told him. "Feeling strong emotions increases my determination and drive."

Apollo nodded thoughtfully.

"Good point. I will give you that. But that doesn't negate the fact that emotions will always cloud your judgment in the end and prevent you from making a rational choice. You cannot argue that, princess."

"I wouldn't dream of it," I answered. "But who says that rational is the best option?"

Apollo shook his head, a slight smile on his lips.

"You speak in circles," he said. "And I grow tired of it. There is no way you can win the game, do you realize that? You are growing weaker by the moment. It is apparent."

I swallowed, because he was right. Everything within me grew weaker, my heart, my soul, my spirit. I needed a soul to feed me. I'd already known that for days now.

Even as I clenched my fists in frustration, I could feel my fingers shaking. My weakness would soon overtake me if I didn't feed. And there was no way I could face-off against Apollo in this condition.

"And therein lies the problem, doesn't it?" Apollo observed politely, as he read my mind. "You must either feed on one of these healthy priestesses, these women who have taken you under their care and trusted you, or you will die. If you don't feed your curse, you will not live to finish the game. You'll never have a life with my son. What a quandary."

I gulped in air, trying to force it into my lungs so that I didn't hyperventilate. He was impassive and calm because it didn't affect him. But me... but me.... *but me.*

Even my thoughts were stuttering and my shoulders slumped limply. It affected me. I had never in my entire existence fed on a healthy mortal, not even one time. It would break a stead-fast, iron-clad rule that I had made for myself. If I crossed that thin silvery line, it would turn me into the monster that I tried so hard not to be.

Apollo read my thoughts, a crease forming across his forehead.

"You do surprise me, Empusa," he mused. "You have a surprisingly pure soul. It truly is no wonder why my son is drawn to you. Not that it matters."

He smiled again, matter-of-factly. "You have a decision to make here today."

It seemed that the wind stilled and even more clouds billowed over our heads. My fingers went numb and my heart slowed as I listened to the melodic sound of his voice. A decision. I knew I wouldn't like it.

"No, you won't," Apollo confirmed. "This is your decision. It is yours to make. You can choose how your sister dies. I can kill her. Or you can."

I gasped as what little strength I had left abandoned me and my knees went weak.

"For what purpose?" I demanded breathlessly, shock rendering me almost speechless. "Why would you kill her?"

"I don't need any other purpose other than wanting to force your hand," Apollo said calmly. He was so detached, so emotionless. I never wanted to become like that. He smiled a little at my thought and leaned toward me.

"No, you wouldn't want to be like me," he agreed. "You are too soft inside. Now what is your choice? Shall I kill her or will you?"

My stomach clenched tightly and I looked at Branwyn. Her green eyes were calm now and she held still, no longer fighting her restraints. Apollo was blocking her thoughts from me, but I could see them in her eyes.

She believed that this was her fate, that she was meant to die for me. I could see it in the tranquility that I found on her face. I gulped. Was she right?

Had my mother truly allowed Branwyn's birth simply so she could serve me in death? It was an unthinkable thought, yet I had it. It was there, hanging in the front of my mind, and I was unable to ignore it.

Because it was true.

The knowledge welled up in me. Whether it was fair or not, it was a truth. Branwyn's entire life had been arranged to serve me in this moment. I didn't know why, but sometimes that's how life worked. The why was forgotten or never understood at all.

Branwyn stood still and strong, her eyes calm and accepting. She was willing. She knew that without a soul, I would die.

And I knew in that instant that she would have offered hers to me even if she was not bound against the tree. If I hadn't been put into this situation, I probably wouldn't have taken it...which was probably why this situation had come about. As Apollo had said, to force my hand. He thought he was calling the shots, making me do something I didn't wish to do. But my mother had foreseen this long ago and had arranged for a plan to save my life.

The breadth of my mother's vision was astounding.

Gratitude and sadness welled up in me at the same time as I walked numbly to Branywn. I could feel Apollo watching me, could feel his amber eyes boring into my back, but I didn't care.

This moment was all that was important. This moment when I would end my sister's life to save my own. I had a purpose. I didn't know what it was yet, but Branwyn must die for me to achieve it. This was *her* purpose.

Pulling the limbs away from Branwyn's face, I murmured to her.

"This won't hurt. I promise you that. I don't want to give Apollo the satisfaction of killing you. Your soul will nourish mine and perhaps I'll live to fulfill whatever purpose there is for me. My mother will provide for you in the Underworld. You will dwell in the Isles of the Blessed. It is the most beautiful place in the world. You'll be happy there. I promise."

Branwyn nodded, her eyes clear and tranquil. "Thank you, princess," she whispered. "I look forward to it."

Pain gripped my chest, wrapping my heart in cold fingers. "This won't hurt," I promised again. "Forgive me, Branwyn."

She nodded wordlessly. Being so near to her in this state caused her aura to appear to me in an explosion of yellows, golds and reds. Her spirit was strong and true and my mouth watered with the need to take it. I was so weakened at this point that I couldn't fight the urge for long. My chest shuddered with the restraint that I was already showing.

Branwyn's purity surrounded us in the air, her strength wrapping around us like a ribbon, tying us tightly together. Loyalty, one of the strongest attributes in existence, flowed through her veins. It was in her blood, in her heart, in every thought that she had.

Bending ever closer, I whispered, "Thank you, Branwyn. Your sacrifice will not go unnoticed."

With one short breath, I started the process. Her lips touched mine and her spirit flowed into my mouth, down my throat and filled me up.

She tasted as beautiful as her spirit actually was. Warm, strong, loyal, proud. Her attributes joined with mine, making me stronger even as her mortal body grew weaker and limp. I continued breathing her in, closing my eyes, until it was finally over.

I opened my eyes and Branwyn was gone, her green eyes staring lifelessly at me. Stepping back, I closed her eyelids gently and then turned to Apollo.

"It is done," I told him.   "You can't have her now."

"Foolish girl," he told me. "I never wanted her. This   was   a   challenge.   And   much   to   my disappointment, you have passed it."

Chapter Ten

challenge?" I repeated shakily. "A challenge?"
My voice rose an octave. I couldn't help it. "My
sister was murdered for a *challenge*?"

Apollo stared at me in amusement. "If she was
murdered, then you are the murderer, darling. Think
on that for a moment."

Red hot anger boiled up in me, so quickly that I
lost control for a moment.

The anger exploded through me and ripped the
weeping willow tree that Branwyn was still attached
to apart. The roots erupted from the ground and the
limbs flew off, landing erratically around us. When
the dust settled, it looked like lightning had struck the
tree trunk. And Branwyn was now lying limply at
my feet in a heap. I didn't look at her. I focused
instead on Apollo and on controlling my emotions.

"I realize that," I said calmly, gripping my fists
at my sides. "You placed me in that position."

"Details," Apollo shrugged. "You made the choice. No one forced you. But you should be happy. You have passed this challenge. You were able to overcome your soft emotions and act as a true goddess. A true goddess must be calculating when need be and not focused on her heart."

"Why do you not sound more upset?" I asked suspiciously. "I just passed a challenge, which means that we have another point and you do not. Shouldn't you be upset by that?"

My foot bumped Branwyn's lifeless body and I cringed, yanking it back. I couldn't help myself and glanced down. Branwyn stared up at me, her sightless eyes fixated on my face. Her back was twisted unnaturally. I gulped.

"What is going on here?"

Brennan's voice thundered from across the creek. My head snapped back and I whirled to face him.

"Brennan. It's fine. Go back to the village. I'm okay here."

Brennan stood on the edge of the water, his face both confused and determined. I saw a muscle tighten in his jaw as he examined the situation. He glanced at his father.

"Apollo, I presume?" Brennan sounded confident and secure, but I could feel his emotions. He was unsettled, nervous. He looked back to me.

"Empusa, this might be an obvious question, but why are you naked?"

The muscle in his jaw clenched tighter and if the situation had been less serious, I would have laughed at his expression.

"Trust me, you have nothing to worry about," I assured him drily. "Please, Brennan. Just go back. I've got it handled here."

In an instant, before I could breathe or move, he stood next to me. Quickly, he knelt and felt for a pulse at Branwyn's neck. Looking up at me in concern, he stood once more.

"Yes, I can see that," he answered. "Completely handled."

"It's not what you think," I started shakily. "This was a challenge. I passed."

"You look infinitely better," Brennan observed. "Branwyn?"

I knew what he was asking...if I had fed on Branwyn to regain my strength. I nodded wordlessly.

"I'm glad you're here, son," Apollo said conversationally.

Apollo stepped forward so that we formed our own little circle. It was too intimate to remain naked, so I quickly imagined myself wearing clothing. Instantly, it was so. I was dressed in a knee-length gray shift, belted loosely at the waist with a black leather cord. Neither man noticed. There were each too focused on each other.

"Don't call me son," Brennan instructed politely but firmly. "I do not know you. And from what I've heard about you recently, I'm not sure that I *want* to know you."

"Oh, Brennan," Apollo replied breezily, seemingly unfazed by his son's statement. "You don't truly know what you want. You're still mortal."

"Again, from what I've seen lately, being mortal is starting to seem like a good thing." Brennan's eyes flickered to Branwyn's body as he spoke and I fought a wave of nausea.

I had killed her. It was unavoidable. I had taken her life. And Brennan was right. If I had been mortal, it never would have been necessary.

"You do not know what you speak of," Apollo answered pleasantly. "Eventually you will learn that all that you currently believe is flawed. Once you are immortal, nothing will seem the same. Trust me."

"Trust you?" Brennan answered incredulously. "Trust you. That's funny. I don't even know you. But I know that somehow you forced Em into a corner here today. She never would have taken Branwyn's life on her own. I know that you want to send Empusa to the Underworld or even worse, you'd like her dead. And for what? Just so that you can control my abilities. Did it ever occur to you that I won't be controlled?"

Brennan was adamant, firm and very, very confident. He stood proud and tall, the wind rustling through his honey-colored hair. I had never felt so proud of him and I took his arm. He was afraid, but fear is what makes bravery possible. In overcoming the fear, you make yourself stronger.

"You certainly are my son," Apollo replied smoothly. "You think just as I do. I would never allow anyone to control me, either, if I could possibly avoid it. You and I are a great deal alike, Brennan."

"I doubt that I am much like you. If you knew me at all, you would have known that you had a greater chance of winning me to your side if you just come to me and explained your position. Trying to strong arm me by threatening the woman that I love... all that did was turn me away from you," Brennan spit angrily. "Go back to Olympus. I don't want anything from you. Empusa just scored a point for us. I daresay that we will win here and this entire conversation will be moot."

Apollo threw his head back and laughed.

"Oh, Brennan. You still have mortal thoughts and naivety. It is amusing, but you will not win. And even if you do, you'll have had to gain that victory by doing unthinkable things... as Empusa has just proven. In the unlikely event that you do actually win, I guarantee that you will wish you had not. You aren't like the gods. Your guilt will weigh you down. You will wish you had never met Empusa at all."

"Never," Brennan answered angrily. "That will never happen. Return to Olympus, Apollo. Tell them that we are ready for whatever they want to throw at us."

"I do like your spirit, son," Apollo chuckled. "But you should learn to never poke at the gods. You won't enjoy it when we poke back."

With that, Apollo disappeared, although we could still hear his laughter for a moment after he left. I stood quietly, facing Brennan while I avoided looking at Branwyn.

"Are you okay?" Brennan asked quietly. I tried to form an answer, but found that I couldn't, not without breaking down. Instead, I shook my head as tears ran down my cheeks. I felt weak, but I couldn't help it. What I had just done was suddenly crashing down around me and it was all I could see.

"Come here," he said quickly, grabbing my hand and pulling me to him. I buried my face against his chest, trying to block out Branwyn.

"You don't understand," I sobbed. "I've taken souls hundreds of times. But this was different. She was alive and vital and healthy. And worse, she would have just given it to me. I think that's what she expected. She thought she was born to die for me. And I think she was right...which makes it even worse."

I cried harder and Brennan stroked my back with strong hands, silently allowing me to cry all of my anguish out. It took awhile, but finally my sobs died off to sniffles and then tapered off completely. Stepping away from him, I wiped at my eyes and smoothed my hair.

"I'm sorry," I told him. "I didn't mean to fall apart on you. I have no right to be upset. Someone just sacrificed her life for me. If anyone should be upset, it should be Branwyn- wherever she is at right now. You must be growing so weary of hearing me cry about my wretched curse."

Brennan smiled at me, a comforting and familiar sight. "Em, I'm here for you- no matter what you want to do with me. If you need to cry on me, so be it. You're so strong that if you want to use my shoulder for that purpose, it's almost an honor that you would trust me so much."

I smiled weakly at him. "You always know what to say."

He shrugged. "I try. Just remember that the next time I say something stupid. Em, whatever happened here today was not your fault. I hope you realize that. You've lived your life the best possible way that you could. Please don't cry. You're amazing. We'll get this sorted out."

He was so confident, so sure that I almost believed him. I knew that at the very least, we would give it everything we had. And that was all we could do.

"Thank you," I murmured, standing up on my tip-toes to kiss his chiseled cheek. "I'm very blessed to have you."

"I'll remind you of that the next time I tick you off," he said with a grin. He sobered up quickly though as he stared at the woman at our feet. "We should take Branwyn back to the village. We'll need to bury her."

I nodded. "I believe they build funeral pyres here. I don't know what to tell them. I have no idea how much she told them... whether she shared her belief that she would die for me, whether she kept that to herself...." My voice trailed off and Brennan wrapped an arm around my shoulders and pulled me to him, kissing my forehead.

"It will be fine," he promised quietly. "We'll just take their lead and roll with it."

I nodded and he stepped away. Kneeling, he gently gathered Branwyn into his arms. I picked up her arms and crossed them over her chest as Brennan cradled her to his. Slowly, we made our way back into the village, stepping carefully through the brambles until we made it back to the trail.

No one said a word as we walked through the village. Each woman stopped what she was doing and stared with wide eyes as Brennan and I walked quietly through the center of the village and toward our hut. It was truly Branwyn's hut and so it just seemed to be the place where we should take her. After one priestess collapsed into tears at the mere sight of us, I focused my attention on Branwyn's dangling legs. Staring at her bare foot, I avoided the gazes of anyone watching us.

Entering our hut, Brennan carried Branwyn straight to our bed. He laid her down gently and I arranged her dress.

"Thank you," I murmured to him. He stood to the side and I found Branwyn's comb. As gently as I could, I ran it through her long, red locks. Her skin was even paler in death and she seemed as white as snow.

The door to the hut opened and without even looking, I knew who it was. The air itself changed as the old witch entered.

"We won another challenge," I told Circes.

"I know, child," she answered. Crossing the room to stand at my side, she laid dried herbs around Branwyn, forming a protective circle. I was silently appreciative. Branwyn would have liked that. The druids felt that circles were sacred.

"You knew, didn't you?" I asked, not looking at her face. "You knew that I would kill her."

"Yes."

There was no apology, no explanation. I glanced at her and found her cloudy eyes fixed on me, waiting for my reaction. I decided not to give her one and instead returned my attention to readying Branwyn for burial. Circes handed me a bowl of water and I sponged off Branwyn's arms and face.

"She didn't deserve this," I said, to no one in particular.

"No, she didn't," Brennan agreed.

Circes said nothing... because there wasn't anything else to say.

"I told you that you must be on your guard," Circes creaked a few moments later as she held Branwyn's arm up for me to wash beneath it. "I warned you, Empusa. As you can see now, I was right. Never let your guard down."

"Lesson learned," I said calmly. "Do you know what the next challenge will be?"

Circes shook her ancient head. "No. I know not whether it will be announced or if it will be unexpected again."

"I'm not that fond of surprises," I said off-handedly. Not that it mattered. I knew that Zeus was going to do whatever he felt like doing. My opinion certainly wouldn't be considered.

Chapter Eleven

Branwyn burned on a pyre that lit up the night. My half-sister lay in the middle of a sacred circle in the center of the stone altar. The priestesses murmured prayers and chants to my mother as they offered Branwyn's soul to the gods. What they didn't know was that Branwyn's soul had already been taken...by me.

We had spent the day solemnly, in silent reverence, as each priestess had come to pay their respects to Branwyn.

Each one offered her something, a trinket, a ring, a smattering of herbs. Each one had cried, each one had hugged her, each one had grieved. I had sat stoically, trying not to reveal my own sadness and despair at what I had done. But with each minute that had passed, my guilt grew.

"Are you alright?" Brennan whispered as he grasped my hand. I knew he could feel my pain, my grief. His fingers were warm and strong. For a moment, they reached the icy depths of my heart, but then fell away. I didn't want to be reached.

"I'm fine," I answered, keeping my eyes on the altar. I wasn't fine. But there wasn't anything Brennan could do to fix it.

As what was left of Branwyn continued to burn, I watched the dark tendrils of smoke curl towards the heavens.

Idly, I wondered where her soul was now. If nothing else, her death just spurred me even more to win this game. Once my curse was reversed, Zeus would release all of the souls that I had ever consumed...from wherever they were being held.

The breeze was cold and it carried with it the scent of burning flesh. Both things combined made me shiver. Brennan wrapped his arm around my shoulders and drew me to his side. I tried to absorb his warmth, to draw strength from his, to ignore the reality that was in front of us lying on the stone.

A pale priestess that was kneeling next to the altar uncurled from her crouch to face me.

"Princess, Branwyn left a bundle for you. She instructed me to give it to you after she was gone."

The woman's face was calm and impassive, as though she didn't know that I was the reason that

Branwyn was dead. They all acted that way, calm and quiet, and completely oblivious to the fact that I had killed their leader. But they knew. I knew that they did. It was in their eyes.

"What is it?" I asked. "What did she leave?" I asked. I was tired, cold and emotionally drained. But this definitely piqued my curiosity.

The woman shrugged. "I do not know. I was instructed not to open it. It is only for you. I also need to reassure you that even though Branwyn is gone, you still have the complete cooperation and hospitality of this entire group. We are at your disposal, princess."

"Thank you," I murmured.

I didn't deserve it and their loyalty choked me up. It wasn't for me, though. It was for my mother. And once again, I was thankful to have her. I'd been blessed in the maternal department. She more than made up for the fact that my father was a psychopath.

One by one, the women filed past Branwyn and within the hour, everyone had finished paying their respects and saying goodbye. Her pyre would burn into the night and throughout the day tomorrow, but weren't going to stay and watch it tonight. I was so physically tired that I felt I might collapse.

The priestesses made their way back into the village while Brennan and I trailed behind them. The moon hung heavy and full in the sky and I lifted my face to it, soaking in its energy. Being a creature of the moon, its rays provided me with strength and I needed all of that I could get these days.

As the women broke apart to return to their individual huts, the one who had spoken to me about Branwyn's package turned back to me.

"Come with me," she instructed quietly.

I glanced at Brennan and then followed her into the trees where the darkness enveloped us like a cloak. The temperature had dropped so much by this point that I could see my breath in the air. I cupped my hands over my mouth and blew on them as we walked further into the forest on the other side of the village.

"Where are we going?" I called to her. "And I'm sorry. I didn't catch your name."

"It's Keelin," she answered over her shoulder. "Just follow me. And don't shout. It attracts the spirits. Samhain is drawing near. The spirits will be gathering."

In spite of myself, goosebumps formed along my arms at her words and I glanced at Brennan. He rolled his eyes and I felt a flash of annoyance. How could he dismiss her statement so easily? He'd seen firsthand lately that reality wasn't what he once thought it was. Many, many things were possible. Ghosts were real. I'd seen them myself all of my life.

"You're right," he apologized to me, having read my thoughts. "I'm sorry. I'm still getting used to all of this."

"I know," I answered. "And it's a lot to get used to. You're doing a fantastic job. Really."

He reached up and grabbed my hand. "Anything for you," he reassured me, jokingly. But I knew that he was serious and his words warmed me more than the sun ever could.

Keelin abruptly stopped in front of us and knelt in front of a massive and imposing oak tree. Its roots bubbled to the surface of the ground, gnarled and twisted. I stepped over them and stood behind Keelin, waiting.

She reached into a small hollow in the tree and withdrew a package, wrapped in cloth and tied with string. Rising from the gound, she turned and offered it to me with shaking hands.

I could swear that the wind died down when my fingers touched it and that realization raised the hair on the back of my neck.

"What is this?" I whispered. My fingertips were cold where they touched the cloth.

"I know not," Keelin answered. But her face was pale and drawn. She might not know, but like me, she sensed the importance and the darkness that the packaged contained.

"I don't like this, Em," Brennan said quickly, stepping forward and laying his hand on my arm. "Just put it back. We don't need it."

"It won't matter if you put it back or no," Circes voice penetrated the small clearing.

I turned to find her creeping toward us, her cloaks swirling around her with an unseen wind.

"It will not matter. That package contains knowledge and the knowledge exists whether you read it or not. A wise person would want to know what they are up against."

Within a second, she was at my side, her yellowed teeth flashing in the dark as she spoke.

"Open it, Empusa," she instructed with fetid breath. "This is something that you need to know."

My fingers trembled and I ached to drop the package and run. It felt icy cold and ominous in my hands and I desperate wanted to release my hold on it, to drop it to the ground and stomp on it. But I resisted the urge and turned toward the old woman instead.

"You know what it is?" I half-asked and half-demanded.

She nodded.

"Your mother left it for Branwyn for safe-keeping, until it was time to give to you. She felt you should know."

"Know what?"

"You should know why you shouldn't sacrifice everything to save Apollo's son. He is doomed anyway."

My heart, already cold in my chest, froze into a block of ice as my fingers ripped apart the strings that bound the package. The cloth fell away and revealed a rolled parchment. With trepidation mounting in my stomach, I unrolled it and held my breath as I read.

As I read the last word, the parchments slid from my fingers and fell to the ground. I couldn't speak, couldn't breathe.

"Em?" Brennan asked, alarmed. I could only shake my head, my eyes wide.

He snatched up the papers and read through the words quickly. I watched his face and I knew the moment when he read the most relevant words. He went completely still and his beautiful golden eyes met mine.

"So, it doesn't matter what we do. I'm going to die anyway."

Chapter Twelve

I refused to move from that very spot until Circes started talking and explained the words that had just been seared into my heart. Her voice, solemn and ancient, did nothing to allay my fears.

"Your mother saw this long ago," Circes explained to me, her voice low. Brennan gripped my hand tightly while the old woman spoke.

"Your mother helped Hades and the Fates imprison the gods in an effort to protect you. They promised that if she did as they asked, you would be released your father's curse. As you know, that is not how things worked out. Your mother has seen that Zeus will soon decide that he is annoyed, very annoyed, with the behavior of the mortals during the two millennia that he and the Olympians were imprisoned. The mortals forgot about the gods and that is not wise. He will lean toward eliminating them completely because he is tired of their ungratefulways."

"But my mother wrote that Brennan will offer his life in exchange for the mortal world. That if he offers his life to save them, Zeus will forgive the mortals for their indifference to the absence of the gods."

Circes nodded.

"Hecate saw this long ago. Zeus himself doesn't even realize that he will consider this as an option. Brennan must make the suggestion... he must offer himself in lieu of the mortal world. Zeus will find the gesture graceful and worthy."

"But why Brennan?" I persisted. "Why is Brennan the one that must die? Did my mother actually foresee this happening or is this wishful thinking on her part? I worry that this is a trick- that she is simply trying to eliminate him as a problem. If I don't fight to stay with Brennan, then my issues here with Apollo are over. The game would be over."

"You cannot see it?" Circes asked me, her cloudy eyes fixed upon with laser precision. "Zeus will find the gesture fitting because it is so appropriate. Your mother conspired with the Fates to imprison him in order to save you. She chose your well-being over that of his. Zeus will find it a just punishment that your very well-being will be decimated with the death of your soul mate. If Brennan dies, it is likely that you will never recover. And Zeus will feel that in that way, justice will be served."

My heart seemed to slow to such a pace that I could feel each individual beat thrumming one by one in my ribcage. I couldn't breathe. I couldn't speak. I couldn't think. I stood numbly staring at the ancient witch in front of me.

"What is the purpose of this game, then?" Brennan asked in frustration. "Why have we been asked to participate in this evil, twisted game if we can't win anyway?"

Circes rocked on her heels, appraising him. "It is because, young boy, Zeus has not come to this decision yet. Hecate foresaw it long prior to the thought even passing through Zeus' mind. It will happen. It just hasn't happened yet. Hecate wants you to have this knowledge now, so that you can stop this game. You have the ability to appear in front of Zeus and make this offer. You will prevent the destruction of the entire mortal world. And you will save Empusa's life. The choice is yours."

"And what a choice it is," Brennan murmured. He still held my hand, tightly enclosed within his.

"Why did my mother not tell us this herself? Why did she leave it on a scroll with Branwyn?" I demanded. "That makes no sense."

"It makes perfect sense, princess," Circes argued. "Your mother knew that it was not something you would wish to hear. She knew, however, that after you saw the brutality of this game, you would see for yourself the lengths that Zeus will go if he so chooses. He *will* end the mortal world. He will not hesitate. He has no human compassion, princess. You have seen that for yourself."

"I know that is true," I told her, resignation bowing my shoulders like a heavy, heavy weight. "I've never denied it or doubted it. Zeus has lived a very long time, always looking over his shoulder to make sure he is not overthrown. That has to do something to a person, even a god such as Zeus. But I am not allowing Brennan to do this. I will not sacrifice Brennan for the mortal world. I'm sorry. That's just something that I cannot do."

Circes, Keelin and Brennan all stared at me. Circes in consernation, Brennan thoughtfully and Keelin in absolute horror. As a mortal, I'm sure my words struck both terror and anger in Keelin. But none of it mattered. The only thing I could think of was the vast sense of loss that was already welling up in me at the mere thought of losing Brennan. It was suffocating and I suddenly felt like I couldn't breathe.

Spinning, I ran as fast I could, blurring into immortal speed. I didn't know where I was going... all I knew was that it needed to be far, far from here.

The scenery around me, the trees, the sky, the waving grasses, all blended together into one big swirl of color. The cold wind washed over me as I ran and it was only then, as I left everything else behind me, that I could take a deep breath. I could smell the heather in the air, I could taste my fear in my mouth, I could feel the despair in my chest. Everything culminated in one big overwhelming feeling.

And then I was tackled from behind.

Before I could even see Brennan, before I could focus my eyes on his face, I could smell him. He brought the smell of sunshine with him wherever he went and I would know the scent anywhere.

"You can't run from this," he told me as he held me gently to the ground. "I know you want to. I know you want to hide and hope that if you do, it will go away. But it's not going to happen. This is something that I need to face."

The ground was wet beneath me, small stones poking into my back. I stopped squirming and lay still, staring up at the man that I loved. At one point, seemingly forever ago, I had thought he was a boy. His mortal age was eighteen, his body was eighteen. But his soul... his soul was a thousand. Ageless. Timeless. Beautiful.

I reached up and stroked his cheek and my eyes instantly teared up, blurring my vision. I brushed the tears away impatiently. Brennan grasped my hand gently.

"It okay to cry," he told me. "It doesn't make you weak."

"Doesn't it?" I asked with a sigh.

"No," he answered firmly. "It does not. Em, we're going to have to talk about this. You know what I have to do."

"No," I answered tiredly. "You do not have to do anything. I won't allow it, Brennan. I mean it. You will not be sacrificed to pacify Zeus for something my mother did. I just need to think on this. I'll figure something else out. I just need to think."

I knew I was babbling, I wasn't making any sense. But Brennan could feel what I was thinking, he could feel the emotions that pulsed through my heart. His face was pained and I realized that for the first time, I couldn't read his mind. He had accomplished a new skill.

"You're blocking your thoughts from me," I pointed out in astonishment. "Of all the times to learn a new trick, you choose that particular trick at this particular moment? Right when I need to know what you're thinking?"

He smiled, a beautiful grin that took the air right out of my lungs.

"Yes. Aren't you pleased? You wanted me to master more of my abilities."

I glared at him.

"No," I grumbled. "No, I'm not pleased."

He grinned again and jumped to his feet. Reaching down, he offered me his hand. I took it, placing my cool fingers inside his warm, strong grip.

"Brennan, what are we going to do?" I whispered. "For the first time in my life, things aren't clear to me. I don't know what to do."

"And for the first time in mine, things are perfectly clear," he told me, his amber gaze focused on me.

"No," I answered firmly.

"Yes," he replied, just as firm. "It's not a question, Empusa. If Zeus wants me and it will save you and the *entire mortal world*, then Zeus can have me. I just need to decide how to go about it."

"Brennan…"

He held up a hand. "Empusa, please. It will be hard enough just walking away from you. I don't know if I can do it if you are begging me to stay. Please. I love you. You know that. Don't make it harder for me."

I gulped. A hard knot had formed in my throat and I was having a terrible time trying to swallow it, to breathe around it.

"Brennan," I whispered. Just saying his name pained me.

"We have to decide how to stop the game," Brennan said calmly. I knew he was trying to ignore my distress so that it didn't do him in.

"The game is going on even as we speak," I reminded him. "There is a chance that it will finish out- that all of those mortals in Zeus' gauntlet will die. Just know that right now. You don't understand. This is entertainment for the gods. They will be ill-inclined to stop it."

"I understand," Brennan answered evenly. "Perhaps more than you think. If we provide them even more entertainment, perhaps they will be inclined to cooperate."

I raised an eyebrow. "Meaning?"

"Meaning, if we drop into the very arena that they are sitting around, if we explain our intentions—

my intentions- right there on the playing field, perhaps they will comply. Perhaps they would rather see me die alone than continue with the gauntlet. It's just shifting their focus, that's all."

"Yes. Shifting their focus to watching you die," I said sadly.

I couldn't even think about it without my heart constricting painfully in my chest. In my head, a vision of Brennan dying in the middle of an arena on Olympus while the Olympians all watched with their strange silver eyes flitted through and I squeezed my own eyes closed. I couldn't believe we were even talking about this, much less considering it a real option.

"Brennan, there has to be another way. There has to be."

"I don't think there is," he said quietly. "And I can't take the risk of waiting too long before I act. I need to take a little walk and clear my head. I've got to think of how to do this."

"Do you want me to come?" But even as I asked, I knew the answer. He wanted to be alone. And sure enough, he shook his head.

"Not this time," he answered, picking up my hand and kissing it with his perfect lips. "I need to focus."

I nodded silently as he kissed my forehead and then watched quietly as he turned around and walked quietly into the night. I felt like he took my heart with him. I bowed my head and cried.

Chapter Thirteen

I felt his presence a scant moment before his voice, as smooth and soft as silk, drifted toward me from the shadows and enveloped me like a blanket.

"Empusa, no man should ever make you cry."

Hades.

His very presence was tangible and my head snapped up to look for him.

Hades possessed a magnetic pull, an innate ability to draw anyone, men and women alike, to him. The longer I was in his presence, the more the strange attraction built in my belly and even though I knew it wasn't real, it was difficult to resist.

As my eyes flitted along the perimeter of shadows, I found him. He was standing just on the edge, half in the moonlight, half in the shadows. As always, his beauty was staggering.

Hades was a dark presence, both physically and emotionally. He carried an air of danger with him, a feeling that lingered in the air around him.

His glossy dark hair curled slightly at his shoulders. His eyes, as black as onyx, glistened in the night. He wore a crisp white shirt with flowing French cuffs, open at the wrist and casually unbuttoned at the collar. His black cape fluttered in the wind and his black leather pants fit him perfectly.

I gulped.

His delicious scent wafted to me on the breeze and without meaning to, I closed my eyes to inhale it. Before I re-opened them, Hades was standing behind me, his hands on my shoulders as he murmured into my ear.

"Why has he left you alone, Empusa? At a time such as this, when you are feeling so very alone and vulnerable, he shouldn't have left you."

I wanted to step away from him. I truly did. The fact that he could reach into my mind and my heart and see what I was feeling was alarming and dangerous. But it was difficult to move. His voice was tying me to him like a ribbon of steel and it grew stronger by the second.

Gathering my most inner reserves of strength, I gritted my teeth and yanked away. Whirling, I faced him from three feet away. For good measure, I took one more step backward. He smiled. He was well aware of the effect that he had on me.

"Why are you here, Hades?" I asked tiredly. I really wasn't in the mood for this. He looked surprised and I had to give him credit for appearing genuine.

"I'm here because I'm concerned for you, of course," he answered. "If you continue on your current path, things will grow very dangerous for you, very quickly."

"And you care because...?"

I knew I was being sarcastic and unfriendly. But I was dealing with the god of the underworld. He always had an ulterior motive and I wasn't in the mood to try and figure out what it was this time.

"Honestly? I care because it's in my best interest to ensure that you win."

And that honestly surprised me.

"What do you mean?" I asked suspiciously. "Are you still under the assumption that if I win, Brennan and I will cause an apocalypse and all the mortal souls will come knocking on your door? That might have been the case, but no longer. I'm sure you are aware of the new developments. You've probably been lurking around here and saw for yourself."

Again, he looked genuinely surprised. "What new developments?"

"You honestly don't know? I find that hard to believe."

"Believe it," Hades answered patiently, his gleaming teeth white in the night. "Please fill me in."

I took a few minutes and explained my mother's visions to Hades and included the part where Brennan thought he should offer himself to Zeus in exchange for my life and that of the entire mortal world. When I was finished, Hades looked flabbergasted.

"Apollo's son would sacrifice himself in such a way?" he asked in surprise. "He doesn't take after his father, that is for certain. Apollo doesn't have the depth for an act such as that."

"I think you are formed more by who raised you than by your genes," I said absently. "Clearly, it is so in Brennan's case. His mortal parents are good people."

"I know," Hades replied. "His mother dwells in the Underworld now. She passed on years ago. I know her personally. She has pure energy."

"You know his mother?" I exclaimed. "You should tell Brennan. He would be happy to hear any news of her."

"I care not, Empusa," Hades said quietly. "You mistake me for having a soft-heart. You know that is not true. Brennan will see her for himself in the near future, I am certain, one way or another."

"No. Not if I have anything to say about it," I answered angrily. "Brennan owes the mortal world nothing. If I can help it, he will not sacrifice himself. It likely will not appease Zeus anyway. He will find entertainment in it, then he will demolish the mortal world anyway. He will certainly carry out this foolish game."

"It is true that my brother has grown hardened throughout the years," Hades acknowledged. "In fairness, it is hard not to become that way. Time turns us calloused, I fear."

"Are you defending your brother?" I asked. "Because that is not like you."

"No. I'm not defending him. I would never do that. I am simply pointing out something that you already know. A thousand years ago, you would have been railing against Zeus and the unfairness with which he handles the mortal world. You would have been anguished over the fates of the poor mortals. But here you are. Not one tear shed, except over *your* precious mortal. Time turns us calloused."

"Time is nothing!" I snapped. "Zeus will not touch one precious hair on *my* mortal's head."

"What would you give to make sure of that?" Hades asked solemnly. "What would you do for him, Empusa? What would you sacrifice?"

I backed up one more step and studied Hades' face. He was very serious, his dark eyes fixed on me.

"What are you asking me to give?" I asked stiltedly. "I think that is the question here."

"You've always been an astute child," Hades observed. "So smart, so impetuous. How will your impetuous nature serve me now, I wonder?"

In a flash, he blurred into motion and was standing behind me once again.

With one slender, graceful hand, Hades grasped the back of my hair and bent my head back. Lowering his face, he ran his nose along the length of my neck inhaling me like a hungry man who hadn't eaten in a thousand years. His chest was rock hard beneath my hand and as I gathered my wits, I pushed against it.

"Get. Away. From. Me!" I managed to rasp. Wrenching away, I stood with a heaving chest, facing him once again. "What the hell was that?"

"My apologies," Hades said quietly. "You just seem so fragile. And I have a weakness for beautiful, vulnerable women...I have a penchant for trying to save them, I suppose. Please accept my apology."

He was completely unbothered, not a hair out of place. I, on the other hand, felt like I had come undone. My breathing was ragged, my hair was disheveled, and my heart was racing. I didn't want to acknowledge the fact that Hades had a weird pull on me. I loved Brennan. My heart knew that. But my body- it was under Hades' spell and I hated that.

"Please control yourself," I told him irately.

"I would tell you the same," he said with a grin, "But we both know how well *that* works."

"Only around you," I snapped. "I never have control issues otherwise. Now tell me, what were you saying before you so rudely accosted me?"

He templed his fingers and stared thoughtfully at me around them. "I was asking you what you would be willing to do to save Apollo's son?"

I returned his gaze unflinchingly. "I would do anything."

"Anything?" Hades raised one dark eyebrow.

I shuddered at the thought of what "anything" might mean to him. But I answered clearly. "Anything."

I had visions of becoming an enslaved bride to Hades, of living in the same house with he and his wife. So his next words truly surprised me.

"So you will help me with Brennan, then?"

"Help you do what with Brennan?" I asked. "I will never allow you to harm him."

"I don't want to harm him," Hades answered, impatience showing for the first time. "I just want to restrain him so that he cannot turn himself over to Zeus. If he can't get to Olympus, he can't surrender."

"You're not taking him to the Underworld," I snapped as soon as I understood what he was saying. "No way. I don't trust you enough."

"And well you shouldn't," Hades nodded. "I don't blame you. I wouldn't trust me, either. I will restrain him here, with your help. We can keep him in the sacred circle, if you'd like. I would just need your permission to breach the circle. Your mother has enchanted it to keep everyone at bay. But with your permission, we can keep Brennan here. He won't have the ability to turn himself over to Zeus. He won't die."

Those three words were really all that mattered. *He won't die.*

Even though I had been running from Hades for eons, even though I didn't trust him at all, I found myself considering the unthinkable. I was nodding before I'd even thought it through, because Brennan's life was all that mattered.

"You grant me permission?" Hades asked.

"Yes," I said quietly. "But you cannot hurt him." But I looked up and found that Hades was gone. I had no idea if he had heard that last part of my statement or not. Shaking my head, I rushed to find him. I knew right where to begin looking.

All I had to do was find Brennan.

It wasn't hard.

I made my way to the sacred clearing with inhuman velocity. I could smell them both before I even broke through the ring of trees.

As I burst through, I found Brennan and Hades circling each other, each watching the other with wary suspicion.

"I'm fairly sure you are breaking a rule by being in this ring," Brennan called out.

He was crouched low and balanced evenly on the balls of each foot, prepared to spring in either direction. I found myself admiring his skill. He'd never had to fight for his life before- and he thought that was what he was doing now.

"That would be true," Hades acknowledged from a similar position, "Except that Empusa granted me permission."

Brennan didn't break concentration. "I don't believe you," he said firmly.

"You should," Hades answered, a slight smile curving his lips. "She told me that I could be here. She wants me to imprison you."

I could see the rage building on Brennan's face and before I could even say a word, he did.

"You lie!" he snarled as he uncoiled and sprung toward the god of the underworld.

Hades grinned and leaped and they collided in midair above the altar. Grappling, they fell to the stone beneath them and rolled, each trying to best the other and come out on top.

I bit my lip. I wanted to interfere, to protect Brennan from harm, but this is what I had wanted. I had wanted Hades to restrain Brennan. If he didn't, Brennan would die. He would die because of his own stubbornness and sense of right.

I bit my lip harder as Hades slammed his elbow into Brennan's face. Blood exploded from Brennan's nose, splattering Hades' crisp white shirt. I cried out.

"You cannot harm him!" I snapped.

I blurred into motion and stood at their side. They both froze while Brennan stood with his mouth agape.

"It can't be true," he murmured, his eyes flooded with confusion. "You wouldn't..."

"I had no choice," I answered pleadingly. "You have to believe me Brennan. I don't trust Hades. I want nothing to do with him. But he's the only person in this entire universe who has as much reason as I do to keep you from surrendering to Zeus."

Brennan returned my gaze in alarm. "Because Hades wants the mortal world to end! You can't help him accomplish that, Empusa. Has your life hardened you so much that you don't care what happens to anyone else?"

"I care what happens to *you*," I answered softly, trying to swallow my pain at the look on Brennan's face. He was appalled at my lack of humanity. It was the first time I'd seen that look on his face. I didn't like it. "That's all that matters."

"It's not all that matters," Brennan answered. He looked away from me to Hades, but Hades had straightened from his defensive crouch and was watching us with interest. He would much rather watch us implode than engage in personal physical violence. He smiled slightly at my thought and shrugged.

"It's true. I'm a lover, not a fighter."

I glared at him. "You were doing just fine a moment ago when you broke Brennan's nose."

"I didn't say that I couldn't fight," he clarified. "I just prefer not to. You wanted me to do this, Empusa. You cannot blame me for my methods."

"I want you do this, yes. But I do not want you to harm Brennan. Keep him here in the clearing. I'll try to finish this game by myself."

"Oh, yes... the game," Hades said. "I may have forgotten to mention one small thing. I am here, in part, as a challenge to your little game. But let us finish this small detail first, shall we?"

With his words, he pointed at Brennan and Brennan flew backward onto the stone altar with such force that his head slammed hard against it. He shook his head once, but then closed his eyes and didn't reopen them. He was limp against the altar.

I cried out again and dashed to his side, picking up his hand. His pulse still beat, although blood trickled from his nose.

"You!" I spit at Hades as he joined me by Brennan's side. "You weren't supposed to hurt him."

Court

"And what was I supposed to do, little one?" he asked innocently. "Ask him nicely to sit on this altar while I tied him here with steel cords?"

What came out of my mouth was more of a growl than a reply and Hades looked properly chastised. He quickly lashed Brennan's wrists and ankles securely to the altar. I conjured some cotton padding and tucked it beneath the cords so that it didn't cut into Brennan's skin. Hades rolled his eyes.

"You've gone soft, Empusa," he observed.

"Only where Brennan is concerned, so you should stay alert," I warned him.

He smiled, not exactly the reaction that I was going for but I ignored him and turned my attention back to Brennan. Dabbing at his bloody nose, I pushed his hair out of his eyes and stroked his cheek.

"I'm sorry," I whispered into his ear. "It's only for a little while, I promise."

He didn't move and didn't open his eyes, although his heart was beating strongly.

"He'd better be alright," I snapped at Hades.

"Or what?" Hades snapped back, losing his perpetual cool for once. "What will you do, Empusa?"

Instantly, the air in the clearing grew charged with his anger. The trees started rustling as the wind picked up from his energy. I quickly remembered who I was dealing with.

Sometimes, it was easy to forget when Hades was trying to woo you. He made it difficult to remember that he had a very dangerous side in addition to his charming one. He was the god of the underworld for a reason. He had the ability to be very cold-hearted and ruthless when needed.

"I'm sorry," I apologized, in order to defuse the situation. "I'm just worried about Brennan and about this entire situation. I didn't mean to snap at you."

Hades visibly relaxed as he regained his cool composure. "It's no matter," he told me. "No harm done."

The wind died back down, a crisis avoided. I breathed a sigh of relief.

"Now what?" I asked him. "Brennan is secure here so he can't travel to Olympus. What do we do next?"

Hades turned to me, his handsome face a perfect picture of innocence. That expression instantly set me on edge.

"Why, Empusa, we continue with the game, of course. And to the best of Zeus' knowledge, that is my reason for being here."

"You know, he could so easily check on us here," I reminded him. "He would see Brennan lashed to the altar and he would begin to wonder why."

Hades was already shaking his head.

"You're forgetting. Your mother, in her infinite wisdom, arranged for that clearing to be sacred for you. Unless Zeus tries very, very hard, he cannot get into it. And trust me, my brother is so immersed in playing this game, he isn't going to put that effort in."

Hades perched on the edge of the altar and looked around at the clearing.

"It's a simple little place," he observed. I followed his gaze. It was simple. It was just a plain little clearing. But there was reverence here. You could feel it in the air. You could just feel that important things happened in this circle.

"What is my next challenge?" I asked firmly, raising my chin. "You said that you are here as part of the game. What does Zeus want you to do?"

Hades looked at me over the inert form of my boyfriend. His dark gaze was smoldering and I felt an instant sense of panic.

"Remember when Brennan had to withstand a siren?" he asked softly. His words instilled an instant horror and foreboding in my chest. I couldn't speak, so I nodded haltingly.

"You must withstand the same. I'm your siren, Empusa. Can you withstand me?"

Chapter Fourteen

"No." Before I could even speak, Brennan had spoken one firm word into the night. I didn't even know that he was conscious but he was staring at me now with a gaze the color of burning embers.

"Empusa, untie me."

His directive was firm, his tone left no room for argument. It broke my heart. I wanted nothing more than to release his bonds and stand by his side. But I knew what he would do the moment that he was free. I shook my head.

"Brennan, I love you. I'm doing this because I love you. I would not be able to bear it if you died. I couldn't live through it."

"So, you're trusting Hades?" Brennan was incredulous. He lifted his head as far as he could to look at me. "You wouldn't trust him with your life, but you will trust him with mine?"

Guilt rushed through me.

"It's not like that," I mumbled. "I have no choice. Please understand that."

"I understand that you're allowing Hades to play you. You don't know what would happen if I stand before Zeus. He might not kill me at all. He might find that my willingness to sacrifice myself is enough. I would rather trust Zeus than Hades. You're foolish if you do not."

I stuck my chin out.

"Then I guess I am foolish. I do not trust Zeus any more than I trust Hades. They both have their own agendas, their own motivations. I am smart enough to know that, Brennan. You need to understand that you cannot trust Zeus, either. He's not a benevolent grandfather. He's a god- the god of all gods, and he didn't get to that status by being a softie."

For his part, Hades was standing by quietly observing. He stared at us thoughtfully before interrupting in a voice as smooth as caramel.

"I understand your angst, Brennan, really I do. However, I think at this point, the best thing to do is to just move forward. We have a task to complete. Empusa, are you ready?"

I shook my head. "No. Not really. What is our challenge?"

In my periphery, I could see Brennan straining at his restraints, desperately trying to break free. But even though he had mastered controlling his immortal strength, he wasn't able to budge them.

Hades strolled to me, stepping into the line of my vision that led to Brennan, effectively blocking him from my sight.

With each step, his tantalizing gift of magnetism drew me to him. I didn't want it, but it happened anyway. It was like warm fingers were massaging my heart, pulling me closer and closer to Hades. But it wasn't real. I knew that. It was simply my mind playing tricks on me.

I don't want him.

I don't want him.

I don't want him.

I repeated the phrase in my head like a mantra and watched the small smile play along Hades' lips as he listened to my thoughts. He stopped in front of me, so light on his feet. He barely made a whisper of noise as he moved. If Brennan smelled like the sun, then Hades smelled like the night- of everything dark and sensual.

"You don't?" he asked softly. I raised an eyebrow. "You don't want me?"

I gulped. "No."

"Liar," Hades smiled. "But that's alright. I like that trait in a woman. Come with me, Empusa."

Brennan started hollering behind Hades, telling me to stay, not to go. But Hades ignored him, staring quietly into my eyes instead. His were fluid and dark, bottomless. I found myself mesmerized by his spell.

"Come with me," he repeated.

"Where?" I asked.

I almost felt dizzy from his nearness to me.

I don't want him. I repeated in my head.

But the words seemed trite now. Because I *did* want him. I might as well admit it. The trick now was remembering that I really didn't, not truly. I wanted Brennan. I loved Brennan. Hades was simply manipulating my mind. But he was oh-so-good at it.

"To a place where we can be alone," Hades answered. "We need to talk, moon princess."

He lifted his hand and placed his long, slender fingers within mine. His were as cool as mine, so different from Brennan's warm body.

"Come," he murmured into my ear. And before I could even glance at Brennan or say even one word, we were gone.

While we were moving in utter blackness for the one split second before we emerged in our destination, Hades closed his fingers tightly around mine, almost protectively. My heart squeezed a little. And then we arrived.

We were standing in a place I'd never been.

It was a place certainly owned by the night, a place where Hades was comfortable and where I would draw strength. The moon hung full and low in the night sky while silky mist swirled around us. The darkness was violet and so velvety that I could feel its whisper soft touch on my skin. The air smelled of freesia and night-blooming flowers.

"Where are we?" I whispered as I pushed aside lush ferns and flowers to reveal a large canopied bed laden with luxurious bedclothes. Next to it stood a small glass table, filled with bread, cheese and wine. My heart began to stutter and then race. This was a seduction scene. That much was clear.

"Don't be so cynical," Hades said with a grin. "We're here to talk. I simply like bread and cheese and I enjoy reclining while I partake in it."

"Right," I muttered.

As I walked along the soft pathway to the bed, I realized that it was strewn with flower petals. And that I was barefoot. I had somehow lost my shoes along the way again.

My bare feet landed in soft, blood-red petals with each step. I was also dressed in a gossamer night dress. It fluttered softly around my body in the perfect breeze, illuminating my curves in the moonlight. I glanced at Hades and rolled my eyes.

"Nice touch."

"Thank you," he grinned confidently. "I thought so too."

I rolled my eyes again.

"Where are we?" I asked. "I don't recognize this place."

Hades shrugged. "It's the Neitherworld. It's neither here nor there. It's in between."

I stared at him. "In between what?"

"In between reality and dreams. While we are here, we can be whatever we'd like. I can be the god of the sun, if I like. You can be un-cursed. If we wish it, it will be so. But only while we linger here. Once we return to reality, everything changes back to what it was. But while we are here...." He slid his fingers along my arm. "While we are here, our problems disappear."

What a delicious thought. I hadn't been physically without my curse in a thousand years. The idea that I could exist peacefully, without blood or souls, was tantalizing.

"But Brennan..." I turned to speak to Hades and found Brennan standing behind me.

"What..." I stammered. Brennan smiled and spoke with Hades' voice.

"You see what you want to see here," he told me. Brennan's mouth moved with Hades' words. It was Brennan's chiseled jaw, Brennan's soft lips, Brennan's dimple and Brennan's smile. He was radiant, like the sun, like the light that surrounded us in the daytime, even though we were standing in the night. His radiance was impossible, yet I was staring at it.

I reached out with trembling fingers and touched his face. "You look just like Brennan," I said with a shaky voice. I found that my knees were shaking, too.

"I *am* Brennan, if that is what you wish," Brennan's mouth said again. The line between reality and fantasy was growing very, very blurred. My mind actually began to grow foggy and I ached to lean into Brennan's arms. But they weren't really his.

"What *is* this?" I demanded. "What is this trick?"

"It is no trick. I am whoever you want me to be."

A thought occurred to me. "And who do I look like to you?"

Hades smiled with Brennan's mouth. "That is the beauty of this place. We can see what we choose. Right now, you are my wife. You are my wife without the baggage that such a long marriage can accumulate. You are my wife without her suspicions and anger. You are as she once was. Hopelessly in love with me."

Twinge.

I couldn't help it. My heart twinged just a little at the vulnerable look on the god of the underworld's face. He loved his wife. Years of bickering and various heartaches had just taken a toll and made him wish for simpler times. Yet, in life- real life-you didn't get do-overs. You didn't get to go back to the beginning when things were fresh and new. Unless you were a god and could exist in the Neitherworld.

"Emmie," Brennan's mouth murmured, his arms reaching out to me.

"Don't do that," I said, but my heart uncertain. It would be so easy to close my eyes and imagine that it was Brennan. But. It. Wasn't.   I gritted my teeth. "Don't call me that. You are not Brennan."

"Let's not debate the details," Hades suggested, seating himself on the soft bed and patting it. "Come sit with me. Let's enjoy this peaceful evening, shall we? And there are a few things we should discuss."

"Things like what?" I felt my eyes narrow suspiciously. Brennan's amber eyes glowed at me in the dark, but they lacked Brennan's warmth. Beneath the surface, coolness dwelled.   It was a dead giveaway.

Hades smiled serenely. "I thought we should discuss why your father was willing to trade your soul to me- why you are so expendable to him."

My heart practically stopped beating. It was a question that had plagued me for a thousand years.

Chapter Fifteen

es. Let's discuss that," I replied weakly as I sank onto the bed beside Hades. He smiled in satisfaction, but I wasn't sure what he was satisfied about... having me near or knowing something that I didn't. Probably both.

Hades stroked my back in between my shoulder blades with Brennan's hands, in exactly the spot that caused me tension. I didn't ask him how he knew, I just leaned limply against his deft palms.

"What do you know about my father?" I asked. I was dying to know and terrified at once, an interesting quandary that made my heart palpitate.

"I know something that you don't," Hades said calmly, still kneading the sensitive skin of my back with his cool fingers. Another dead giveaway. Brennan was blazingly warm.

"Are you going to share that information?" I twisted away from him and turned to look into his eyes. Brennan's beautiful eyes.

I shouldn't be here. I should be with Brennan. The feelings overwhelmed me as quickly as I had them, filling me up with panic. I shouldn't have left him- no matter the reason.

"Just tell me," I pleaded. "I need to leave here."

"Why ever would you leave here?" Hades asked innocently. "Life is perfect here. Watch this."

He turned and gestured toward the sky. Vines instantly grew across the canopy, lush and green, their spindly tendrils spreading down the legs of the bed. He snapped his fingers and the vines instantly bloomed, exploding into color- the bright blue of Olympus Lotus Blossoms. They were the food of the gods, the manna that kept them young and beautiful, along with the nectar.

The blossoms hung above us now, beautiful and vibrant. Hades reached past me and plucked one perfect bloom from the vine. Leaning into me, he held it to my lips.

"Eat," he urged me. "Lotus blooms are truly the most delicious things in existence."

The soft blue petal lingered against my lip, resting as it waited for me to eat it. I could smell its heady scent beneath my nose and it drew me in, tempting me to bite.

"Just try it," Hades added. "I know you will love it."

I glanced at him suspiciously. Something about his tone set me on edge. Why did he want me to eat it so badly? I asked him as much.

He looked innocently at me, his eyes widened. "I just thought you would like it," he shrugged. He tossed it onto the mossy earth and ground his heel into it. "We're not in the Underworld," he told me with a smirk. "I'm not going to try and trick you into eating here so that I can keep you."

"Well, you'll have to forgive me for doubting you," I told him wryly. "It's sort of your MO."

He threw back his head and laughed, a hearty, throaty sound that warmed my heart yet again. It was the first time he had sounded sincere in all of my dealings with him. Hearing this genuine reaction from him, this true and honest emotion, pulled me closer to him when I really just wanted to back away.

"Why?" he looked at me with lucid and glistening eyes. "Why do you resist me so much, Empusa? Am I so horrible?"

My heart twinged again. Something that I had learned in my thousand years was that rarely was someone ever completely horrible. People were varying shades of gray. Only in rare circumstances, like my father, were they completely evil.

"You're right," Hades stared at me thoughtfully. "And that's a very insightful belief. Very few people in this world are all good or all bad. I've said that for eons. I should definitely know."

"Yes, you would know," I agreed. "And there's probably a lot more to you than meets the eye, but I don't have time to discover it right now. Can we talk about my father, please?"

Hades' expression hardened just a little. I could practically see the clouds rolling across it. He didn't like that I had cut him off when he was trying to connect with me. I backtracked.

"I'm sorry," I amended. "I'm just curious at what you know. I've been curious about Mormo's motives for so long. I've always wondered how he could treat me as he has. I've never done anything to him."

"Of course you haven't," Hades agreed, his tone softening now. "Mormo is the type of person, the type of creature, who doesn't need a motive. He's conniving, heartless and cold. But this time, this once, he does have a motive. A very valid motive."

"And what is his motive?" I asked through gritted teeth.

My patience was growing very, very thin. This was so important to me, even though I'd like to pretend that it wasn't and I felt like Hades was trifling with me...playing with me a like a cat does a mouse.

"You're not a mouse, Em," he smiled. "You're more like a kitten. A fragile little kitten. What do *you* think Mormo's motive is? Have you given it any thought?"

"I'm not fragile," I snapped. "And don't you think that I've given this subject quite a lot of thought? Of course I have. I have no idea what his motive is. I've never done anything to him."

"Empusa, I'm surprised at you," Hades drawled. "You're such a smart girl. Surely you've thought this through. So often on Olympus, people are punished not for what they do themselves, but for what those close to them do. Their husbands, their wives, their parents, their children... hasn't that occurred to you?"

"Of course it has," I answered. "But I don't have a husband and my mother hasn't done anything to Mormo. She angered Zeus, but not Mormo. Not to my knowledge. She's the one that should be upset with him. He's abandoned her periodically for thousands of years. He just goes away and doesn't come back for years and years. She should be the one angry at him. For that and for cursing me, of course."

"Hmm, you could be right," Hades said thoughtfully. "But you could be wrong, too. Perhaps she has done something to upset him that you don't know about. Did you consider that possibility?"

And I hadn't. In my mind, my mother was perfect. Perfectly wise, perfectly loyal, perfectly brilliant. It had never even once occurred to me that she might have done something to infuriate Mormo to the point where he would exact revenge on me. And Hades sounded like he knew something. My eyes instantly narrowed again.

"What do you know?" I asked. "You know something."

"I know many things, darling," he answered smoothly. "Many, many things. But I'm sure you can figure this out for yourself if you just think on it. Trust me, it is ever so much more satisfying that way."

"I've been thinking on it for a thousand years," I argued. "Just tell me."

"You're impatient," he smiled. "I like that about you. I used to be...once. So long ago , it seems like.

I've grown patient. Being immortal does that to a person. I'm surprised you haven't wielded to it just yet."

He reached up and plucked another Lotus blossom from the vine and chewed on it thoughtfully as he studied me with his dark and dangerous eyes. His magnetism was strange and interesting. It wasn't sexual per se, but it was oh-so-strong. I wanted to be near him, I wanted to touch him, I wanted to hear his voice. It was a compulsion that I couldn't control and I hated that.

"Yes, my dear. You are a woman who craves control. I think that is a direct result of the life that you've been forced to lead- how so much has been taken from your control, don't you agree?" Hades asked, in response to my thoughts.

"Perhaps," I answered grudgingly. No one liked to admit a fault, least of all me. "But that is really neither here nor there."

"True," he nodded. "It is not. I have to admit, I enjoy being in control, as well. I could never cast stones for that."

I couldn't help but laugh. The god of the underworld certainly did have a few control issues. You could just ask his wife, Persephone. He wanted her so badly as his wife that he tricked her into staying in the Underworld with him.

Hades appraised me silently. "Glad I can make you laugh," he said wryly. As I stared at him, his face shimmered for a second, like a mirage in the sun, and then his appearance changed back to his own. "Let's be ourselves, shall we?" he suggested. "I am no more Brennan than you are Persephone."

"That's what I've been saying all along," I reminded him. "I have a sense, though, that you never wanted me to be Persephone in the first place."

Hades smiled again, his teeth beautiful and white against his olive skin.

"You're very perceptive," he said. "I simply wanted to see Persephone's face for a moment- while it wasn't wearing an expression of disappointment or anger. I'm sorry that I used you for that."

Twinge.

I ignored my heart.

"Stop trying to make me feel sorry for you. By all accounts, Persephone is a good wife to you. Has she had dalliances? Yes. But so have you. Have you disappointed her? Probably. But who among married couples hasn't disappointed their partner, particularly when they've been married for eons? It's bound to happen. I'm sure she has disappointed you too. But the important thing is that you still love each other. And I know that Persephone loves you."

"You're not heartless after all, little Empusa," Hades observed. "I'm sure that's a little known secret. Don't worry. I won't share it. You do have empathy. It's an admirable trait, if you don't let it go too far."

"And what would you say is too far?" I asked curiously. "Having human emotion?"

Hades rearranged himself on the bed. He was sprawled leisurely against the cushions, as nonchalant and relaxed as he could be. With the gauzy drapes hanging from the sides of the canopy and the vines hanging low from overhead, he could practically be on a postcard. It was a picture-perfect, relaxing scene. I was the opposite. I was bouncing my foot in agitation, in a hurry to wrap this up and get back to Brennan.

"You must learn patience, kitten," Hades chastised, reaching around me for the wine on the side table. He poured a glass for himself and then one for me. Offering it to me, he noticed my shaking fingers.

"Surely you don't need blood already, do you?" he asked, examining my face. "No, you still have healthy coloring. Why are you shaking?"

"I'm not," I answered. "I'm just anxious to return to the real world."

"I don't see why," Hades drawled, relaxing again. "What is there for you besides a curse?"

"The man that I love," I answered coolly.

"Details," he replied with a grin. "Love is over-rated, you know. Kingdoms have been lost because of it."

"And kingdoms have been won," I reminded him. "People will move mountains for love."

"True," Hades acknowledged. "And I've known people who traveled to the depths of hell for it. And they perished there."

I rolled my eyes. "Pleasant thought."

He shrugged, unbothered.

"It's true. People will do insane things for love and it usually comes back to haunt them. Take Orpheus, for example. When he traveled to the Underworld and stood in front of me to beg for his wife's life, I conceded to his pain and torment. I allowed him to return to with his wife to the mortal world—something that is very unlike me. I don't let people leave the Underworld, as you well know. But Orpheus was so haunted that I gave him a chance. His only condition was that he must walk ahead of her on the way back to the mortal world and that he should never look back. He was so distracted by the love and concern that he felt for his wife that he forgot and turned to check on her. I had to take his wife away for the second time. He lived out the rest of his life in anguish... all because of love."

"No. All because of you," I snapped. "You didn't have to place such a ridiculous constraint upon him. I've heard the stories. Orpheus loved his wife. Of course he would turn to check on her out of habit. It wasn't so great an offense. Certainly not so great that you should condemn his wife to a second death. I've never understood why you did that."

"Because he didn't do as I asked," Hades answered smoothly, as though it explained everything. "I asked for a small thing. He couldn't comply. But enough about that. Let's talk about you."

"No," I said quietly. "Let's talk about Mormo."

"Oh, we'll get to that," Hades said, munching on another Lotus blossom. "But first, I'm curious about you- about a few things. Do you function the best at night, in the dark?"

I shook my head in bewilderment. "What does that have to do with anything? You know that I do. I function best in the light of the moon. My mother is the goddess of the moon, after all."

He nodded. "And you are rather altruistic at times, not evil at all, although others might not realize that?"

"I do drink mortal souls and blood," I acknowledged. "That tends to sway opinion."

"Do you find solace in the shadows and feel comfortable there?"

I stared at him. "What are you getting at?" I demanded. "You know these things are true. I'm a child of the night. Of course I feel comfortable in it and around everything that it contains. Why are you asking me these questions? I would rather you answer mine instead."

He leveled a dark smoldering gaze at me. "Fine. Ask."

I gulped. It was the moment of truth. I knew that when I asked my question, Hades would answer it. He held the answers that I had waited so long to hear. I could see it on his face as he waited expectantly, his dark features thoughtful and still.

"Why does my father hate me enough to curse me?"

I could hear the vulnerability in my voice and I hated it. I tried so very hard to be strong. But this aspect of me, this thin, sheer facet of me, was fragile. I usually protected it, hid it from everyone so that they couldn't use it against me. And here I was exposing it to the god of the Underworld, of all people.

"Do you truly want to know?" Hades asked me. "Are you ready to hear the answer, even though you might not like it- even if it changes everything that you know to be true about yourself?"

I nodded. "Yes," I whispered.

"So be it," Hades said firmly. "Here is the answer that you seek. Mormo abhors your presence, the very idea of you in fact, because he is not your father at all."

My breath caught in my throat as I stared into Hades' dark eyes. My heart practically stopped beating with his next two words.

"I am."

Chapter Fifteen

"What?" I stuttered. I suddenly felt dizzy and faint and sick. The colors around me swirled together and I felt Hades' hand on my back.

"Breathe," he instructed me. "Breathe, Empusa. It really isn't so bad."

I glanced up at him. The blood had all rushed from my face and I knew I must be as pale as a ghost. My fingertips felt numb. If a goddess could experience physical shock, this must be what it felt like.

"Not so bad?" I repeated. "Isn't it?"

He shook his head. "No. Why would it be? The man you believed to be your father condemned you to the Underworld in his own stead. I would never do that. By default, I am a better choice."

I stared at him, my mouth agape.

"You condemned me to the Underworld, too," I reminded him. "What kind of father does that?"

"A father who wanted you near," he answered quietly. "I happen to live in the Underworld."

I ignored the strange look on his face, the vulnerable expression. I didn't want to feel emotion toward him at all right now. I just wanted answers.

"How long have you known?" I asked. "Has my mother always known or did she believe me to be Mormo's once?"

"Your mother believed you to be Mormo's at first. You were born with gray eyes, after all, just like his. But when you were small, still a toddler, she took you outside one night to look at the stars.

"While you were outside, you grew tired and cranky and began crying. You accidentally turned the moon dark with your distress. Hecate knew right then that you possessed more magic than was possible of a child of Mormo. She and I had been together only one time, but it was enough."

"She's known for so long and never told me," I muttered, as the realization came crashing down around me. "Why? Why didn't she want me to know?"

"She didn't want Zeus to know," Hades clarified. "She thought that Zeus might use it against her at some point. She was right about that. I agreed with her. And it didn't truly matter to me if you knew who I was or not, to be honest. Being a father is not something that I've ever cared about. But now that you are here, in front of me, and I can see how much magic and power you possess, I must admit. It is fascinating to know that I sired that... I sired *you*."

"That's exactly right," I snapped, yanking away from him and scooting backward on the bed. "You sired me. You haven't been a father. And *I know you*, Hades. Your only interest in me now is my magic. You've seen that I possess strong abilities and you want to control it, just as Apollo wants to control Brennan."

"First of all," Hades began. "You don't know me. Not truly. No one does. Second, Apollo wants Brennan so that *I* can't have him. Apollo, along with a few others, have long since suspected that you were mine. Brennan has made it clear that he will go with you wherever you may go, which is admirable. But Apollo will not stand to have Brennan with me, fighting for me. Everyone has seen the magic that the two of you possess when you are together. It is stronger than we've seen in a long time. Does that magic fascinate me, as well? Yes, it does. I won't lie to you."

I suddenly felt more confused than I had ever been. Mormo, the blood-sucking psychopath that I had always believed to be my father, was not related to me at all. Hades, the god of the Underworld himself, was. I almost couldn't believe it. But it certainly would clear up so many things. I realized now why he had been asking me so many questions about myself. He was drawing parallels.

"You feel more comfortable in the shadows, too, don't you?" I asked. Hades nodded.

"Of course I do. And I am a creature of the moon, like you. You have that tendency from both of your parents, so you are a true child of the night. It is no wonder that you draw such strength from it. Come look."

Hades snapped his fingers and a giant, ornate mirror suddenly appeared in the vines at the foot of the bed. The greenery wrapped around the legs of the mirror, making it seem as though it had always been there as a part of this enchanted forest.

Hades stood in front of it and gestured toward me. "Come and see our similarities," he urged me. Grudgingly, I rose from the bed and joined him in front of the beautiful mirror next to Hades...my father.

His hair was darker than mine. His eyes were almost black, while mine were gray. But the contour of my cheek matched his. He reached out and traced it with his fingers and our eyes met in the mirror.

"Look at the shape of your brow," he instructed. And I did. It was the same as his. The shape of my chin matched his, as well as the peak of my hairline.

"I'm so pale while you are so dark," I pointed out.

"True," he acknowledged. "But look at our hands." We each held out a hand and I saw that we shared the same long slender fingers. "And look at the way we're standing."

Sure enough. We were both balanced mainly on our left foot, with our hips slightly angled to the right. Exactly the same stance. I sucked in my breath.

"Let me see your wrist," I demanded. He smirked slightly. He knew what I would find. He was going to smell just like me. I knew it before I lowered my nose to the skin above his pulse point.

He smelled like the night, like velvety darkness and the moon, like heady night-blooming blossoms and musk. Exactly like me.

"Are you satisfied now?" Hades asked quietly. I nodded silently, my eyes dropped to the ground. I couldn't bring myself to look at him and I didn't know why.

"It's not so bad," he assured me. "It's not as though you enjoyed having Mormo for your father. And now that the cat is out of the bag, so to speak, things will change."

"Zeus knows?" My eyes shot up to meet his. He shook his head.

"Not yet, but it's only a matter of time."

"You're going to tell him yourself, aren't you?" I narrowed my eyes.

Hades grinned. "It's true that no one knows me. But you might know me better than most."

"This is not funny and it is not a joke," I snapped. "Why would you share this with Zeus? Nothing good can come out of it."

"Not true," Hades argued. "Allow me to show you a couple of things, Em."

The mirror in front of us clouded and then cleared, forming into an intriguing scene. Brennan and I relaxed on cushioned lounges, each sipping cool drinks from sparkling crystal goblets. We were happy and carefree and Brennan threw his head back and laughed. Persephone appeared on my left and leaned down to whisper in my ear and then kissed my cheek. And then the fog overtook the mirror once again. I turned to Hades incredulously.

"We were in the Underworld? And you truly think that Persephone would just accept me like that? Not hardly."

"You've just seen the future, or your future as it will be if you join with me and fight against Zeus."

The very idea of fighting against Zeus left me stunned. "And if I don't?"

Hades motioned toward the mirror once again. "See for yourself."

The mirror swirled in fog once again and another scene formed. Mortals were screaming and wailing. Dust was everywhere as the world had withered into a dead and horrific place. The only moisture appeared to be blood and it was everywhere. Bodies were piled in the streets, children wept in the gutters. It was the apocalypse scene that Brennan and I had already seen. I squeezed my eyes closed.

"Open them, Empusa," Hades directed. "You need to see this part."

Hesitantly, I opened my eyes, afraid to look back into the enchanted mirror.

My trepidation had been justified. Brennan's dead eyes stared back at me, wide open and sightless as he was trampled in the street by angry mortals. I watched someone stomp on his dusty hand before I squeezed my eyes closed again and turned away, my hand pressed to my mouth.

"Why?" I managed to eke out without vomiting.

"Why?" Hades seemed surprised at my question. "Because their world that they knew ended because of you and Brennan. You couldn't control your powers and you ruined it all for them. Brennan tried to sacrifice himself to Zeus, but it was too late. Zeus killed him and left his body to the mortals and he did nothing to restore the mortal world. Do you want to know what happens to you?"

I shook my head. "It doesn't matter what happens to me. If Brennan is dead, I may as well be also."

Hades took my hand and led me back to the bed. We sat on the edge, my hands shaking. The picture that I had just seen hung heavily in my mind and laid on my heart like a dead weight. My tongue felt like a lump of wood in my mouth and suddenly nothing seemed to matter anymore.

Hades squeezed my hand and nudged my shoulder. "It doesn't have to be so," he reminded me. "Remember the first vision? You are the true princess of the Underworld. You can take your rightful place

and fight against Zeus by my side. You and Brennan
can reside in my world without worry of harming the
mortals- the Underworld will buffer your abilities. It
is safe there for you."

As I stared at our hands, my moonstone bracelet
caught my eye. In all of this other craziness, I had
completely forgotten its importance. My soul was
tied to it. It couldn't be destroyed or I would be
destroyed as well. And Hades had once said that he
wanted it destroyed because it was a danger to all
creatures of the night. Whoever held it could control
any child of the moon, including me.

Hades read my mind before I could even say
anything.

"There is a way around that," he said
thoughtfully. "I was always correct in my assertion
that your moonstone's existence is not safe for the
inhabitants of our world. However, I would relent on
insisting that it be destroyed if you would entrust its
care to me. It would be guarded night and day, I
assure you. And if you decided to come live in the
Underworld, you could keep it yourself. As long as it
remains in the Underworld, I will agree to let it stay
with you. It's a solution to think on, Empusa."

"Everything has become so convoluted," I said weakly. "I almost can't decide what the true issues even are anymore."

"The issues are simple," Hades answered solemnly. "You want to figure out a way to stop Zeus' game, to save the son of Apollo, to learn how to harness your powers so that you can be together, to find a release from the curse that Mormo put upon you and to live a normal life. You'd like to figure out a way to do all of these things without confronting Zeus outright and without losing your life or Brennan's."

"I guess that about sums it up," I replied tiredly. "And when you list them like that, our issues seem insurmountable."

"Nothing is impossible for you anymore, Empusa," Hades said firmly. "You've got to remember your new identity. You're the daughter of the god of the Underworld. Combined with your mother's witchery, you are unstoppable if you put your mind to it."

"I don't even know where to start," I said uncertainly. "I really don't. It's all so overwhelming."

"You must start at the beginning," Hades said wisely. "You must choose what side you are on. If you stand with me, your rightful father, I will help you achieve that which you want the most. And in doing so, you will help me achieve what *I* want the most."

"You want to rule Olympus."

Hades shook his head. "No. I've never wanted that. Think on that, Empusa. You are like me. Would you rather live on Olympus in the sun and the light or would you rather live in the peaceful shadows of the Underworld? The Underworld is my home. When I imprisoned the other Olympians, did I sit on a throne and reign in Zeus' absence? No, I did not. I simply went on about my business at home. But I did it without the interference of my brother. He has no right to try and inflict his control over me. I simply want to be free of that."

I believed him. With a start, I found that I truly did believe Hades. And if I believed the god of the Underworld and was willing to fight with him against Zeus, what did that say about me? I decided that I didn't want to put too much thought into that.

Hades held out his hand. "Are you with me?"

I paused, completely still and uncertain.

"Well?" Hades prompted. "Are you with me? I am the only way to save Brennan."

My thoughts flashed to the vision of Brennan being trampled in the streets, his sightless eyes fixated upon me. I gulped and put my hand in Hades' cool grip.

"Your word is your bond," he reminded me.

I nodded. "Yes."

I shook his hand.

And that is how I made a deal with the devil... my father.

Chapter Sixteen

ades and I tumbled from the Neitherworld back into the Druids' sacred clearing and I stood for a moment as I gained my bearings and my vision sharpened. It was always a little bit disconcerting. This time, if only took a minute to realize that we weren't alone and that Brennan wasn't the only one here.

The priestesses were all in attendance, each dressed in a dark hood and standing in a circle around the large stone altar. They were chanting incoherently and I couldn't understand their words. But I understood the fierce tone of their voices and the absorbed expression on their faces. This couldn't be good.

"What the hell?" I murmured quickly, turning to Hades as we emerged from the tree line. "What is going on here?"

"It's hard to say," he said quietly, his dark gaze frozen on the scene in front of us. "But we should probably break this little party up."

"Agreed."

We crept quietly into the clearing and Hades pushed two of the women apart without aplomb so that we could enter the circle.

I glanced sideways at them as I passed by, but didn't say a word. They were clearly annoyed with our interruption, but they didn't speak aloud. I could see that they sensed who Hades was as a quiet pall fell over the circle.

"Dark lord," Keelin bowed her head in deference. I could see, though, that she resented our presence.

"What is going on here?" I demanded, pushing through the circle. "Brennan, are you okay?"

I was finally able to see him after pushing through the women and he seemed to be fine. He was still bound since no one but Hades was able to break the restraints. At the look of surprise and then dismay on Brennan's face, I realized that was exactly what they were trying to do.

"Were you trying to break free?" I asked incredulously.

A shadow passed over him and he clenched his jaw as he looked at me. And then he nodded.

I felt the air rush out of me. "You didn't trust me," I murmured in disbelief. "You didn't trust me to come back for you?"

He shook his head. "No, that's not it. I want to save you, Empusa. And I know you won't let me go. I have to do what I have to do to keep you safe. And in saving you, I'll also save the mortal world. It's the right thing to do."

"You don't understand," I said through clenched teeth. Turning to the priestesses, I announced, "You can all go. Your services are no longer required."

They remained still, each eye fixed upon me.

"Did you not hear me?" I demanded. "You may leave now."

Keelin stepped forward. It seemed that she had taken a leadership role now that Branwyn was gone.

"I'm not sure that we can," she answered quietly. "You see, we were called here, we believe by the goddess herself. We were all waked from the same dream and we were all led to this clearing, where we found Brennan tied to the altar. We have a purpose here."

Out of the corner of my eye, I caught Brennan's eye. He looked almost bemused and fairly satisfied with himself, triggering a memory.

One of his gifts was willing something into existence. If he tried hard enough, he could sometimes make things happen... like giving all of these priestesses the same dream and making them come to the clearing. Of course they would believe that 'the goddess', my mother, had summoned him.

"Well done," I told him grudgingly. He grinned.

"Thank you."

"What do you mean, princess," Keelin asked. As she moved slightly, something silver flashed in her hand.

"Why do you have a knife, Keelin?" I asked her. She pulled it from the folds of her dress.

"I know not," she admitted. "I simply have it with me."

I whirled and glared at Brennan. "Really? Without even saying goodbye to me? I mean so little to you?"

His grin was gone now and he looked pained.

"It was the only way I could bear it," he admitted. "If I saw you, I knew my resolve would disappear. I have to do this, Em. I have to."

"No. You. Don't." I was gritting my teeth so hard that I could hear the enamel on them groan. "You don't understand."

I turned back to the women. "Leave."

"I don't think we can," Keelin answered quietly. She was brave, I'd give her that much. I looked her straight in the eye and practically growled.

"Leave."

"No."

"Yes," Hades interjected.

With his one word, the women began flying out of the clearing, tossed carelessly by something unseen. Hades. I glanced gratefully at him and took a moment to calm myself while he evacuated the women. After a minute, only Keelin remained, standing uncertainly in front of me.

"I'm sorry, princess," Keelin offered limply. "We only sought to please your mother. I hope we haven't offended you."

"No, you have not," I assured her. "You were trying to help and I understand that. But leave now."

She nodded curtly. "Yes."

She turned and joined the women huddled in the treeline, leading them away. None of them looked back. Circes remained.

"You can leave, too," I told her. "I'm not sure who exactly you were trying to help or what you were trying to do. But you are relieved of it now."

"You know," she observed, studying my face. "You know the truth. Your truth."

"Yes. I know that which has been kept from me for so long. Now please leave us."

Circes crept around me, without another world. I think she could see on my face that I was in no mood for further discussion.

"What do you know?" Brennan asked curiously, his voice husky.

Glancing at Hades, I asked, "Can you give us a minute?"

He nodded silently and disappeared, leaving Brennan and I alone.

"What do you know?" Brennan asked me, his beautiful amber eyes trained on my face.

He was at once impatient and reluctant to hear. I could feel it. I sank wearily down beside him on the stone, picking up his warm hand in mine. He was so warm, so very vital and beautiful. It felt as though I had been absent from the sun and now it was once again shining on me. It was such a warm and wonderful feeling.

"I learned something.... Something important," I told him, stroking his fingers.

"Which is?" Brennan prompted.

I lifted his head and propped it on my lap, hoping it would make him more comfortable. I found myself wishing I could free him. But instead, I explained what had just transpired in the Neitherworld. After a few minutes, my story had left him astonished. I could only imagine that I had looked the same way when I first discovered my true paternity.

"No," Brennan breathed.

"Yes," I nodded. "It's true."

"What does this mean?" he asked. "And can you please release me? I won't do anything until we discuss it. You have my word."

"When Hades comes back, we'll release your bonds. Please forgive me for tying you. I just knew that you would try to sacrifice yourself. And I was right."

I couldn't keep the chastisement from my voice and he met my gaze firmly.

"You know I would do anything for you," he said quietly. As quiet as he was, he voice still echoed in the night.

"I know," I sighed. "Which is how I knew what you would do. Please, Brennan. You have to trust me. Going to Zeus isn't going to save me and it certainly won't save the mortal world. I've seen it. Hades showed me two versions of what will happen. One if we stand with him and one if we try to go it alone in the mortal world. Trust me, the latter ends very, very poorly."

"Did he show you what would happen if I go to Zeus?" Brennan asked plaintively.

"No, he did not. Because I'm sure he knows that it isn't an option for me," I replied firmly. "It's not an option, Brennan. I won't lose you. Whatever we face, we're going to face it together."

"So, you're just going to trust Hades now, without even a question?" Brennan asked doubtfully. "You've been running from him for so long. And your mother has been pushing you to go to him... do you think this is why? Do you think she really wanted you to know?"

"Probably," Hades answered for me as he stepped into the ring. "I'm sorry to interrupt. I thought I had perhaps given you sufficient time for discussions."

"It's fine," I told him. "I've just explained everything that I've learned to Brennan."

"And Brennan is questioning your decision?" Hades asked, one dark eyebrow raised. I glared at him.

"Why wouldn't he? You're not exactly the first choice that comes to mind when I think of someone who I can trust."

"I'm hurt, kitten," Hades said glibly. But then he turned to Brennan. "Let me lay it out for you, son of Apollo. If you want to live and if you want Empusa to live, you will stand with me. You cannot trust Apollo. The sole reason that he is trying to keep you and Empusa apart is so that he can control your magic rather than have you under my influence. While I can understand his concern, it is still not a fatherly one. He doesn't care about you and probably never will. Apollo is known for being superficial and shallow. You cannot trust my brother, either. You simply cannot."

"Yet we cannot trust you, either," Brennan pointed out. "Now can you release my bonds, please?"

"Well, since you said please," Hades answered drily. He was kneeling beside Brennan before I could even blink, releasing the restraints.

Brennan sat up and rubbed his wrists, rolling his eyes at me at the same time. "If you wanted to tie me up, I can think of better ways, Em."

He swung his legs off the altar and stood, nimbly stretching. "I wish I could say that was fun, but it wasn't."

"I'm so sorry, Brennan. Really."

He stared at me. "Come here."

I was at his side in a flash and he pulled me to him, crushing my lips with his own. He kissed me like I was the most delicious treat on earth, so soundly that I felt dizzy when he finally pulled away. As he did, I noticed a tree burning to our left and I glanced sheepishly at Hades.

Hades just shook his head. "You give new meaning to the term 'explosive relationship'."

I rolled my eyes. "What's next? What should we do now?"

"Well, first we need to ascertain whether your boyfriend will be fighting with us... or against us."

Hades looked pointedly at Brennan. I almost gasped aloud.

"Brennan would never fight against me," I snapped. I twisted my head quickly and looked at Brennan. "Right?"

Brennan returned my gaze drolly. "Of course not," he assured me. "I would never fight against you. Not ever, for any reason."

I turned back to Hades in satisfaction. "There you have it. He's with us."

"What a relief," Hades said smoothly, with a sarcastic edge. "I was so worried. Now, back to the matters at hand. I was sent here at Zeus' behest as one of your challenges. Empusa, your challenge was to withstand temptation... me. I believe that Zeus purposely sent me as your challenge because he suspects your true paternity. He knew that if it was true, I wouldn't follow through. Any moment now, he will realize that the challenge was not met. Which, as you know, means that a mortal will fall into the gauntlet. I care little about that, but I know that you do. Or, at least, Brennan does. Of larger consequence to me is that Zeus will soon know the truth, that I am your true father. As you know, it changes everything. We need to determine how we will move forward."

"How do you think Zeus will react?" I asked him. "You know him the best."

"My brother will be instantly threatened," Hades replied. "And that is the most dangerous frame of mind for him to be in. When Zeus is threatened, he becomes proactive and defensive. We need to keep a step ahead."

"I hate this," I said miserably. "Will he do anything to our supporters in Olympus... like Harmonia and Cadmus? And my mother?"

Hades studied me, his dark eyes glittering. "I know not," he admitted. "I wouldn't be surprised. It is doubtful that he will harm Harmonia and Cadmus. They saved the Olympians from my trickery, after all. But your mother... I believe that he would welcome the excuse for retribution."

I swallowed hard. I knew he was right.

"So, now what?" I whispered.

"That is a very good question," Hades said. "We need to carefully think on it and plan our first move. Let us sleep here for the night and plot our next steps. We'll move on the morrow."

"Agreed," I nodded. "We're protected here in the circle."

"Yes," Hades agreed. "For now. Zeus won't allow that to stand forever, but for tonight, it should still be safe. I have a matter to attend to in the Underworld and it will not take long. Do you feel comfortable staying here in my absence?"

I nodded. "Of course. "We'll be fine."

"Very well," Hades answered, buttoning his cloak at his neck. "I will return shortly." And he was gone.

Brennan and I stared at each other in the night. The moon was full in the dark sky above us and the stars twinkled brightly. If the fate of everything that we knew wasn't hanging in the balance, I could almost enjoy this moment, this sudden and unexpected alone time with Brennan. But as it was, the air was filled with tension and our fate was uncertain at best.

I sighed and leaned my head against Brennan's strong chest. His arms automatically closed around me, holding me tight.

"It will be okay," he murmured into my hair. "I won't let it be anything else."

"Says the man who was willing to die a moment ago," I said wearily. He sighed in response.

"Yes, I was willing to die—for you. I'll do anything it takes."

And that was what worried me.

Chapter Seventeen

We woke to fire. I knew it before my eyes even opened. I could smell the thick smoke and hear the popping cracks.

I leaped to my feet, pulling Brennan with me. Whirling around, I found everything around us in flames. The trees, the grasses, the village containing the priestesses. I could hear their screams, both screams of sadness and screams of agony. I squeezed my eyes closed for a scant moment, before I reopened them and squared my shoulders.

"Zeus knows," I said needlessly. Brennan nodded. "Hades isn't back," I added. Again, Brennan nodded. "I wonder what is keeping him?"

I was running toward the village now, to see if I could help. I didn't know how long the fire had been burning while I slept. When I reached the edge of the clearing, right before the ring of fire began, I hit an invisible wall and was thrown backward into the air.

I landed hard, with my head and shoulders slamming against the altar. I sat up, shaking my head to clear it.

"What the hell?" I muttered.

Brennan tried to get through, but he was prevented as well. He patted the air, feeling the invisible barrier.

"It's a wall," he announced. "A see-through wall."

"Zeus," I said quietly.

A movement to my right caught my eye and I turned.

Hades was approaching the wall. He stood directly in front of me and his mouth was moving, but I couldn't hear a thing. I held up my hands as if to tell him and he nodded quietly. He knew. His face was clouded over. He was not a happy god.

I watched him try and break down the wall with magic for several minutes before he shook his head again. He couldn't touch it. Only Zeus could.

"Did you truly think you could deceive me?" a voice boomed.

It seemed to come from nowhere and everywhere at once. Thunder boomed and lightning flashed and the burning trees began to blow. I felt a chill run down my spine. I had always thought it would be Hades that did me in. But I realized now that I was wrong. It would be Zeus.

Brennan jumped onto the altar and looked into the sky.

"We meant you no harm," he shouted. "We didn't know that Empusa was Hades' daughter until last night. She didn't even know. This is not her fault."

An apparition appeared in front of us then, a perfect rendition of Zeus himself. It shimmered in the night and broke up slightly as he walked toward us before becoming whole again.

"You have plotted with Hades to stand against me," Zeus said, his voice as loud as ever. "That is treason."

I dropped to my knees and bowed my head. Reaching up, I tugged on Brennan to do the same. He quickly joined me.

"Forgive us, uncle," I said quietly. "We meant no disrespect toward you- none at all. We were simply brainstorming ways to survive and remain together. I have never wanted to stand against you. I only wish to live in peace. I've been cursed so long that I have forgotten what that is like."

"You act as though your intentions mattered," Zeus replied. His silver eyes flashed with anger in the night. His wild mane of gray hair waved in the breeze, standing on end. He wore ancient Greek dress; a silver toga belted at the waist with an ornate, jeweled belt. Beautiful silver sandals laced up his calf. In all, he was a vision of glimmering silver.

"*Intentions* do not matter," he continued, ignoring my veiled appraisal of him. "Actions matter. Words and oaths matter. You intend to stand with my brother Hades against me. You felt you couldn't trust me to assist you, to stand behind my word. That vexes me, Empusa. If it weren't for my granddaughter Harmonia's interference, you would be dead right now- the both of you. She has stood up on your behalf and pleaded for your life."

"What about the game?" I asked, my voice small in the night. An instant smile widened across Zeus' lined face. I was instantly uneasy. A turn in the game had brought Zeus pleasure which didn't bode well for us.

"Obviously the game still plays on," Zeus said. "You and Hades didn't complete the last challenge, so a mortal died. One point for Apollo."

He was indifferent about the mortal and pleased about Apollo's point. I was filled with instant rage and I knew that he could sense it. A small smile played at the corners of his mouth.

"You're such a feisty one," he observed. "I do not know who I wish to win this next challenge. You're feisty and strong, but yet you use your spirit to try and work against me. You would be guilty of treason right now if I had not interfered and prevented it by containing you in this very clearing. You should thank me. And Brennan, the handsome son of Apollo. He's loyal and strong- very dedicated to you and that is commendable. He seems to have more substance than Apollo, but that has yet to be determined."

"What do you mean, 'who will win this next challenge'?" I asked uncertainly. "The game is surely over- everything has changed."

"The game is over when I say it is over," Zeus boomed. "In case you haven't noticed, you are at my mercy right now. You cannot leave and no one else can come in to save you. There is an invisible barrier completely surrounding you. It is absolutely secure and cannot be penetrated. You will complete the next challenge or you will both die."

"So the rules have changed?" Brennan asked quietly. He reached over and grasped my hand in an effort to comfort me. I was so furious that I didn't even really even need comforting. I wasn't upset or sad or distressed- I was unbelievably pissed off. I could feel the anger pulsing through my veins, flooding through my heart and flushing my cheeks. Zeus smiled.

"Such spirit," he said, gazing upon me. "Use it now, little one. Your challenge, your test, is to fight each other. You wished to stand against me? That is not going to happen. But you can use your skills against each other. Only one of you will leave this clearing. When a victor emerges, the mortals in the gauntlet will be released unharmed. The mortal world will continue as before. I will accept the death of one of you as repentance from the mortal world."

"The mortal world never knew that you were imprisoned!" I snapped. I was so angry that my vision almost blurred. "They never knew- it wasn't their fault. It was Hades and the Fates. The blame should rest directly on their shoulders."

"And your mother, Hecate," Zeus pointed out. "She participated, as well. And that, young one, is why I am allowing this game. You should know by now that the best way to seek retribution from a god is to gain it from those who they love. You are Hecate's most valued treasure. You are correct. The rules and object of this game have changed. No matter who wins here in this clearing, you or Brennan, I will consider your mother's transgression against me wiped clean. If Brennan dies, you will forever live in misery. If you die, your mother will. Either way, justice will have been served."

"Justice?" I spit. "Justice is not sick and twisted. You are."

"Such spirit," Zeus repeated, shaking his head. "If only you had chosen to use it for me, rather than against me."

"You speak as if I ever had a chance!" I lashed out. "I never did. I've been cursed by the man I thought was my father and you never interfered on my behalf. And now I will pay a debt that isn't mine."

"The life of a god is never fair," Zeus leveled a silver gaze at me. "You should know that by now." He turned to Brennan.

"If you are the victor here, I will grant you immortality. You will reside in Olympus with all of the glory that you deserve. If you lose valiantly, you will live in the Underworld in the Isles of the Blessed. Either way, you future will not be unpleasant."

"If I lose valiantly?" Brennan asked. "What does that mean?"

"It means if you lose after fighting me with everything that you've got," I interrupted. "Zeus wants us to fight to the death. He wants to see blood."

"I *deserve* to see blood," Zeus replied angrily. "Do not forget that."

"Perhaps," I acknowledged. "But not ours. We did nothing to deserve this."

"It is no matter," Zeus answered, once again calm and impassive. "Haven't we already discussed that? This is your lot. Now, the new rules have been explained to you. They are simple. One of you will survive. You will remain in this clearing until one of you is dead. I have taken away Empusa's immortality. If she wins, I will restore it and I will remove her curse. No one can assist you. You will each stand alone." He waved a hand toward our right and the arena in Olympus appeared to us.

"We will be seated in the Arena watching you," Zeus continued. "You will be able to see us, as well. Unfortunately, no one can interact with you or offer you advice. You will each be completely on your own. Do you understand these rules as I've explained them to you?"

Brennan nodded silently.

"I understand the rules," I answered coldly. I gazed at the vision of Olympus. My mother sat next to an empty seat, her shoulders slumped. I assumed the empty seat was Zeus' since Hera sat on the other side.

"My mother?" I asked. "What will happen to her?"

"Why nothing of course," Zeus answered. "You will pay her debt. Your mother is a unique goddess in that her magic is very, very powerful-"

"More powerful than yours!" I interrupted.

Zeus continued as if I hadn't spoken. "But she will not use it against me or to assist you since she knows that you are at my mercy right now. With my whim, you will live or die."

At his words, pain like I'd never experienced ripped through my body, causing me to drop to my knees and writhe in the dirt. It literally felt like someone was using a hot poker to rip my internal organs to shreds and pull them out through my belly button. It was so intense that I couldn't stand it. I couldn't breathe...I couldn't see. Everything turned to black and then nothing.

When I opened my eyes again, I found Brennan clutching me to him, murmuring anxiously to me. Zeus stood to the side and observed us. I realized that I had passed out from the pain and then just as quickly realized that the horrible pain was gone.

"Do we understand each other?" Zeus asked quietly. I nodded silently. His message was clear. He could annihilate me or Brennan in the blink of an eye if he so chose. We were nothing to him, no more than a speck of dirt beneath his heel. He nodded at my thought, confirming it, and then he was gone.

Brennan and I were left alone or as alone as we could be with the Olympians watching us from the arena. I turned my back on them and faced Brennan, focusing solely on him and ignoring the fact that any of the Olympians could be watching us this very minute.

Brennan's face reflected all of the horror that I felt inside. He was silent, his expression tortured. He reached over and wiped a tear from my cheek. I hadn't even realized that I was crying. I leaned into his hand and he pulled me close.

"I will never harm you," he whispered. "I will not do it. They cannot force me."

Pain seemed to shatter my heart into a million jagged pieces.

"They have ways," I whispered to him. It was difficult to speak past the lump that had formed in my throat. "Trust me, they have ways."

Brennan held me for the longest time. I listened to his heart beat in his chest, slow and rhythmic. I felt his warmth, smelled his masculine scent, felt the softness of his skin and the rigidity of his muscles. I could stay within his embrace forever. But it couldn't happen.

I knew that if we didn't act, they would find ways to force us into action. It was simply how Zeus operated. I glanced at the vision of the arena and found Zeus smiling in reaction to my thought. It appeared that even though we were isolated from the world and could not hear them, they could still read our minds. And from his knowing smile, I could see that I was right.

Zeus would eventually force us to act. We couldn't hide here forever. It would be better for everyone if we just got it over with right now and didn't drag it out.

I pushed away from Brennan and took a ragged breath, watching it form in the air in a puff as I breathed it out in the cold night. After a thousand years of running and hiding in self-preservation, I couldn't believe the words that came out of my mouth next.

"Brennan, I want you to kill me right now."

Chapter Eighteen

rennan stared at me in disbelief, then shock, then horror, and then finally back to shock. His mouth was slack, his eyes wide. He stood motionlessly, his arms limp at his side. I could hear the jumble of thoughts in his head as he tried to make sense of my words and my intentions.

"No."

One word, spoken with finality as he finally came to his senses.

"I can't believe you would expect that out of me," he added in a hurt tone. "I could no more hurt you then I could kill an infant with my bare hands. I never want to live without you. I want you to kill *me* instead. Right now. Do it."

He held his hands up, palms up to the sky, his eyes fixated on me. "I love you, Emmie. Just do it. Please let me save you."

I only thought my heart had broken before. I had been wrong. Because it was breaking now, all over again, as painful as anything I'd ever felt. It was excruciating. I shook my head from side to side, not able to breathe enough to speak.

"Then what will we do?" Brennan asked softly. "I can't kill you and you can't kill me. But we're trapped here until one of us is dead."

"Well, they took away my immortality," I said. "Perhaps we can just see who starves to death first."

Brennan shook his head. "I doubt that will be enough for him. He will force us to act—somehow."

Brennan was a fast learner. That was exactly what would happen.

"I don't know what to do," I admitted in a whisper. "I don't know what to do."

My shoulders slumped as though the weight of the entire world was on them. It was a heavy, heavy weight.

"We need to think on this," Brennan said firmly. "There has to be a way. There has to be something we can do. Nothing is ever hopeless, Em."

He pulled me into his arm and we sank to the ground together with me in his lap. I rested my head against his chest. I should be trying to think of a way out of this mess, some possible way that I could save the man that I loved, but all I could do was lay limply in his arms, inhaling his scent and absorbing his warmth.

The night closed in around us and I could smell the dew in the air. I could hear the fire continually burning, the screams still emanating from the village. But it didn't matter. Nothing mattered anymore.

I closed my eyes.

Chapter Nineteen

Blackness

Chapter Twenty

Blackness

Chapter Twenty-One

ξ mpusa, you've got to wake up." Gaia's clear voice penetrated the black fog of my sleep. I had been dreamless and peaceful until she interrupted my solitude. I growled and tried to ignore my ghostly friend.

"Seriously, Empusa. Listen to me. If you don't wake up, Zeus will kill you and Brennan both. Wake. UP."

I opened my eyes.

At first it was difficult to focus and I couldn't see. Everything around me was blurry. A golden shape formed in front of my face and I focused sharply on it, trying to see what it was.

"Empusa?"

Brennan's voice came from the shape and he was concerned, relieved... and slightly empty. Hollow.

I quickly tried harder to see and Brennan's anxious face came into focus, directly in front of my own. He grabbed me to him before I could even think.

"Oh, my god. Thank god. Thank god. Thank god."

He was talking into my neck, his voice muffled and I couldn't understand why he was so upset. What horrible, catastrophic thing had happened?

I pulled away and stared at him.

"What happened, Bren?"

He looked at me, completely shocked.

"Empusa, do you know how long you've been asleep?"

I stared at him again, confused.

"All night?"

He shook his head. "No. You've been asleep for at least two months. Maybe longer. I can't tell- time runs together nowadays. It's like you were in a coma. I didn't know what to do."

Shock slammed into me. A month?

Brennan held onto me tightly. "I did everything I could think of. I even tried appealing to Zeus, but that clearly didn't help."

He motioned toward the vision of Olympus. A smattering of Olympians, including Zeus, were seated in the arena seats. They were all watching us, with varying expressions in their silver eyes. My mother sat next to Zeus, and although she was calm, I could see the concern in her eyes. Her gaze held mine and I saw a million things in it. But nothing that she could put a voice to. An invisible wall saw to that.

"What was wrong with you?" Brennan asked anxiously, patting down my arms as though he was checking for broken bones. I stared at him.

"Nothing's broken," I told him wryly. He actually smiled, a sight that made my heart flutter. How I had missed that...his beautiful face.

He actually had a beard now, a blonde scruff, which I was sure was a result of our being trapped in this clearing. I was not normally a fan of beards, but Brennan could even pull that off.

"What is wrong with you?" he asked again. His eyes were still full of worry and concern. "Are you alright now?"

I shook my head. "I don't know. Nothing like that has ever happened before. I was so overwhelmed, so sad at the thought that things are not going to end well for us that I just wanted to sleep."

"Well, you certainly did that," Brennan answered, shaking his own head. "I guess we see now what happens when a goddess becomes depressed. You get your own personal coma-like getaway."

"Don't knock it," I told him as I shakily got to my feet. My muscles felt like they hadn't moved in a year, slightly like gelatin. "I'd like to go back. I had no worry there, no pain. I wonder if that is what death is like...true death? Because I somehow doubt that Zeus will allow me to live in the Isles of the Blessed if I lose. I'd like an eternity of nothingness instead."

"Don't talk like that!" Brennan snapped. "Do you have any idea how hard it is has been for me all of this time? I couldn't reach you, I couldn't help you. No one would help me, we're trapped in this god-forsaken clearing. To hear you talk about giving up, when I haven't given up on you this entire time, it's a slap in the face, Empusa!"

He turned his back on me and crossed the clearing, sitting on the edge of the stone altar. He stubbornly refused to look at me, glaring at the ground. If looks could kill, the grass beneath his feet would be dead.

And he was right. I had no idea what it had been like for him, but I could imagine how it would have been for me if the tables had been turned.

Seeing him in a coma-like state for months without being able to help would have been excruciating.

I weakly crossed the clearing, my legs shaking the entire way, and sank to my knees between his. Cupping his face in my hands, I stared him in the eye.

"I'm sorry," I said simply. "I didn't mean to leave you and I didn't mean to belittle it. You are everything to me. It kills me that I left you alone."

"It's alright," Brennan said gruffly. "You're back now and that's what matters."

"It's not all that matters," I argued. "But it's what we have to work with right now. We've got to form a plan. No one can come to our assistance here. It's just you and me."

"And me," a small voice announced.

I spun around, leaping to my feet as I looked for the voice.

"I'm here," it said softly. I narrowed my eyes as I looked for it, for *her*. The voice was female.

And then I saw her. So transparent that she was almost invisible, Gaia hovered by the edge of the clearing, just inside the invisible wall. She was so faded that she almost blended into the backdrop of trees and I realized that she was purposely camouflaging herself to avoid detection by the Olympians.

I quickly tore my eyes away from her so that Zeus didn't see me looking at her and I knelt once again in front of Brennan. Trying to be inconspicuous, I spoke to her from the corner of my mouth.

"What are you doing here?" I hissed. "If Zeus sees you, you're dead."

"I'm already dead," she answered calmly.

"Fine. You'll be worse than dead."

"Impossible," she answered. "Do you want my help or not?"

"How are you even here?" I asked. "Did my mother send you? How did you get through the wall?"

"Ghosts can't be contained," she sniffed. "I'm here to bring you news. Zeus is keeping your mother close to him at all times. She will not be able to help you. He has threatened your life if she tries. Your father sent me."

Instantly, Mormo's face clashed into my eyes and I cringed.

"Hades," Gaia clarified. "Your true father."

I expelled a breath slowly. It was going to take me quite a while to get used to that, I could tell. Mormo had been my 'father' for a thousand years. Old habits died hard.

"What did he have you risk your life to tell me?" I asked quietly. I glanced up at the vision of Olympus. Zeus was engaged in a conversation with Apollo and was not even looking in our direction. I felt a brief feeling of relief. "Why exactly are you here?"

"Well, he had me wake you up for one thing," she pointed out. "If you hadn't, Zeus was going to kill you today."

Her entire tone had changed when she mentioned Hades' name and I narrowed my eyes.

"Don't tell me that you trust Hades now," I rolled my eyes and then glanced up at Zeus again.

He was still speaking with Apollo, who was waving his arms around. Apparently, Apollo wasn't enjoying their conversation. I imagined that he was probably trying to get Zeus to just kill me outright rather than allowing this game to continue. I turned my attention back to Gaia, who was studying me with ghostly eyes.

"No, I don't," she answered. "No more than you do. But I might have been slightly wrong about him. He hasn't condemned me to the Underworld yet, at any rate."

"Don't turn your back on him," I warned. She nodded.

"I won't. For now, I'm just going to concentrate on you," she said quietly. "You've been my friend when I had no one else. I can't leave you here like this."

"What message did Hades have for me?" I asked, trying to ignore the lump in my throat. I was strangely melancholy today for some reason. Perhaps because I was awake for the first time in two months. That might do it to a person.

"He wants you to know that the deck is stacked in your favor. That long sleep that you just had? That was your body's natural reaction to being rendered mortal. Further, you may have been rendered mortal, but your curse has not been removed. You will soon begin to crave human blood and souls so badly that you won't be able to control it. You will kill Brennan without meaning to. You won't be able to help yourself."

Horror slammed into me. I was trapped here like a rat in a cage with the person that I loved most in the world. And very soon, I would turn into a monster with no self-restraint. Brennan would stand no chance.

Chapter Twenty-Two

y *father* might feel that it is good news," I replied to Gaia icily. "But I do not. Return to him and find out how I might be able to avoid this fate. I don't care what it takes. Since I am now mortal, bring me back poison. Give me a dagger. Hell, I'll take a noose. Anything."

"No," Gaia said, shaking her luminescent head. "I can't do that. I won't help you kill yourself."

"Do you love me?" I demanded harshly. "Do you?"

She hesitated, knowing where I was going with this. "Yes."

"Then you will do it."

"I'll go speak with Hades," she answered, without addressing my mandate. And before I could say another word, she was gone.

Brennan was staring at me. "Gaia?"

I nodded.

"How could you see her? I mean, now that Zeus has taken our abilities?"

That was a good question.

"I don't know," I shrugged. "Maybe I'm still naturally inclined to see ghosts because of my connection to the Underworld? I truly don't know. Gaia seemed very faded to me, almost transparent. I thought she did it on purpose but maybe it was simply because of my weakened vision."

"What did she say?" Brennan asked, stroking my arm gently. I literally felt sick as I relayed Gaia's message, every hateful part of it. Brennan's touch on my arm never faltered.

"So it is done, then," he said when I was finished explaining. "You won't have a choice. You will have to kill me." He sounded satisfied and relieved which promptly annoyed me.

"I don't have to do anything," I snapped. "Mortal or not, I have more self-restraint than anyone I know."

"You used to," Brennan agreed. "But you've never been mortal. You don't know what toll it might take on you. Mortals are far weaker than you think."

"In some ways," I agreed. "And in some ways, they are not. Mortals have souls and spirit and a zest for life that some of us- those of us who have been alive for eons- lack. That counts for something."

He looked at me. "It won't count for you," he observed. "You've been alive for eons."

"True," I acknowledged, looking around us.

I hadn't really examined our surroundings since I had woken up. I found that winter had descended upon us. Frost had turned the grass into glass-like shards and the temperature had dropped substantially. And I was cold. Really, really cold.

I hadn't realized that until just this second.

We had no provisions; no blankets, no heavy clothing. In fact, I was still barefoot. Brennan caught my gaze.

"Food and water appears on the altar once a day out of thin air," he said grimly. "Other than that, they give us nothing."

"How kind of them," I muttered.

Now that I had realized how cold I was, it was all I could think of. My feet were so cold that they almost felt hot as I stood in the frost.

Brennan picked me up into his arms and held me against his chest. He sank onto the altar and rubbed my hands within his as he cradled me on his knees.

"This is a lot easier now that you're awake," he pointed out, moving to rub my feet. And even though I was freezing, warm flooded my heart at the thought of him rubbing my body to keep it warm while I slept. It was the sweetest thing anyone had done for me in a while.

"I love you," I told him quietly, my cheek pressed against his heart. He stilled for a minute, then grasped me even tighter.

"I know," he told me gruffly. "I love you, too."

"I know," I whispered.

Brennan's heart beat reverberated in my ear and I imagined all of the blood flowing through his veins... his warm, sticky blood, flowing in and out of his heart like a delicious fountain. I gulped as hunger exploded within me.

Ba-bump.

Ba-bump.

Ba-bump.

The loud thud of his heart might as well have been an advertisement for a fast-food restaurant...because that was suddenly all I could think of.

Drinking.

Brennan's.

Blood.

I shoved away from him hard and retreated as fast I could across the clearing.

"What the—" Brennan started to follow me, but I cried out to stop him.

"No. Please don't."

He froze uncertainly, watching me.

"Are you in pain?" he asked in concern.

"Don't be worried about me," I said, turning away from him. "Worry about *you*. You stay on that side of the altar, I'll stay on this side."

"No," he answered, as he began to walk toward me.

"You're making it worse for me," I snapped as I caught a whiff of his scent in the breeze. He instantly froze.

"I'm sorry," he answered quietly. "I certainly don't want to do that."

"Thank you," I whispered.

I curled up on the ground and hugged my knees, trying to shield myself against the cold and protect what little warmth I had. I averted my gaze from Brennan's. I didn't want to see the pain that I knew I would find within his.

"It's not going to end like this," he said softly, staring at me from across our prison. "I'm not going to stand here and watch you shiver to death in a ball.

If you're going to kill me anyway, just do it now. Do it now before you can suffer any longer, Empusa. I know you don't want to. But I'll go to the Isles of the Blessed, Em. Perhaps, if you win, Zeus will allow you to accompany me there."

"Don't be ridiculous," I hissed.

It was growing more and more difficult for me to withstand the temptation to sink my teeth into Brennan's fragrant flesh and drain every drop of blood from his body. I gulped from the sheer idea, the saliva pooling in my mouth.

"Don't be ridiculous. They are punishing us both for crimes that we didn't commit. You for crimes of the mortal world as a whole and me for my mother's transgressions. They will never let us have a happy ending. They simply won't allow it."

I could see his shoulders slump slightly as the weight of my words bore down upon him and I felt guilty that I had done that to him. But it was best if he just accepted it now. There was nothing I could do to get us out of this- it simply wasn't going to end well. I closed my eyes to the black ugliness, reveling instead in the darkness behind my own eyelids. I took a ragged breath, then another.

I suddenly felt almost as though I could feel my mother's presence. I felt the same sense of calm as I always did when she was near. I felt certain that if I opened my eyes, she would be gone, so I kept them closed and focused on her presence. She was somehow projecting herself to me. I knew that if I opened my eyes, I would see her sitting next to Zeus. But it didn't make her presence in my mind any less real.

She was here. I knew it beyond any doubt. By the second, her presence got stronger and stronger, like an approaching light, until I finally heard her voice.

"I love you, Empusa," she murmured.

The first thing my mother did was to profess her love. An errant tear slipped from the corner of my eye. It didn't matter that I was here because of her- she had only done what she had to try and save me. I knew she was in agony over my situation right now. I could hear it in the tenor of her voice.

"I'm so proud of you," she said. "You're so strong and brave. I only have a moment, Empusa. You need to know something. It's your bracelet that can save you... your bracelet. Your soul is tied to the moonstone. As long as the moonstone survives, I can save you. Your father, Hades, can save you. And I'm sorry for that too. I'm so sorry for so many things."

I squeezed my eyes tightly closed as hot tears filled them up.

"Don't cry, my sweet," she whispered. "They will see. Zeus will see. Do with this information as you will... but just know that no matter what happens to you on that altar, I can save you if your moonstone survives. I love you, Empusa."

And she was gone. I felt her absence immediately It was as though a breeze had blown through and then stilled. I felt a vast emptiness, but even still, my heart was buoyed. She had just given me a kernel of hope. I touched my bracelet, but then dropped my hand. I didn't want Zeus to notice it.

It was astounding to me that he didn't realize the importance of my bracelet. He himself had been saved from the clutches of Hades because he had embedded his blood within Harmonia's bloodstone...a simple jewel. It had saved him from imprisonment in the Underworld. And now mine, a pretty trinket, might save my life.

I opened my eyes.

Because I had been granted a bit of hope, everything looked brighter now. The snow blanketing the ground looked beautiful, even though it was frigid. The sun shining down through the clouds and tree branches reflected off the ice crystals and send glittering prisms of light everywhere. And Brennan.

Brennan was as beautiful as ever, proud and strong. I ached to touch him, to run my fingers over the smooth expanse of his muscled arms, to feel the stubble on his face. I squared my shoulders and marched over to him. I could do this.

As his scent filled my nose, unquenchable thirst filled my consciousness. I had never wanted anything so badly in my life than I wanted to drink Brennan's blood right now. It was warm, it was wet, it would be delicious. But even more than that, I wanted to protect him, to save him. Because of that, I knew that I could do this. At least long enough to save him.

Stretching up on tiptoe, I brushed my lips against his. At the mere contact, his aura appeared to me and I found that with each breath that I took, his soul threatened to suck away from him and into me. With regret, I stepped away from his slightly, just enough to keep him safe, but still enough to whisper. If I kept my hands running along Brennan's arm and chest lovingly, Zeus would just think we were whispering as lovers.

Brennan's amber eyes were trained upon mine. He knew something had changed. He knew me well enough to sense it. But he stayed calm and quiet, trusting me enough to wait until I shared it with him.

"My moonstone," I whispered to him, as quietly as I could while I ran my fingers along his shoulders. "It is tied to my soul. As long as it is intact, my mother can save my life."

"You know this for certain?" he asked, as he grasped one of my hands and casually drew it to his lips to kiss it. We were making quite the effort to appear relaxed and I was certain it was paying off. We looked every inch like a pair of imprisoned lovers who were was just trying to steal a moment alone while being watched by a group of people.

I nodded. "Yes."

Brennan sighed a heavy sigh. He knew what that meant. In order for us both to survive, I would have to die here and now. He would have to kill me.

However, before we could say anything else, Zeus' loud voice boomed throughout the clearing.

"I grow weary of this monotony. The game will change."

My eyes met Brennan's as I sucked in my breath.

It was hard to say what Zeus would throw at us next.

"I am tired of watching this stalemate. You think that you have outsmarted me? You will soon learn otherwise. Your opposing abilities have always fascinated me, the idea that your very existence could snuff out that of the other. I will play on that today. Know this, the longer you delay action, the more mortals will die. This is true now more than ever. One of you will die today and justice will be served."

Zeus sat back down, my mother at his side. Her face was calm, but I could see her hands twisting in her lap. Her fingers were turning white. Whatever Zeus had in mind, it wasn't going to bode well for Brennan and me.

I noticed that Harmonia and Cadmus had slipped into the stands. They sat behind Harmonia's parents, Aphrodite and Ares. Harmonia's face was pale and distressed and Cadmus had his arm wrapped comfortingly around her shoulders. Whatever Zeus was planning, it certainly wasn't good.

Harmonia leaned over and murmured something to Zeus, but it didn't faze him. He shook his head almost imperceptibly and Harmonia slumped back in her seat. Clearly she had tried to intervene on our behalf and it hadn't been successful. There was nothing to do now but to wait for whatever came.

And we didn't have to wait long.

The sky suddenly darkened, causing Brennan and I to look up. The moon was moving in front of the sun, darkening the sky. The sun turned gold then orange then fiery red before its light was finally snuffed out and all went dark.

An eclipse.

Chapter Twenty Three

"What does this mean?" Brennan asked uncertainly as we both craned our necks to peer into the sky. The only light now was a blood red rim of the sun peeking from behind the darkened moon and the flickering light of the stars scattered overhead.

"It's an eclipse," I said woodenly. "Think about it, Bren. You're from the sun and I'm from the moon. Our spirits are tied to those energies. If the sun and the moon block each other, they cancel each other out. Our energy is going to fade soon. Zeus is trying to force our hand."

I couldn't see his face in the darkness, but I could feel that he was shocked. His silence attested to that.

"What do we do?" he asked quietly.

"You know what we have to do," I answered. "You know what *you* have to do."

Silence.

I strained to see him, but could barely see my hand in front of my face. I looked to my right. The vision of Olympus was gone. Apparently Zeus had wanted to extinguish all forms of light around us. We were left with nothing but the eerie red ring of the sun.

Without the energy from the moon, I instantly felt weaker, although I wasn't sure if it was my imagination at this point. Surely my strength wouldn't drain so quickly. But I was still hungry. I knew that for sure.

My throat was as dry as a bone, so dry that I constantly felt like I needed to cough. I was at a distinct disadvantage. Not only was my energy draining at an exponential rate, I had to deal with my curse as well. I could only pray that Brennan would kill me before I killed him.

And then I had to laugh at myself. I had to pray? Pray to whom? The gods? No one there would help me. None of them could. The only one who could wanted my head on a spike for the world to see. I laughed a humorless laugh and then fell as silent as Brennan.

"Brennan?" I said quietly.

No answer.

"Brennan?" I asked, this time in concern. Why wasn't he answering?

Finally, his low voice came from the shadows. "I'm here," he replied.

"Why weren't you answering?" I asked. My heart had started a slow slam against my ribcage. Was this it? Was he finally coming to his senses and he was going to kill me? Was I going to die soon?

"It's hard to speak," he said, his voice heavy. "There's a weight on me. I can't move very well."

"A weight?" I asked quickly, rushing through the darkness to find him. I tripped on the altar and went sprawling across the stone. I lay still for a moment, rubbing my throbbing shin before I climbed to my feet again.

Feeling my way carefully around the altar, it didn't take long for my fingers to brush against Brennan's warm body. My first thought was that his normally very hot body wasn't nearly as hot as usual. It was back down to a normal body temperature. Secondly, his skin was clammy. I fumbled for his face and pushed his damp hair away from his forehead.

"Come sit down," I instructed him, pulling him toward the altar.

"I don't feel right," he mumbled. I gently pushed him onto the altar and curled up with him on the stone, stroking his arm. I gritted my teeth at the frustration of being so close to his tantalizing smell, but I had to stay with him. He needed me.

"I think the absence of light is harder on you than the absence of moonlight is hard on me," I observed. "It's affecting you more quickly. It probably has something to do with the fact that moonlight is only a reflection of the sun or something. God knows we've been warned about that enough."

As I spoke, a thought occurred to me, a thought so horrible that it stilled my hand immediately and I pushed Brennan away as I leaped to me feet.

"What is it?" he asked groggily. "What's wrong?"

"I think I steal your energy," I said uncertainly. "Do you feel better the farther I am away from you?"

As I spoke, I backed up, further and further until I was against the invisible wall.

"Do you feel somewhat better now?" I called to him.

"A little," he answered. His voice wasn't quite so sluggish. It was true. I absorbed what little energy he had left. I would have to stay very far away from him.

"Brennan, you're going to have to end this," I said wearily. "Soon, you will be too drained to function. You have to kill me and end this now. Please."

"I can't," he answered sadly. "I honestly don't think that I can. I don't think I can make myself hurt you."

The despair in his voice caused me to weep. I couldn't help it and I felt so weak, but I couldn't stop the tears that streaked down my cheeks. My shoulders shook with my sobs and I thought bitterly that Zeus was probably vastly enjoying my sadness. Even that thought couldn't stop the flow of tears.

"Please don't cry, Emmie," Brennan begged from across the way. "I can't stand it. Please. It's tearing my heart out."

"There's a way to end it," I pointed out dryly.

More silence.

Brennan was ignoring me now as he tried to ignore the effect the eclipse was having on him. I knew exactly what he was doing, because I was doing it myself. I was trying not to think about the discomfort that my curse was causing me or the pain that sprung forth every time I thought of not being with Brennan.

I curled up into a ball on the icy cold of the stone altar and closed my eyes. The blackness of sleep consumed me quickly.

* * *

"Empusa."

I opened my eyes. It was still blacker than the blackest night. The trees were still, there was no wind. I couldn't see Brennan anywhere, but I knew he was here.

"Empusa," the voice whispered again.

Gaia.

I sat up, the stone of the altar cold beneath my hands. It was so very cold here. I shivered without meaning to. I hated to show Zeus my discomfort and I gritted my teeth together in an effort to keep them from chattering. I couldn't see her, but Gaia's voice was right in my ear.

"Don't turn around," she cautioned me. "Zeus is watching."

I glanced towards where the vision of Olympus had been, but it was still black. I couldn't see them, but I had no doubt that Gaia was right and that they were watching me at this very moment. I could practically feel their silver eyes on my skin.

I tried to look as casual as possible as I stretched, then tucked one leg under me as if I was just trying to get comfortable in the cold. I stilled, waiting for Gaia to speak again. When she did, it was a feather-soft whisper in my ear.

"Hades sent me to remind you of something," she said hurriedly.

In my mind's eye, I could picture her glancing toward the Olympians, worrying that Zeus would discover her presence. Gaia was a survivor. She would never put herself in danger unless she considered the reason to be very, very important. I gulped hard. She was putting herself into danger for *me*.

"Brennan can will things into existence," she reminded me. "Use that. You will need to replenish your strength- so drink from each other. Then act, while you are at your strongest."

"But Zeus took our abilities," I reminded her quietly.

"Empusa, are you or are you not Hecate's daughter? Are you or are you not Hades' daughter? It is being whispered that you might just be the most powerful goddess that any of us have ever seen...just as soon as you realize your full potential. Why do you think that Zeus is so intent on punishing you in your mother's stead? He wants to ensure that you will never become a threat to him. He knows that

Hades will use you against him at the very first opportunity.

"But that's neither here nor there right now. Right now, you need to realize that while Zeus is powerful, you might be more so. Concentrate on your powers. Bring them back. Have Brennan do the same. Mind over matter is a very powerful thing. Have Brennan will you into the Underworld. Hades will be waiting and you can take your rightful place at his side. You don't have to die."

I couldn't believe my ears. This girl had been trying to outmaneuver Hades for thousands of years. And here she was wanting me to stand at Hades' side. I was just shaking my head with bewilderment when the little clearing lit up like a football stadium.

I blinked hard, trying to see. My eyes had been away from light long enough that the presence of it now was blinding. But before I could see, I could hear.

Scuffling.

Scraping.

A blood-curling scream.

A ring of Olympians came into focus, all standing in a circle around the clearing. Zeus was in the front, Apollo and Hera at his sides. Their brightness was indeed blinding, beginning with their silver eyes and silvery clothing. White light seemed to emanate from their very persons. Harmonia and Cadmus stood nearest to me, with my mother next to them. They watched me anxiously. Helplessly. I watched their eyes move from me to a spot over my head. I looked up and gasped.

Gaia hung suspended in mid-air over the altar. She had materialized and no longer looked ghostly. She looked as flesh and blood as I did. Her bare feet were shaking, her skin as pale as mine. She was terrified, but defiantly jutted her chin out as she hovered in the air.

"Empusa," Zeus boomed. "This is what happens when someone tries to circumvent my wishes by way of devious means. This girl's blood is on your hands."

I watched in horror as Gaia exploded into flames. Her tortured shrieks filled the night and I tried to pull her out of the sky, but Brennan pulled me back. There was no way I could help her.

I pushed my face into Brennan's chest until Gaia's last scream had faded. I hesitantly turned around in time to see Zeus snap the lid down on an ornate black box.

The box of murderous souls.

I had heard legends of it. The box contained the blackest souls of the most heinous mortals. And now, it apparently housed my friend Gaia's. Her charred remains were motionless on the altar, the acrid scent of burning flesh still heavy in the air. I squeezed my eyes closed again.

Gaia had been so terrified of the Underworld. And now, because she had tried to help me, she would forever be imprisoned in a box with the worst mortals that the world had ever known. Guilt pressed on my heart and I knew I would struggle with it forever.

"We'll fix this," Brennan told me firmly. "We'll fix this."

"You cannot, son of Apollo," Zeus called. "It cannot be repaired. It is done. The traitor's transgressions have been punished. All that is left is for you to finish the game."

The game. The wretched, twisted game. I was tired of it. My weariness caused me to lose any sense of caution. Whirling, I faced the crowd of Olympians.

"Take me now, Zeus. Just kill me now. You know that's the outcome that you want, anyway."

"Empusa, no!" My mother stepped forward, her hand help up in caution. But too late. My mouth was already open and Zeus was listening.

"Kill you now?" he asked, his lip curling in thought. "Right now? But that would be so unfair. I revel in justice, moon princess."

I swallowed my ire and walked to the edge of the clearing, standing almost nose to nose with the ancient god. Only the invisible wall separated us. I ignored my mother's protests and Brennan's calls from behind me.

"Kill me now," I implored Zeus again. "Please."

I held my hands palms up, signaling that I was not a threat. I was surrendering without a fight. Zeus smiled.

"While I appreciate the gesture, Empusa, killing you would be too easy. You need to figure out a way to die all on your own. But you need to hurry, time is ticking. If you don't figure it out, I'm sure you will be overcome with temptation and will kill your lover. You don't want that, do you?"

I stared into his cold silver eyes and I'd never hated someone so much. Anger filled me up in waves and I suddenly saw red.

My fury burst several trees that were still standing around the clearing into flames. I thrust my hands into the wall. I had almost reached Zeus, I could feel the thick material of his clothing, when I was thrown backward with unfathomable force.

I hit the opposite wall on the other side of the clearing and slid to a crumpled heap on the ground. I saw a fuzzy outline of Brennan kneeling over me, murmuring to me, but I couldn't understand his words.

Then there was blackness.

Twenty-Four

I opened my eyes.

Was I dead?

I was in a shadowy place; dark and safe. There was no sound but for a faint trickling of water. I couldn't see its source. I was lying amid grass and wildflowers and freesia. There was a garden to my left, filled with violet blossoms on long, flowing vines. The night fell on my skin like velvet, like the softest silk. I sighed, half in resignation and half in relief.

I must be dead.

"No, you're not." Hades' smooth voice came from nowhere and everywhere. He stepped out from behind a willow tree and was beside me in a millisecond. His dark hair hung just-so over his eye and he flipped it away casually.

"Where am I then?" I asked, looking around once more. "Am I in the Underworld?"

He shook his head. "No. We're in your mind. You summoned me. You've managed to tap into your immortal strength and break the barriers that Zeus built around your abilities."

"How did I do that?" I asked. "And if we're in my mind, then my body must still be in the clearing. We're at an impasse. What will I do?"

I couldn't believe I was asking Hades for advice. But truly, I didn't know what else to do. I was at a loss and I was so ready for it to end.

"You got angry," he shrugged. "You caused another forest fire. Zeus threw you across the clearing where you hit your head. You're now unconscious, but you broke the mental barrier surrounding you. When you awake, you can finish this."

"But how?" I whispered. "I don't know how."

"Yes, you do," Hades insisted quietly. He stepped closer to me and I felt his normal charismatic pull. It made me want to step closer to him, to allow him to comfort me. It was like being sucked into a magnetic vortex. He smiled at my thought.

"I'm glad your views about me are changing," he commented wryly. "At least you now acknowledge that I might have a few redeeming qualities."

"I've never doubted that," I answered carefully. "What I doubt are your motivations."

Hades threw back his head and laughed, his hair shiny in the dark. There was a moon here and I reveled in its energy, watching it shimmer across my arm. I sighed again.

"Empusa, you are my child, a child after my own heart. Surely you can see now what Zeus is capable of. I will stand with you. Come with me- take your rightful place by my side in the Underworld. All you have to do is awaken and finish this."

I was suddenly considering the inconsiderable.

It didn't seem so bad to me now, a life in the serene quiet of the Underworld. Perhaps Gaia had been right. Maybe my magic would eventually become even stronger than Zeus'... which meant that I would always be in danger until I learned to stand up for myself. For that, I would need an alliance.

"And so you have one," Hades answered my thought, bowing slightly at his trim waist. "I'm at your service."

Staring into his eyes, I knew it was the only thing I could do. And oddly enough, rather than feel trapped, I felt at peace. Comfortable. It felt right, like it was where I belonged.

Hades smiled and held out his hand. I took it, grasping his long fingers as he leaned forward and kissed my forehead lightly.

"Awaken, daughter," he murmured. "Finish this so that you can begin your new life."

"And Brennan?" I asked softly, my eyes trained upon my father's.

"You'll bring him, of course," Hades answered simply. "And we'll exact revenge upon Zeus and Mormo for everything they've done to you."

Satisfaction welled up in me and I nodded.

"Awaken," Hades said again.

So I did.

I opened my eyes and I instantly felt differently than before. I was stronger, that much was true, but it was a mental strength that buoyed me. I knew it immediately. Brennan crouched beside me, holding my hand. He was worried and as beautiful as he'd ever been. My stomach tightened with the love I felt for him.

"Empusa," he breathed. "You're alright?"

I nodded.

"How long have I been out?"

"A few minutes," he answered.

I glanced around him.

"They're gone," he told me. "Something is different. What happened?"

"I'll explain later," I answered. "For now, we both need to be as strong as possible." I lowered my voice to a mere whisper in his ear. "You're going to will us into the Underworld, alright?"

He pulled away and stared at me. "I don't know if I can," he said uncertainly. "I haven't mastered that yet. Sometimes it works, sometimes it doesn't."

"You're going to try your absolute best," I whispered. "And I know that you can do it. But first, we need to be at our strongest. We have to act soon before this eclipse kills us both."

Brennan glanced overhead at the red ring of the sun.

"Zeus said before he left that the mortal world was going to be affected soon. Crops would begin to die from absence of light. The tides would stop moving because of the absence of the moon. He also said that the absence of tides and light would trigger the fault lines to begin moving. We're going to cause an apocalypse after all, I'm afraid."

"No, we're not," I replied bitterly. "Zeus is. We aren't doing this. We're not taking responsibility for it."

Pulling him down beside me, I twisted around until I was straddling him. Bending, I kissed him, softly at first and then more fiercely. His mouth tasted like honey. He groaned and pulled me to him, his hands clutching at my back.

"Let me see your wrist," I whispered against his mouth. I pulled my own to my mouth and bit, breaking the skin. I offered it to him. "We have to," I told him. "It doesn't matter anymore what we hurt or if we stay in control. It really doesn't matter. Drink now and restore your strength. We can do this, Brennan."

"I trust you," he told me, his amber gaze frozen on my own.

Without hesitation, he drank from my wrist. I could feel the blood gushing in my arm toward his mouth. I picked up his wrist and drank as well. Just as it had happened last time, it happened again.

As our blood mingled and mixed, I felt an overwhelming sense of strength and power. It surged in my veins, filling me up in swells. The sensations that coursed through me were almost unbearable, they were so strong and fierce.

Brennan stopped drinking and looked up at me, his eyes slightly unfocused as my blood streaked down his chin.

"This is incredible," he uttered. I nodded, unable to speak, unable to stop drinking his oh-so-succulent blood. He was the most delicious thing I had ever tasted. He was the sun and the earth and everything pure and good in the world. And I so wanted every bit of him inside of me.

Without another thought, without even thinking it through, I dropped his wrist and kissed him again, hard.

His mouth tasted metallic, like my blood, mixed with his own sweet taste. I plunged my tongue into his mouth and his hands were suddenly everywhere. He needed me as much as I needed him.

I couldn't breathe.

I couldn't see.

I couldn't think.

All I knew was that every cell in my body needed this man. I needed to touch him, taste him, feel him, consume him.

Now.

I took a ragged breath and stripped off my clothes. His heat enveloped me and I ripped his shirt to remove it. His skin pressed against mine and I could no longer form any coherent thought. I knew that the Olympians could see, but I suddenly didn't care. All rational thoughts faded away as the colors of the rainbow exploded around us and our auras materialized to me. Normally, this would be where I stopped, where I forced my hands to still so that I didn't take Brennan's soul.

But today, I felt stronger than I ever had when I really should be at my weakest because of the eclipse. I didn't know what internal well I was drawing from, but I wasn't going to question it.

I kissed Brennan, all of the fire in my veins transferring into my kiss as I bit his lip.

"I want you," I told him hoarsely. "Right now."

From the corner of my eye, I could see the trees on fire again and the oranges and yellows of the flames swirled into the colors our auras. My own fire raged within me and I innately knew that only one thing could quench it. And at this particular juncture, we didn't have anything to lose anyway.

Brennan's hands were everywhere, his breath on my skin. His tongue licked the soft skin of my neck, right before he bit.

He drank more of my blood before dragging his mouth to mine. I felt weak with wanting him, but stronger than I'd ever felt at the same time. We were meant to be one. It was as natural to us as breathing. It was what we were both racing toward now. There was no turning back.

Suddenly, his fingers found the most sensitive part of me and I cried out. The intense pleasure overtook me and the solid granite altar beside us crumpled into rubble from the burst of energy.

My cheeks were flushed and hot, my breaths panted raggedly. Brennan's hands were on my back, my legs, my breasts. And where his fingers touched, his mouth quickly followed suit. Only one thing mattered now.

Only.

One.

Thing.

I pulled Brennan to me and I could feel his hardness, his maleness, his need for me. It was overwhelming, earth shattering, mind bending. I struggled to breathe and everything was a blur. We were moving, but I couldn't define it anymore. I couldn't control it or myself. And then suddenly, before I knew it, we were physically one.

I gasped and Brennan cried out.

In that one moment, with Brennan inside me, I had never felt more complete or at peace. I arched against Brennan as he moved in the ancient, old-as-time rhythm and I felt tears slipping down my cheeks. Sadness didn't move me, an uncontrollable happiness did. There had never been anything so *right* in my entire life. Why had I resisted it for so long?

We moved toward an unseen precipice and I braced for what would come. It built up and built up and as Brennan exploded within me, so did the sky above us. Colors and pops and cracks and supersonic booms came from every direction and suddenly, the sky was on fire.

We froze and watched in wonder for several minutes as the sky burned.

And then, as the clouds and smoke moved and parted, we saw the sun and the moon separate, moving back into their rightful places in the sky. The eclipse was over. Our power, the energy that we had created together, had torn the eclipse apart.

I collapsed onto Brennan's damp chest and cried...from happiness, from relief, from love. He held me close and whispered sweetly to me, cradling me against him. Whatever happened to us next almost didn't matter.

"Use your will now," I whispered to him. "Take us to the Underworld, Bren. We'll never be stronger than we are right now."

The last thing I saw before I closed my eyes was the sky opening up and the Olympians descending upon us. Then we were gone.

Chapter Twenty-Five

I had never been as comfortable as I was right now. I came to that realization as I stirred, as I slowly regained consciousness.

I opened my eyes and found that I was wrapped in red silk bedding, situated in the middle of a massive, soft bed. Ebony bedposts as thick as my body framed each of the four corners and billowy gauze floated above me.

Brennan sat in a chair next to me. He was clean and shaven, and was dressed in linen trousers and a white silk shirt. He practically glowed with his own brand of health and beauty. His eyes lit up when he saw that mine were open.

"Empusa," he smiled. "How do you feel?"

"Like I've been asleep for a thousand years," I admitted, moving my arms gingerly. "How long has it actually been?"

"A few days," he said quietly, pulling my hand to his lips. "Our strength was completely drained. I slept for a solid day, myself. But I'm awake now and I feel better than ever. Do you feel better?"

I considered that. I stretched each of my hands, then my legs. I felt strong. My mind was sharp. I seemed to have made a full recovery from the effects of the eclipse. To be honest, I hadn't felt so good in a long time.

"And Zeus?" I asked hesitantly.

"Seriously pissed off," Brennan confirmed. "There's a storm brewing now, Empusa. But we're together and we're both alive. Hades tells me that the game has changed. Your significance has changed everything."

"Yes, indeed it has," Hades added as he glided into the room. Everything about him was so fluid, so polished. So refined.

"I knew from the moment that I first saw you that you were special, Empusa," he continued, as he poured nectar into a sparkling goblet and handed it to me. "I just didn't know how significant you would actually become. I do believe that you will be the key that will change everything."

"Well, no pressure, or anything," I mumbled sarcastically. Hades smiled at me, his teeth bright white in the cool darkness of my bedroom.

"Do you like your rooms?" he asked casually. To be honest, I hadn't looked at them. From my bed, I could see silken tapestries, thick woolen rugs, chandeliers, mahogany, gold. He had certainly spared no expense in decorating.

"You also have a sitting room and a Greek bathing room," he added. "If something isn't to your taste, simply let Persephone know and it will be changed at once."

"Persephone?" I raised an eyebrow. "How does she feel about my presence here? I'm assuming we're in your palace."

"Of course we are," he confirmed. "And Persephone loves guests. Although, you aren't a guest, of course. This is your home. Please treat it as such."

"Where are Brennan's rooms?" I asked.

"Right next to yours," Brennan interrupted. "In fact, they adjoin."

"You seem to have thought of everything," I told Hades. He shrugged.

"I try."

"What will happen now?" I asked. "If Zeus is angry, there will be hell to pay. We outmaneuvered him. He won't stand for it."

"Of course not," Hades agreed. "Only the time has come that perhaps he will have no choice. You are a game-changer, daughter. And I think Zeus knows it."

"I never asked to be a game-changer," I pointed out. "And where's my mother?"

"Well, whether you asked for it or not, it is what you are," he answered. "And your mother is gone. The second that Brennan willed you here, your mother disappeared. I'm sure she is safe. In fact, I wouldn't be a bit surprised if she doesn't turn up here very soon. She certainly won't stand on Zeus' side. Not now."

"Zeus' side?" Brennan asked. "You talk like there will be a war."

"Of course there will be," Hades answered, completely unconcerned. "Finally."

He was pleased. Brennan and I could both see that. I found that I was actually indifferent. I didn't care about angering Zeus any longer. As long as my mother was free of his hold, it no longer concerned me- not as long as Brennan and I were together.

"So be it," I replied carelessly. "It matters not."

"Of course it doesn't matter," Hades agreed. He pulled the covers back on the bed and pulled me to my feet. "You look well rested, daughter. We must feast this evening, in your honor."

"I cannot eat here..." I began out of habit. And then I caught myself. This was now my home.

"You are princess here," Hades reminded me. "You can come and go as freely as you would like."

"And Brennan?" I asked expectantly.

"Brennan will enjoy the same freedoms once he is your husband," Hades answered.

Brennan's eyes snapped to mine and held in an unwavering gaze.

"Married?" I breathed.

"Of course. Once you are tied together, he will enjoy the same freedoms and privileges as you."

"And until we're married?"

"Until then, he will be as any other person who enters the Underworld," Hades said matter-of-factly. "If you choose to not get married, Brennan must drink from the river Leche to forget his mortal life and he will remain here. I'm sorry, Empusa, but I'm sure you know that I am a very fair god. Rules for one apply to all. I can treat Brennan no differently. But that doesn't concern you, does it? Weren't you planning to marry?"

Were we? Brennan had asked once upon a time, but so much had happened that it hadn't even crossed my mind in so long. We were together. That was all that mattered to me. Making it official wasn't a concern.

Until now.

"Brennan?" I asked.

"You already know that I want you to be my wife," he answered. "And it appears that in marrying me, you will save me from a lifetime of amnesia."

It was true. Drinking from the river Leche would render him without memories. He would forget who he was, who I was, who we were together. Suddenly, it was no longer a question. It was inevitable.

"We'll be married at the soonest opportunity," I told Hades.

"Wonderful," he dipped his head. "Congratulations. I'll tell Persephone. She can ready the feasts and the ceremony can commence tonight. There is no time like the present."

He walked toward the door. "I'll leave you alone," he said over his shoulder. "I will send your maid to ready a bath."

He stepped out and closed the heavy door behind him. I stared at the ivory inlay. They were carved with scenes from my life, beginning with my birth. They stopped at the present point, where Brennan and I stood together in marriage. There was blank space left to fill on the bottom half of the second door. Hades had truly spared no expense or trouble in preparing my suite.

I turned to Brennan. "So, this is your last afternoon of being single. You should ask Hades for a bachelor party."

Brennan laughed. "I would marry you this minute if I could. I don't need a bachelor party."

"I worry that you are so young," I told him. "You haven't even lived yet."

"My soul is old," he reminded me. "And when I'm not with you, I'm not living anyway."

"Good answer," I told him with a smile.

"I try," he shrugged, mimicking Hades. It was a perfect impression and I laughed.

"I should be nervous," I told him seriously. "I'm sure that Zeus is planning a battle of epic proportions, but all I can feel is relief that we are out of the clearing and here together. I feel safe for the first time in…ever."

"Me too," Brennan admitted. "I think it just feels good to know what side we are on, finally."

"What about your father?" I asked him. "Apollo will not be happy with you."

"He's not truly my father," Brennan answered brusquely. "Not really. He fathered me and gave me immortal gifts, but he's nothing to me."

I nodded, but before I could say anything, there was a soft knock and then my door opened. A small woman entered, quiet and plain. I had heard that Persephone only had plain houseservants. She was a very jealous woman.

The woman approached me and bowed low. "Princess, I'm Simone, your maid."

"I'm pleased to meet you, Simone," I answered. "I would practically kill for a hot bath right now."

She startled, then smiled when I did.

"I would never hurt you, Simone," I assured her. "I know that there are many things said about me, but I would never hurt you."

"You are legendary, princess," she answered, without going into the sordid details of my curse. I appreciated that. "I'll just go run your bath."

She curtsied once and left the room.

"Can I stay for this?" Brennan asked softly, running his fingers lightly along my arm. Electricity tingled where he had touched. We had been in survival mode for so long that simple acts like this were truly wonderful. And I found that I wasn't ready for him to leave my side just yet.

"Of course," I told him. "Please stay."

He stuck his arm out for me to hold and I was suddenly glad for it. Lying in bed for days tended to make legs a little shaky. I discovered that when I took a few steps and faltered.

"Careful there," Brennan laughed, holding me up. I leaned into him and he wrapped his arms around me. He smelled heavenly and I stood still, simply inhaling him.

"Did Hades say anything about my curse?" I asked softly. Brennan shook his head.

"No. But one way or the other, Em, it will be fine. We know that we can handle it, so it doesn't matter now if you have it with you forever, right? That's the worst that can happen."

And he was right, I realized with a start. I had lived so long with the sole goal of having my curse removed so that I could live a normal life that I was suddenly at a loss when I realized that it didn't truly matter anymore.

I'd like for it to be removed so that I didn't have to be quite so cautious when I was around Brennan, but I knew now that I could control myself and not kill him. That was the most important thing.

"We're getting married tonight," I told him with a smile. "I think it might be bad luck if you stay here while I get dressed."

He looked disappointed.

"Truly?" He raised an eyebrow.

"Truly," I confirmed. "I'll get ready and then come downstairs and meet you. I want to look beautiful for you."

"You always look beautiful," he assured me, leaning down to kiss my nose. "But if you'd like some privacy, I'll meet you downstairs."

He strode toward the door, turning once he reached it. "I love you, Em."

"I love you too," I answered.

He was gone then and I was alone.

Simone poked her head back into the room. "Your bath is ready, princess."

I smiled and joined her. I couldn't help but stare around me in wonder. The Greek bath was something out of a history book, straight from an ancient royal palace.

Marble floors glistened under my feet. The tub was sunken into the floor, inlaid with jewels on the bottom. Rubies, sapphires and amethysts sparkled in the light. The room was large and a hundred candles burned. Fresh flowers sat in vases all around us and I had never seen such a lavish bathroom.

Simone helped me undress and before I knew it, I was sinking into the luxurious bathtub. I laid back on the inclined seat and the water rose to my chin. Simone dropped perfumed oil into the water and then stood back.

"You can go," I told her. "Thank you. I'll call you if I need anything else."

She nodded. "I'll be right outside, princess."

"You can call me Empusa," I answered. She looked mortified.

"Or princess will work, if you prefer," I added. She looked infinitely better at that. I certainly didn't want to make her feel uncomfortable. She bowed and left the room and I closed my eyes. The flickering candles certainly were relaxing.

I soaked and soaked, reveling in the warmth, the clean feeling of the water, the safety that I felt here. I was just about to finally open my eyes when a voice hissed in my ear.

"If you hurt my husband, I swear to you that I will rip your heart out and eat it like an apple."

I startled, then relaxed before opening my eyes. It seemed that Persephone had found me.

Chapter Twenty-Six

As I opened my eyes, I felt Persephone's thin fingers on my temples. My head was leaned back against the marble tub edge and she massaged my head, harder than she needed to.

"I know who you are," she continued, her voice icy and calm at the same time. "I know what you've been through. It might have done a weaker person in which is impressive. None of that concerns me now though. What does concern me is my husband's well-being.

"I do not wish him upset or harmed in any way. I do not wish for his hopes to be raised in relation to this war with Zeus by someone who does not intend to follow through with her promises. If you disappoint him, in any way, I will pull your eyes out of your head and feed them to you. Do you understand?"

I stared into her cobalt blue eyes which were glittering intensely at this moment and then sat up, shoving her hands away from my face.

Turning, I stared at her once more.

"I understand that you think that I am a threat to the god of the Underworld. I understand that as a wife, you are concerned. What I do not understand is why you underestimate your husband so much or why you feel that you are skilled enough to threaten me."

Bright red spots of color stained Persephone's alabaster skin and her lips pinched together. But before she could speak, I continued.

"Regardless of those things, I want you to know that I bear no ill toward you at all. I would like nothing more than to enjoy a healthy relationship with you. There is enough drama in the world without creating it when it is unnecessary, don't you agree?"

I could see Persephone's buxom chest, clad in tight gold satin, rising and falling as she quickly breathed. As she gained control of her emotions, it slowed. And finally, she spoke.

"I would like nothing more as well. It appears that you will be here for a while, if not forever. It would make things easier if we got along."

"Agreed." I stared at her, almost daring her to look away first. She did not. We stared into each other's eyes for an uncomfortably long time, before I finally smiled.

"I hear that you are putting together a feast for me this evening. I greatly appreciate that and I hope that you haven't gone to any trouble."

"You are my husband's daughter and a true princess of the Underworld," Persephone sniffed. "It is no trouble."

She and my father had a very strange relationship. She knew of his dalliances and she had her own, yet they were as loyal to each other as two people could possibly be in every other way but sexual. And they loved each other fiercely. I knew that if I proved worthy and true, her loyalty would eventually extend to me.

She smiled back at me and offered me a hand. An olive branch, so to speak, a very tenuous olive branch. I took it and stepped out of the tub, dripping scented water on the marble. Persephone wrapped a soft towel around my shoulders.

"You have a wedding to ready for," she said knowingly. "And I have just the jewels for you to wear. They will look stunning with your gray eyes. Will you be wearing white?"

I hadn't thought of it, to be honest. But I did want to look beautiful for Brennan. Theoretically, we would only be getting married once. I should wear white. I nodded.

"Perfect," Persephone nodded. "You will be lovely. Just let me bring you the jewels. I'll be back in a moment."

She slipped out and I toweled my hair dry. I briefly wondered where Brennan was, but didn't worry too much.

We were in a strange new world now, one where everything was backward from the way it used to be. We were safe in the Underworld. Hades was an alliance. He was on our side and he needed me as much as we needed him.

Plus, he was my father. That was a fact that I hadn't allowed myself to think on just yet. Not really. But soon enough, I would have to sort out my feelings on that matter.

For now, I concentrated on making myself as beautiful as possible for my wedding.

I envisioned the most beautiful wedding gown I had ever seen, a long, flowing silken creation with thousands of pearls and iridescent beading and a simple train. It was slightly off the shoulder with an open back that reached the very small of my own. I pictured it clearly in my head and instantly I was wearing it.

The silk was butter soft against my skin and looked lovely against my dark hair. The beading glittered in the light of the candles and I found myself twisting my arm to make them sparkle.

Simone returned and sat me in front of her, patiently twisting and curling my hair into an elaborate up-do piled on top of my head. Wispy tendrils escaped from the front and framed my face and when she was finished, I gasped at the reflection in the mirror. I honestly did look stunning.

And I didn't care for myself. In fact, I could scarcely care less. But I wanted to be beautiful for Brennan. I wanted him to remember this night forever, no matter what we would have to face in the future. He deserved that and so much more.

Persephone re-entered my bedchambers carrying a velvet box of jewels and a glass bottle with an ornate ruby stopper.

"I've brought jewelry and the most beautiful fragrance oil you've ever smelled," she announced. "It was a gift from Hera a long time ago. The perfume oil conforms to the woman who is wearing it, creating an exquisite, unique scent for each who wears it."

She dabbed some at my neck, cleavage and wrists and I had to admit that she was right. I drew my wrists to my nose and inhaled. I smelled...ethereal. Beautiful. I smelled like the loveliest of night-blooming flowers, which suited me completely. I was a creature of the night.

Persephone dipped her head in and sniffed at me, nodding. "See? I told you."

She opened her velvet box and withdrew a sparkling, chunky amethyst necklace and draped it around my neck. It was elaborate, which perfectly offset the simplicity of my dress. As I stared into the mirror, I found that the deep purple stones seemed to bring out small purplish flecks in my eyes. I hadn't even known those purple flecks were there, but Persephone had noticed. She was very perceptive.

She fastened the matching bracelet on my left wrist and I left my moonstone on my right. She didn't question it so I assumed that she already knew what it was and the importance of it.

The earrings were the last touch and then she turned me to face the mirror. I was a vision in white, I could honestly say that without any conceit. While white usually washed out pale people, it went perfectly with my dark hair and gray eyes. My cheeks were unusually flushed, my eyes sparkled. I would do. I would make a fitting bride for Brennan.

"You're beautiful, princess," Simone whispered to me. She seemed in awe and dropped in a low bow. I smiled and grabbed her elbow, pulling her back upright.

"Thank you," I told her. Turning to Persephone, I asked, "What time is dinner?"

"Directly following the ceremony," she answered, reaching around to tuck a stray piece of my hair into the updo. Strange how an hour ago she was threatening to rip out my heart and now she was doing my hair.

"I still would do it," she replied to my thought. "If you ever hurt Hades."

I shook my head at the absurdity of the situation and changed the subject.

"What time is the ceremony?"

Persephone looked at me like I was insane. "When you get there, of course," she answered. "We cannot start without the bride."

"Do you know where Brennan is?" I asked her uncertainly. She laughed.

"Do you think that he ran away after all of this?"

I shook my head. "No. But I just haven't seen him in a few hours."

"He went to get your ring. He should be back by now."

"My ring?" I was a goddess. I didn't need a ring.

Persephone read my thought. "It was his mother's, I believe, and it means a great deal to him."

Warmth flooded my heart. Of course. Brennan was just that sweet that he would want to honor his mother on our wedding day. And honor me, too, by offering me his mother's ring. I was suddenly overcome with love for him and couldn't wait to see him.

I made a beeline for the door and Persephone followed suit. I could hear the rustle of her silk dress behind me as she hurried to keep up. I knew that she wanted to see Brennan's face when he saw me. I didn't care about that. I just wanted to see Brennan's face.

As I flew through the halls of Hades' palace, I blurred into superhuman speed. I was on the ground floor within a minute and out the back terrace doors that led to the gardens within a few seconds more.

Hades was standing there amid the flowers, vines and fountains. He was drinking from a one of the fountains, from a nondescript metal cup. He looked up when I approached and I saw the appreciation on his face.

"You look beautiful, Em," he acknowledged, setting the cup back down on the stone. "Truly, you are a vision."

"Thank you, Hades. The terrace looks beautiful, as well."

And it did. I had never been out here before, but I had to imagine that the twinkling lights that were strung above our heads and the hundreds of paper lanterns were put here specifically for my impromptu wedding. It was a beautiful setting and it was absent of only one thing.

My future husband.

I turned to Hades, and he was speaking before I could even form the question.

"He'll be back soon, Empusa. He is simply getting you a gift. A ring, I believe. It's a mortal tradition, but it is an endearing one. We need a moment alone, anyway, you and I."

"We do?" I asked curiously. "Has something happened while I was in my rooms?"

Hades shook his head. "No. Zeus will carefully plan his attack. It will be awhile. It will give us time to plan, as well. No, what I have to speak with you about involves Brennan."

I raised an eyebrow. "And?"

"And we need to talk about what will happen to Brennan here in the Underworld while he is separated from the light of the sun."

My breath froze in my throat. Because while it was so obvious and simple, it was a problem that hadn't occurred to me yet. There was no sunlight in the Underworld. And Brennan needed it to survive.

Chapter Twenty-Seven

'm such an idiot," I murmured. "I didn't think of that. I should have, but I didn't. Of course we can't stay here. He needs the sun."

I pivoted and rushed for the doors, but Hades flashed ahead of me and blocked the way.

"Empusa, it isn't the end of the world. We can work around it."

"How?" I asked dubiously. "There is no sunlight here and Brennan needs it. We can't stay here without it."

Hades rolled his eyes.

"Who are you? Who am I? Do we not have enough magic between the two of us to think of a way to bring the sun to Brennan?"

That did give me pause. He was right. There was always a magical solution to any problem. We just had to think on it.

"Here," a voice called out faintly.

Hades and I both turned to find my mother making her way toward us from the fields of Erebus that lined the boundaries of the castle.

"Mother!" I cried and rushed through the gardens to meet her.

She looked exhausted, with lines of fatigue forming on her beautiful face. She was pale and had dirt smudges on her cheeks and her clothing was dirty and torn. But she was here. And she was safe.

I flew into her arms and she embraced me, clinging to me tightly.

"You made it here safely," she murmured into my hair. "I've been so worried for you, Em. So very worried."

"There is no need, mother. I'm here, you're here and everything will be fine."

She stepped away from me and looked at me.

"You look breathtaking, sweetie. Absolutely beautiful. Brennan is a very lucky mortal."

I cringed at the word. "Don't say that. We'll figure out a way to gain his immortality. Someday. After all is said and done. I'm so happy you're here, mother. I've been so worried about you. Was it horrible on Olympus? Was Zeus furious?"

She nodded. "Yes, he was furious, throughout most of the game. I've never seen him quite so agitated. I think he had an inkling long ago of your true parentage. It all makes sense now. He's been afraid of you for a very long time."

"There is no need," I said coldly. "I mean him no harm. I just want to live my life and be happy with Brennan."

My mother nodded. "I know. But you know Zeus. He is ever suspicious of those who will threaten his crown. That is not going to change now or ever."

"This is just the beginning, isn't it?" I asked cautiously. "Zeus isn't going to stop until I'm finally dead."

My mother looked at me seriously, her dark blue eyes somber. "He won't stop trying," she corrected. "But we will stop him. We will find a way."

I decided to stop thinking on it at the moment. I was getting married just as soon as my groom returned. And as soon as I figured out what to do about his little sun problem.

"Here," my mother said, thrusting something warm into my hands. "It is my wedding gift to you."

I looked down and found a sparkling citrine globe, cut with a thousand prisms, in my hands. It was the size of a softball and it was glittering so brightly that I could barely look at it. So I looked instead to my mother...for an explanation.

"It contains the light of the sun," she explained with a shrug. "If Brennan keeps it with him here, it will keep him healthy and safe."

A sunstone.

I stared at her for a moment longer before I flew back into her arms.

"How did you know to get me the most perfect gift ever?" I cried into her neck. "I only just realized that he would need the sun here... I don't know why I didn't think of it before. And you came with the perfect gift. Thank you so much, mother. Thank you."

Her beautiful eyes filled up with tears. "I would do anything for you," she answered. "I only hope you know that. If Brennan is what you want, if you're willing to risk so much for him, then so be it. I'll help you in any way that I can. I wish you many, many years of happiness and love with him."

"I couldn't help but hear my name," a low voice said from the terrace.

I turned to find Brennan standing next to Hades. He was golden and beautiful and I had to be with him right now. Turning, I flew to him, crashing into him with enough force that he stumbled backward.

"You're stronger than you look," he observed with a smile. "Has anyone ever told you that?"

"Once or twice," I answered, leaning up to kiss him, then kiss him again. "Don't leave me again, Bren."

He grinned a crooked grin that took my breath away. "I had an errand to run," he explained.

I didn't tell him that I already knew what it was. Instead, I watched as he dropped to one knee on the garden path. I stilled, my breath frozen on my lips. In front of both of my parents, Brennan proceeded to profess his love for me. I might have been embarrassed if I wasn't so focused on the beautiful words coming from his lips.

"I love you, Empusa. I love your humor and your sarcasm and your beauty. I love how you roll your eyes at me but you still blush when you're embarrassed, even though you are a thousand years old. I love that you know me, that you really get me, and that you are so patient with my faults. I love that you're so small, that you fit in the crook of my arm. I love that your eyes are the color of rain on a Fall day. I love that you could kill me in a second, but that you don't. I love everything about you and I have from the moment I first saw you. But most of all, Empusa, I love the way you love me. It completes me in a way that I never thought anything could. I didn't even know that something was missing until I found you and now I feel like I am home. Please be my wife. Let me know that even though I don't deserve you, you will never leave my side. I promise you, I'll love you every minute for the rest of my life."

Brennan paused, his amber eyes sparkling as he waited for my answer. I found that I couldn't answer him. The knot that had formed in my throat prevented any kind of speech. Instead, I yanked him to his feet and kissed him thoroughly on the mouth.

"Is that a yes?" he asked when he could breathe again. I nodded, then kissed him again.

"Yes," I breathed. "It is."

"Then I now pronounce you husband and wife," Hades announced. I looked at him in surprise and he smiled. "What did you expect? A catholic mass? We're gods. We're married when we say that we're married. Brennan, do you have the ring?"

"Yes," Brennan answered, fumbling in his pants pocket for a small blue velvet box.

He snapped it open and I inhaled sharply. It might have been created for his mother, but this ring was perfect for me. Thin ribbons of white gold intertwined to form a band, including one thin thread that was made from amethysts. It was beautiful in its simplicity and so important in sentimental value. I found myself holding my breath as Brennan slid it on my ring finger. It fit perfectly.

"It looks beautiful on you," Brennan said quietly, staring into my eyes.

"Thank you, Bren. It's perfect. And I love you for trusting me with it."

"You may kiss your bride," Hades interrupted. I barely spared him a glance before I wrapped my arms around Brennan's neck and kissed him like the world was ending. Because truly, in our current circumstances, it could end at any given time.

We didn't come up for air for a full minute.

"I love you, Mrs. Delacorte," Brennan said simply. I squeezed his hand.

"I love you, too."

"Now," Hades interrupted once again, rubbing his hands together. "Let's eat."

He spun on his heel and headed for the loaded down banquet tables directly inside the doors. Persephone had prepared for an army. I eyed it suspiciously.

"Is there an army coming?" I asked hesitantly. Everyone laughed so I had to assume that there wasn't.

"I wanted to be prepared for unexpected guests," Persephone explained as she filled up a crystal plate and poured a goblet of nectar. "You never know who might turn up."

"Okay," I answered uncertainly.

They all acted like they knew something that I didn't and it made me nervous. But I followed suit and filled up a plate, poured a glass of nectar and followed Brennan to a nearby table. We sat alone on the edge of the terrace, with only a candle between us.

"How do you feel?" I asked him. "My mother brought a stone that contains sunlight. It should keep you healthy down here."

"I was never worried," he answered, as he took a bite of roasted pheasant. "Your mother is amazing, though."

"Yes, she is," I answered. I watched her speaking with Hades and Persephone. None of them acted like it was weird at all, even though Hades and my mother had once had an affair that had resulted in my birth. Things were beyond strange at times. I returned my attention to Brennan.

"So, we're married now," I pointed out awkwardly. He stopped mid-bite and looked at me.

"Does that bother you?" he asked seriously. "Are you okay?"

I picked up his hand and watched the way his fingers fit over mine so easily.

"No, it doesn't bother me," I answered him quietly. "It feels perfect. Since this was all so last-minute, I don't have a ring for you and Hades is right- it is a mortal custom. Would you like one?"

Brennan shrugged. "If you think of it at some point. There's no need to rush out to a jeweler's."

I smiled. "Okay. I'll surprise you someday."

"Speaking of surprises..." Brennan trailed off, his gaze fixed behind me. I turned in my seat and almost cried out.

Harmonia, Cadmus, their daughter Raquel, Ares, Aphrodite and the entire army of Amazons led by Ortrera stood directly inside the room. Little Raquel's eyes lit up when she saw me and she took off running across the room like a jackrabbit, leaping into my arms when she got close enough.

"Em!" she squealed. "Mama said you're here to live forever! I can't wait. There is so much we can do. We can go watch the hydras, we can ride Ortrera's Pegasus, we can go dragon hunting with daddy..."

I caught Harmonia's gaze above Raquel's head. Harmonia's eyes were loving and soft as she stared at her daughter. The rest of her looked tired and anxious, much like everyone else that she was with. I hugged Raquel and told her that we could catch up in a little while and then I joined the other adults. Brennan followed.

"Not that I'm not happy to see you," I began uncertainly, "But why are you here? Zeus is not going to be happy. There is no reason for you to become involved."

"No reason to be become involved?" Cadmus raised a dark eyebrow questioningly. "I seem to recall that you were there when we needed you. Now we are here when you need us. That's how these things usually work, little one."

A knot formed once again in my throat at their kindness. Brennan could sense my emotion and he rubbed a circle on the small of my back.

"Your kindness is appreciated," Brennan answered, shaking Cadmus' hand. "We sincerely hope that it won't be necessary."

Harmonia looked at him, puzzled.

"Of course it will be necessary, Brennan. Zeus will retaliate. You have outmaneuvered him in front of every Olympian. That, in combination with the fact that Empusa possesses some very formidable magic is enough to ensure that he will wage war. But we will be ready. My husband is a skilled warrior and my father is the god of war. We stand with you, Empusa."

Everyone around us nodded in affirmation. They were here to defend me. It was amazing. I had never witnessed such camaraderie, much less in a show of support for me.

"Thank you," I whispered.

"More will follow," Hades said as he drew up on my right. "I have allies in many places throughout the world and many people who owe me favors. We will not stand alone and for the first time, my brother's reign will truly be threatened. His injustices will be over."

I felt extreme trepidation at the thought of waging war against the god of all gods. But as I looked around and remembered that for once, I wasn't alone, I felt stronger and more confident than ever. It was a feeling that I would have to get used to....not being alone. But as Brennan's fingers found mine and we mingled with our unexpected guests, I knew it was something that I could definitely grow accustomed to.

Chapter Twenty-Eight

The night was chilly on our balcony. Earthy smells surrounded me on the breeze as I stood at the railing looking down on Hades' many gardens.

Brennan's things had been moved into my bedchambers during the wedding feast and so now we were truly a married couple in the eyes of Hades' court.

"Are you coming to bed soon, Emmie?"

Brennan's husky voice came from behind me and I turned to look at him.

He was wearing black trousers and was shirtless, his muscled chest and abs rippling in the candlelight. His blonde hair caught the light and once again, the term "golden boy" came to mind. He was truly magnificent on so many levels. And he was mine forever.

I reached up and touched his face, nodding.

"Yes. But only if you promise that you'll be there."

He grinned.

"I wouldn't be anywhere else."

"I have something for you," I told him. He paused, waiting. I held out my hand and opened my fingers.

A cut black titanium wedding band rested on my palm, glittering mutely in the light. It had beveled edges and its dark metal would look amazing against Brennan's golden glow.

"It's inscribed," I told him. He picked it up and peered at its inside.

Time is nothing...Love is everything.

Brennan smiled. "Agreed."

He slipped it onto his ring finger and of course, it fit perfectly. I had imagined that it would, so of course it did.

"It must be nice to be you," he observed. "You can conjure anything that your little heart desires."

"Not everything," I corrected. "I was never able to conjure someone like you."

"That's because there is no one else like me," he boasted jokingly. "Thank the gods for that or the world would be in trouble."

"You've got that right," I smiled. "Now, what were you saying about bed?"

He smiled and grabbed my hand, leading me back to the bed.

I sank into the softness of the silken bedclothes and the fluffy pillows. Brennan hovered over me, tucking my hair behind my ear.

"You are so beautiful," he murmured. "I'm a very lucky man."

I leaned up and kissed him softly.

"Does it still bother you to be so close to me?" he asked in concern.

"Yes, a little," I told him honestly. "But hopefully we can resolve that little issue someday and we'll never have to worry about it again. Until then, I'll deal with it. All that matters is that I'm with you. Everything else is just a detail."

"Cadmus and Harmonia must think a lot of you," Brennan mused. "They're risking everything to help."

I considered that for a moment as I traced the outline of Brennan's hand with my fingers.

"I think that Zeus' arrogance is coming to a head. I think many Olympians have grown weary of his tyranny, but there was never a catalyst...something that was forcing them to act. I guess that's what we are. And this has been an eye-opening incident for everyone involved."

"So, I'm married to the Princess of the Underworld," Brennan said, smiling as he leaned in to kiss my neck. "I think that might take some getting used to, your highness."

I laughed. "Trust me, I know. It's new to me, too. I still don't know how it's truly going to affect us."

"It won't," he told me firmly. "I'm still me, you're still you. They're not going to change that."

"I hope not," I told him honestly. "But it is unrealistic to expect that nothing will change. Things always change. I just hope the changes are for the better."

"Well, so far... I like them." Brennan grinned. Then he leaned over and silenced me with his lips. There were no more words for the rest of the night.

* * *

When we woke the next morning, I was curled into the crook of Brennan's arm. He was sleeping peacefully, his face boyish in slumber. I reached over and brushed his golden hair away from his face and studied him as he slept. His chiseled cheekbones drew me in and I kissed them one by one. He opened an eye.

"Do you see something you like?"

"Perhaps," I answered lightly, propping myself up on one elbow.

"I certainly hope so," he said. "Because you're stuck with me."

"Ha," I sniffed as I threw the covers off and got out of bed. "Don't push me. I know how to suck your soul out."

He laughed and threw a pillow at me, striking me squarely in the back. I whirled and pounced on him, pummeling him with the pillow that I had left behind. He finally threw his hands up.

"Truce! Truce!" he called. "I mean no harm. I come in peace!"

"Whatever," I laughed. "Let's try this again. I'm going to get ready for the day. I suggest you do the same. We've got a war to wage."

I said it lightly, but we both knew there was truth to my words. There truly was a war to wage and I was certain that the others were already meeting to discuss it.

I hurriedly got dressed and washed up, then together with Brennan walked downstairs to the banquet hall. The magnificent tables were set for breakfast with food of every kind steaming from the tabletop.

"Are we late?" I asked as we stepped into the room. It seemed that everyone else was already here. My mother rose from her chair and crossed the room to kiss my cheek.

"No, sweet child," she told me. "We've just begun discussions. You're right on time."

Everyone continued chattering while Brennan and I prepared our breakfast plates and found seats at the table.

"Well, the Olympians are down by three," Hades announced. "Ares, Aphrodite and myself decrease their headcount."

"That will be useful," Ortrera reasoned. "And we've got my entire Amazon army, plus all of the beasts of the Underworld. I'm sure we could round up the heroes of the Isles, too, could we not?"

Hades nodded. "I'm sure we can. I'm certain that Hercules and Achilles will welcome the excitement."

Their strategic planning droned on in the backdrop as Brennan and I ate our breakfast. Talk of war didn't interest me at all. I had never been interested in military strategy. It was interesting, though, to watch some of our group talk about it.

Ares, in particular, grew extremely animated during the discussions. I supposed that it had to do with him being the god of war. He thrived on it.

At one point, even though I wasn't listened to their words, I caught Ares' dark eye. He was studying me intently and I lowered my fork.

"What do you think about that, Empusa?" Ares asked. I was embarrassed to admit that I hadn't heard the question. I could feel the heat in my cheeks as I asked them to repeat it.

"We're certain that Zeus is still pondering the idea of a mortal apocalypse. None of us are sure how that would affect us, including Zeus himself. But we're fairly certain of how it would affect *you*."

Ares' voice was strong and carried throughout the room easily. But it took a moment for his words to sink in.

"What do you mean... how it would affect me?" I asked uncertainly.

Ares looked at me curiously, and ignored my mother's requests to stay silent. He glanced at her and continued speaking.

"We aren't sure how a mortal apocalypse would affect you, moon princess. We're fairly certain that if Zeus destroyed the moon and the sun in order to destroy the mortal world, it would mean a slow death for you and Brenan... but it would also certainly kill Apollo and it would affect many others, as well. We're not certain if Zeus would do it, if he would risk it. He doesn't know how the absence of the mortal world would affect us a whole. We have long since known that our emotions and actions affect the mortal world. How much does it truly affect *us*, though? No one knows."

Ares' words started running together as soon as he had made his point about Brennan and I. Why had I never considered that option? It was the most simple of plans... but Ares was still correct. No one knew how it would affect the Olympians and because of that, we might be safe.

"Without the sun or the moon, there would be no light," I said haltingly, my heart beating a little faster now at the mere thought. "There would be utter darkness everywhere. Surely Zeus can think of a better way to wage war than that."

"Oh, most likely," Ares said, biting into a huge leg of turkey. "He will most likely not try it. There are a hundred other things he could do." And Ares turned his attention back to the others, discussing these many ways that Zeus could try to kill us all. Ares was excited by the notion, I could tell.

I was not. I suddenly felt sick that Zeus could dim the light of the entire universe with a whim. No wonder Hades had been saying that his tyranny needed to end. I pushed away from the table.

"I need some air," I told Brennan, leaning down to kiss his forehead. "I'll be back in a minute."

"Do you want me to come?" Brennan asked in concern, starting to get up.

"No, I'm fine. Finish your breakfast. I'll be right back."

He nodded reluctantly, but let the matter drop. I could feel his eyes on my back as I walked out onto the terrace. I inhaled the fresh air deeply, enjoying the scents of the many different flowers. But none of the delectable scents or the beauty surrounding me could take my mind off of what I had just learned.

Brennan and I could quite literally be obliterated at Zeus' mere whim. He had never needed us to kill each other at all... he simply thought that would be more entertaining. He could wipe us out so very easily. It was sickening and disheartening.

"A penny for your thoughts?"

Hades stepped onto the terrace, a glass of nectar in his slender fingers.

"You wouldn't want my thoughts," I told him. "They aren't pretty or entertaining."

"I can imagine," he told me sympathetically. "It will be alright, Empusa. Together, we will stand against him and finally, we will prevail."

"How can you be so sure?" I asked him doubtfully.

He looked at me thoughtfully as he crossed the terrace. "Have you ever heard of the Fountain of Truth?" he asked.

"No."

"It is a fountain that I happen to have in my possession...on this very terrace in fact. It has the ability to show truth to those who drink from its refreshing waters. It might show things that have happened, or are happening or will happen in the future. But whatever it shows you is relevant in some significant way to you."

I remembered seeing him drinking from a fountain just yesterday, from a plain tin cup.

"You drank from it yesterday, didn't you?"

He nodded. "Yes, I did. And that is how I can be so sure that we will prevail."

"What did you see?" I asked hesitantly. "Do you know if any of us die fighting Zeus?"

"I didn't see that," he answered solemnly. "Although the odds would suggest that some of us will die. But this fight is worth the risk, Em."

I knew that was true. But it didn't keep me from wanting to know if any of my loved ones would perish.

"What did you see?" I asked again.

Hades was silent for a moment as he stared pensively into space. He swirled his nectar around the bottom of his glass before he finally spoke.

"I didn't see the actual war," he admitted. "I saw what life appears to be like afterward. It is peaceful and pleasant... perfect, really."

"Perfect?"

"Yes. It seems to be so. At least for me. I couldn't see anyone else. Would you like to drink and see what it will show you?"

I nodded. I both wanted and didn't want to see what it would show me.

I approached the old fountain hesitantly with Hades and stood as he dipped the plain cup into the icy cold waters. He brought it to me, the water dripping down the sides of the cup. I took it from him and without hesitation, I sipped the water.

For a moment, nothing happened.

Then, my thoughts were consumed with visions so clear that they seemed to be happening right in front of me.

I saw Ares swinging a sword, fighting in a bloody battle.

I saw Aphrodite crying on an ornate chair, her eyes red and bloodshot.

I saw Harmonia and Cadmus fighting side-by-side behind Ares.

I saw the Amazons yelling as they rode into battle.

The scene was most certainly one of war. There was screaming and blood and the loud clang of weapons being hurled and struck. In the sky, a blood red sun hung low. It was as crimson as it could be and as I watched, blood dripped into the sky and leaked onto the earth below. This vision was strange. Clearly the bloody sun was a metaphor for something. The sun couldn't actually bleed.

And then I saw Brennan.

He was fighting as hard as anyone else, his muscular body glistening with sweat as he heaved a heavy silver sword. Blood streaked down his arms from wounds that he had sustained, superficial, non-threatening wounds. I covered my mouth with my hand as I watched the fierce expression on his face. War had changed him into a man, that was for certain. His eyes were jaded as he fought, something

I'd hoped I would never see. I had wanted him to always keep his youthful outlook.

And then I gasped. More startling than Brennan's skills in war was the person whom he was fighting beside.

Armed with an identical sword, Apollo fought by Brennan's side.

My eyes flew to Hades as the tin cup fell from my hands and clanged on the stone terrace tiles. Apollo was on Zeus' side. Why would Brennan be fighting with him?

"I know not," Hades answered my silent question. "And I believe we will not know for some time to come, until all of the truths of this war are revealed to us. Come, do not dwell on it now, daughter. Let us rejoin the others. There is much to discuss."

I nodded silently, still not able to trust my voice. Surely Brennan wouldn't defect to Zeus' side. Surely, he wouldn't. He would never leave me. He promised.

I walked slowly back to my seat and Brennan smiled.

"I was starting to worry," he said, stroking my hand lightly. "You were taking awhile."

"Oh, I'm fine," I answered. "I was just talking to Hades."

Brennan nodded, satisfied, and continued to stroke my hand. I watched his fingers moving absently as I thought about what I'd seen. There had to be an explanation for it, something that I just didn't know yet. Brennan would never forsake me. Not ever. If he was fighting with Apollo, there had to be a valid reason. Hades was right. All would be revealed in due time. The only thing certain right now was that there was going to be a war.

And I knew who would be fighting with me. I looked around the table at each earnest face. That much was certain, too. Everyone here would fight for me.

I looked down at Brennan's hands again and focused on his black wedding ring.

Time is nothing...Love is everything.

Time would tell. Time would tell who would live, who would die and who would turn against us. Until then, we just had to hold on to those we loved and everything that we held dear. That was all that we could do. And then when the time came, we would fight for what we believed in... we would fight for our lives.

Hopefully, we would win.

About the Author

Courtney Cole is a novelist who live near Lake Michigan with her small domestic zoo (aka family), her favorite cashmere socks and her pet iPad. To learn more about Courtney, please visit her website: www.courtneycolewrites.com

If you are enjoying the Moonstone Saga, please watch for the exciting conclusion, *Princess of the Night*.

In the meantime, you might also like The Bloodstone Saga... the stories that started it all. Please continue reading to read an excerpt from *Every Last Kiss*.

Book One of The Bloodstone Saga

Every Last Kiss

PROLOGUE

Alexandria, Egypt
The Mausoleum of Queen Cleopatra and Marc Antony
30 BC

"Charmian! Is there any sign of her?"

I hurriedly rushed back from the outer room of the mausoleum, looking nervously over my shoulder as my bare feet padded lightly on the cool stone floor.

"No, my queen. Only the guards."

Queen Cleopatra nodded solemnly, her golden armbands glistening in the lamplight. She rose from her perch on a jeweled chaise lounge and gazed sadly at the golden sarcophagus that glittered mutely in front of her. Ornate and beautiful, it held the remains of her husband. Lovingly, she slid her hands along the golden shell that would protect him for eternity.

From the open windows of the outer chambers, the tangy sea breeze blew softly into the inner rooms and I found myself wishing that it could carry me away, somewhere far from here. I fingered the birthmark on my wrist. It was not throbbing, not even an ache, and I knew that I would not be leaving this crypt.

A sudden, soft knock on the doors echoed in the quiet room, causing both of us to whip around. Tension immediately formed in my neck. This was it. It had to be. Cleopatra squared her shoulders, then bent to brush a soft kiss on the golden mask covering Marc Antony's face.

"Forgive me, my love," she murmured.

There was another low knock and I felt my shoulders ripple with the stress that they carried as Cleopatra reached out to grasp my hand.

"Iras, love... could you answer that?" Cleopatra whispered. She squeezed my hand tightly, but I barely noticed.

Cleopatra's other handmaiden nodded obediently and slipped silently from the room to answer the door. She returned a scant moment later with a tiny shriveled woman who looked not a day younger than 200 years old. The glinting eyes that stared from under her brown hood were ageless, full of wisdom and I felt my heart begin to race. It was time. There was no doubt.

Cleopatra squared her shoulders, her face a perfect regal mask as she walked purposely toward the old woman.

"Do you have it?"

"Yes, your highness," the old woman rasped throatily.

She held out a woven reed basket. I wouldn't have thought it was big enough to conceal anything and apparently the Roman guards hadn't either. Nowadays, they checked everything that came in for the queen.

I rushed to Cleopatra's side and we peered into the interior of the basket together. It was full of plump figs and I inhaled their sweet, heavy scent. My eyes raised questioningly to the old healer.

She nodded at my unspoken question. "It is hidden under the figs."

"How long will it take?" Cleopatra whispered, her voice not reflecting even a bit of the fear that raced through my veins.

"Only a few moments. No longer." The healer's faded eyes searched Cleopatra's bright ones. "You must be certain, your highness. Once the poison enters your body, there can be no turning back."

Cleopatra nodded. "No, there is no turning back, old woman."

The healer nodded gravely and held out the basket as if it were an offering. Cleopatra took it and sank back into her chaise lounge, staring absently at the opulence surrounding her as she reached into the basket, withdrawing a fig. Slipping it into her mouth, she chewed it delicately, then smiled.

"Delicious," she announced, swallowing calmly.

She eyed the basket again pensively. I sucked in my breath. It was time. I felt it coming, the air crackled with it. Death was an unseen presence in the room, waiting for our last breaths.

Reaching into the basket once again, Cleopatra withdrew a long, thin black snake. It draped itself along her arm and she stared into its black slitted eyes.

"You will take me to the afterlife," she instructed it firmly. "And do it quickly."

Leaning back into the silk cushions, she shook the snake lightly. It hissed, its large mouth yawning open ominously, revealing glistening fangs. As it stared at her, one drop of deadly venom dripped from its mouth. Nothing more. Impatient, Cleopatra shook it again. It struck her so quickly that I barely had time to register the movement before I heard her gasp.

"It is done then," she murmured, dropping the snake once again into the basket. I flew to her side, my arms around her slender shoulders. Two drops of blood dripped from her breast.

"Cleopatra..." My voice broke as pain flooded through me.

"Charmian, do not fear. We have done what we must. All is well."

Her obsidian eyes met mine and I saw peace in them. My breath caught in my throat just as she drew her last. Her lips quivered and then she was still, her dark eyes staring sightlessly at me. My heart shattered silently.

Courtney Cole

"All is well," I whispered as I reached out and gently closed her eyes. "Is it? Is it well where you are now, my queen?"

Her face was peaceful and even in death, she was beautiful. I swallowed hard as I looked up at Iras. She was shaking her head in grief as she rocked back on her heels. The old woman watched me silently, waiting to see what I would do, waiting to see if I would follow our queen.

Shakily, I picked up the basket and reached inside. The snake's body was surprisingly dry, not scaly in the slightest. It writhed beneath my hand, agitated already. My fingers closed around it determinedly, pulling it back out into the light.

Staring into its flat black eyes, I implored it softly.

"Please be quick."

And it was.

CHAPTER ONE

Pasadena, California
Present Day

The country music singer's spunky voice ripped through the silence in my room as she began singing loudly from my nightstand, causing my phone to vibrate against the espresso colored wood. I smiled. The lyrics about demolishing a cheating ex-boyfriend's car with a baseball bat was tempting. Too tempting. I answered my phone before I got any more ideas.

"Stop obsessing."

Jessa's voice was authoritative and bossy. And so on the money that it was ridiculous, not that she needed to know that. Even as she spoke, my eyes were glued to my computer screen where Derek's face grinned at me. His perfectly mussed blonde hair draped just-so over his green eyes, and I shuddered. *Cheater.*

"I don't know what you mean," I sniffed, trying my best to sound both innocent and offended at the same time.

I could practically hear my best friend roll her eyes through the phone.

"Macy." One word, perfectly conveyed disbelief. I sighed.

"Okay, fine. There might be a small amount of obsessive behavior going on. How did you know?"

"Because I've known you since kindergarten, that's how. Mace, seriously. Anyone who would do what he did isn't worth the time that it takes to obsess over him. Instead of wasting your time going over every detail, and yes, I know that's what you are doing, you should be plotting your revenge. And I mean, in a big way."

Apparently, she hadn't heard my new ringtone. I was way ahead of her on that one.

"Yeah, I should totally get on that." I tried to sound innocent again.

"Have you showered yet?"

I looked down at my unwashed body clad in old sweats and nodded.

"Yep. Why?"

Loud sigh, long pause.

"Macy, jump in the shower. I'll be over in two."

And she was gone. And since she only lived two streets over, I knew that I literally only had two minutes to shower before she arrived and saw for herself that I had lied. I dropped the phone and ran for the bathroom.

2.5 minutes later, I was still rinsing the conditioning balm out of my hair when her smug voice drifted through the steam.

"So, how's that shower coming along?"

Did I mention that my BFF is a total snot?

"Does the word 'annoying' mean anything to you?" I shot over the shower wall.

"Yeah, um, I would think that after taking a pumice stone to yourself last night, that that hot water probably feels pretty *annoying*, doesn't it?"

She was right again. Yesterday, after someone had 'mistakenly' texted me a video of my boyfriend Derek doing the nasty with Tara Wilson at Haley Beckman's party last weekend, I had felt the urgent need to vigorously (and I mean vigorously!) wash every place that Derek had ever touched me.

It had taken a while.

I had stayed in the shower with my loofah, scrubbing myself until the water turned cold and my skin was bright pink, until I was certain that I had scrubbed away any memory of his touch. And Jess was right. My skin was a little sensitive (and still pink) today. The hot water was annoying right now, to say the least.

I turned it off and took the thick blue towel that Jess handed to me.

Toweling off, I stepped into a clean bra and undies and pivoted on the stone tile to face my friend. She tucked her light brown bob behind her ear as she watched me contemplatively with her lips pursed.

"Why are you here, anyway? I was perfectly happy obsessing alone. And don't roll your eyes. They're going to get stuck one of these days." I tossed my wet towel in her face as I walked back into my room to get dressed.

"I came to plot revenge. I already told you that," she reminded me as I dug through my drawers for a pair of jeans and my favorite comfy tee-- the light purple one that said MAN EATER across the boobs. It was perfect for my mood.

"What makes you think I need help with that? Trust me, that part's coming pretty easily right now. I need *you* to reign me in."

She grinned her ornery Jessa grin at me, the one that lit up her entire face and made me instantly nervous about the fate of mankind, with an emphasis on the *man*. Women probably didn't have much to worry about, well, except for maybe Tara Wilson.

"Yeah, don't count on me for that part. I already have plans."

As she spoke, she dug through my closet, pulling out Derek's favorite red hoodie that I had borrowed after our last swim meet, his letter jacket that I wore to make him feel good even when it was too warm outside, the oversized stuffed bunny that he won for me at a carnival, the pink hoodie that he bought for my birthday... and threw it all promptly into a pile in the middle of my room.

As she moved to my dresser to continue her search, I stared at her in confusion.

"What the hell are you doing, Jess? Have you lost your mind? I'm going to have to clean all that up!"

In answer, she tossed the lacy black bra that had also been a birthday gift from my lying ex-boyfriend onto the pile. I was beginning to sense a pattern.

"Hey, I like that one..." I stepped forward to rescue it, but she silenced me with a stare and I stopped in my tracks.

"The *asshole* bought it for you, Mace. We're not keeping it. We'll get you another one."

I stepped back silently, marveling at the way she said *we'll*, as if it was *her* bra that she was throwing out. As I moved, my attention was snagged by the lovenotes taped to my mirror. His sprawling, bold script mocked me now.

I love you today.
You're the best thing that has ever happened to me.
You have the most beautiful eyes I've ever seen.
My heart is the property of Macy Lockhart.

Lies. All of it.

I suddenly saw red, something that has never happened to me in my entire life. I was literally so pissed off that my vision blurred together in a swirl of inky red shades and I couldn't think straight. In my mind, all I could see were his lips; the luscious, soft lips that had kissed me so many times, kissing a trail down Tara

Wilson's neck right after whispering obscene dirty-talk into her ear. And I was seeing red again.

In my underwear and bra, I furiously ripped every single note off the mirror one-by-one and threw them violently onto the big pile on the floor. Jessa watched with a satisfied grin as I got further into the spirit and added his favorite CD to the top of the heap and then another. A few minutes later, I gazed at the large mound in satisfaction. I felt a tiny bit better seeing his things littering my floor like unwanted garbage.

Staring at the pitiful pile of bad memories, I realized that I desperately wanted to set fire to it. But, obviously, that would be crazy. And probably against some sort of city ordinance. Plus, it would also burn my house down. So, I settled for pulling on a pair of boots and stomping on it instead…like an insane Italian woman making wine. After the very last cd had been adequately smashed and my legs were literally shaking from the effort, I finally turned to Jessa.

"Okay, now I'm ready to go," I announced, slightly out of breath from the exertion and still almost naked…except for my boots, of course.

She stared at me wide-eyed and then burst into laughter. I couldn't help but giggle too, as I imagined what I must look like…face flushed and half-naked and insane.

"Go where?" she gasped as she laughed.

"To Derek's house, of course," I answered matter-of-factly. "I need to drop a few of his things off."

I stared pointedly at the broken pile of his belongings and then cracked up again in a high-pitched giggle that bordered on hysterical. I should feel guilty for ruining his things, but I SO didn't. It almost seemed like Poetic Justice since he had broken my heart. I really just hoped he wasn't home when we got there. In the mood I was in, I might be tempted to slash his tires.

I quickly pulled on my MAN EATER shirt and we piled into Jessa's little blue Volkswagen bug because she didn't think I was up to driving, even the short distance to Derek's house. She was probably right. Two minutes and three streets later, we pulled up onto his driveway right behind his little black Ford Ranger with the dent in the fender.

He was home. I fought the itch in my fingers to dig a tire iron out of Jessa's trunk and give it a matching dent on the other side. It was so very tempting. But I resisted, using an extraordinary amount of self-restraint.

We climbed out and I reached into the backseat to pull out the trash bag filled with his broken belongings as Jess watched me in anticipation.

"What are you going to do with it?" she asked curiously, her light blue eyes developing a sadistic gleam.

Without hesitation, I marched straight to the bed of his truck, emptying his things out over the side. Everything tumbled out, small pieces of his CDs scattering onto his bed liner like the trash that it was. My battered black bra settled to a rest on the top of the pile, a garish reminder of the intimacy we used to share. Grabbing it, I looped it around his antenna, letting it hang as a limp banner for everyone to see. I could only imagine his mother's face when she saw it.

I smiled in grim satisfaction as Jess started laughing again. And then I remembered his class ring. Pulling it off of my middle finger, I tossed it in as well, listening to the metallic clink as it bounced along the truck bed. It tumbled to a stop, the blue stone glittering in the light.

And then his front door creaked open. I froze in panic as he stepped onto the porch, bare-chested and in a pair of running shorts. It hadn't occurred to me that I might actually come face to face with him. Now what?

"Macy?"

He stepped lightly from the porch and walked towards us, his handsome face hopeful. My heart started racing as he approached, his blonde hair wet from a shower. He smelled so clean and masculine. I steeled myself with the reminder that I hated him now. He was no longer my perfect, green-eyed Poseidon.

"I'm so glad you came," he sighed as he reached for me. "I was afraid that you were never going to speak to me again."

I side-stepped out of his reach and glared at him.

"I'm not planning on it," I spit, beginning to see red again.

Did he seriously think I was such a pathetic push-over? That he could humiliate me in front of the entire school and I would just forget about it? That his little frownie-face on his 'please talk to me' text yesterday had worked? Not hardly. Not even close.

"I had some of your things at my house and needed to return them." I gestured toward the back of his truck. He circled the fender and peered inside.

"What the..." his astonished gaze flew to my face.

I couldn't quite blame him for being surprised. I was normally such an easy-going person. I wasn't accustomed to fits of rage. I had to admit though, it was pretty satisfying. I stared directly into his green eyes.

"See you around," I murmured coolly, walking past him and dropping into the front seat of Jessa's car.

She quickly started the engine and backed out of the driveway before Derek could say another word. As we pulled away, he stared after us dejectedly. I desperately pushed down the guilty feelings. He deserved nothing less than this. He had broken my heart by impaling it with one of Tara Wilson's tacky stiletto heels.

As we pulled back up to the curb in front of my house, Jess turned to me.

"Do you want me to come in?"

Her voice was doubtful because she knew me well. She knew that after the huge rush of revenge, I was going to crash down hard and would want to mope alone. And she was right.

I shook my head.

"No thanks, Jess. I'm just going to suffer in silence tonight." I looked at my driveway, where my mom's shiny silver car was now parked. "And I won't be alone, so you don't have to worry. Thank you for coming over."

The smile that I gave her was starting to get a little watery. Uh-oh. I needed to make a run for it before I started bawling. I reached for the door handle.

"Okay," she reached over to hug me. "But don't forget, Mace... this is his problem, not yours. You're perfect and he's an idiot. Call me if you need me."

I nodded and got out, rushing without a backward glance toward my brightly lit house.

I'd barely stepped in the back door, though, before my mom waylaid me. So much for suffering in silence. My chattery mother didn't know the meaning of the word.

"Macy, is that you?" she shouted from the kitchen.

"Yes," I called as I kicked my shoes off inside the door.

Who else would it be? My dad hasn't stepped foot in this house since last year, something he complained about regularly since he still had to pay half of the mortgage payment. Mom appeared in the doorway with a piece of half-wilted lettuce in her hand.

"Was that Jessa?"

I nodded.

"She missed her check-up today. She probably hasn't been flossing and was afraid to see me."

That was probably exactly right. My mom had been Jess and Jenn's dentist since they had cut their first teeth- and she regularly slapped them on the backs of their heads when they didn't floss. Literally smacked them. Italians are colorful people.

"Oh, hey. While I'm thinking about it... this was on the porch for you."

She ducked back into the kitchen and re-emerged holding a small brown box out to me. It had my first name written on the top in bold black marker and nothing else. I didn't recognize the writing.

I raised my eyebrows as I stared at her questioningly.

"What is it?"

"I don't know, honey. It's yours. I didn't open it. Maybe Derek left it for you as an apology."

She shrugged nonchalantly, but the interested expression on her face betrayed her. She was dying to know what it was.

I carefully opened the top and peered inside. For all I knew, Tara had left me a bomb. But it was harmless. A necklace glittered within tissue-papered folds.

"It's a necklace," I stated simply.

Mom gave up on subtlety and yanked the box from my hands, pulling the odd necklace out to examine it in the light. It was the most unique stone I had ever seen... a dark red quartzy looking thing, the size of half my fist with veins of black running through it. It was beautiful. I'd never seen anything like it.

"It's a bloodstone," mom observed. "You don't see these much anymore. And they're usually green, with only a little red. This one is very unique. It has to be from Derek. He knows how much you love old things."

And I did. I loved retro jewelry, vintage dresses, old movies. But I had just come from Derek's house and this box had hadn't been on the step when I left.

I shook my head. "Why wouldn't he have left a note? Besides, it couldn't be from him. I just came from there and he didn't mention it."

Surprise filtered across her face as she studied mine.

"Really? Do you want to talk about it?"

My rebellious chest started to quake. No, I didn't want to talk about it. And I didn't want to break down, either. *He* didn't deserve my tears. I took a few shaky breaths before I spoke, gripping my own hands tightly so that my mom wouldn't see them shake.

"No, thanks. I don't want to waste any more time on him."

The words sounded wooden, my voice flat. I was surprised at my own ability to get through them without screaming or throwing something through the window. I was also surprised and overwhelmed by the level of emotions I had been consumed with today. For being an easy-going person, I was feeling uncharacteristically violent. It was mildly alarming, even if I did have a very good reason. My mom looked concerned at the look on my face. I rushed to reassure her.

"I'm fine, mom. I'm just really tired of dealing with it right now. We can talk about it later, if you want. But I need a break from thinking about it. And if he comes here, please don't let him in. I don't want to see him. And the next time he comes in for a cavity, if he has the nerve to face you, that is... don't give him any Novocain."

She nodded quietly and stepped forward to hug me. Her dark hair, just like mine, swung forward and brushed against my shoulder, bringing with it the scent of apples and strawberries.

"I'm sorry, sweetie. You didn't deserve this. But it will be okay, I promise. If you need anything..." her voice trailed off uncertainly and I nodded.

"I know. If I need anything, I'll let you know."

How about a baseball bat for his car? Or a tire iron for his femurs?

But obviously I didn't say those things. If I did, my mother would stick to me like Velcro for the rest of the night. Instead, I just walked calmly past her and trudged toward my room.

"Honey?"

I turned back around.

"You forgot this." She put the necklace back into the box and handed it to me. "It must be from your dad or something. It looks expensive."

I nodded as I turned around again and trudged away. I needed to get far, far away from her pitying looks.

Tossing the box onto my bed, I dropped next to it like a sack of bricks, my breath whooshing out of me. Regardless of the fact that it was only 6:00, I was bone-weary. I didn't even take the time to take my clothes off or stop to pee. I knew that if I thought about this mess for one more second, I might start screaming. Ramming a pillow over my head to block out the dying sunlight, I closed my eyes and slipped mercifully into the silent oblivion of sleep.

But sleep betrayed me. Dreams of Derek cheating on me plagued me off and on as I tossed and turned, slept and woke. Pissed off and frustrated at my subconscious psyche, I crammed the pillow over my head again, inhaling the cool, cottony smell of my sheets as I tried to ease myself back into slumber.

Before long, a pair of dark eyes stared at me. Blinking, I walked toward them, and they morphed into a man. A breathtakingly beautiful man. I literally couldn't breathe as I stepped up to him, the sunlight bouncing off of his angular handsome face. His dark eyes, almost black, sparkled in the sun as he pulled me close, his strong arms wrapping around my back. His scent was intoxicating and familiar and I buried my face in his chest.

"You're so beautiful," he murmured into my ear, his voice husky against my cheek. "Don't leave me again..."

My eyes snapped open and I stared at the green numbers on my alarm clock. 2:00 a.m. Who the heck was that? I had never met that man...but I knew him. The familiarity was unmistakable. It was so strong that it was overwhelming. And I was annoyed that I had woken up.

But something had woken me. Something had pulled me from my delicious dream. And I knew it wasn't a noise or a light that had disturbed me. It was a feeling. A *strange* feeling.

It took me until 2:01 to wake up enough to realize that I was clutching the bloodstone necklace in my hand. Apparently, I had grabbed it in my sleep. The cool stone was polished and smooth in my palm and as I turned it over, vivid images assailed me like a lightning bolt. Sloe-eyed, dark skinned people, the heavy scent of jasmine and blue eye paint. I gasped just as soon as I could breathe again and dropped the stone onto the floor.

What the hell was *that?* I could swear that I still smelled jasmine.

I pulled my knees up to my chest and stared at the necklace in the corner. If I didn't know better, I would think that the red splotches were glowing, rising above the surface of the stone and pulsing. But that would be impossible. Or I was crazy. And that was entirely possible.

I waited until my raspy breathing returned to normal and then curled up in bed. Every two seconds, I glanced back toward the necklace. It was laying motionlessly on the floor, as innocuous as ever. And it was not glowing. Either I was crazy or I had imagined it. I finally drifted back off to sleep as I desperately tried to convince myself that I had dreamed the whole thing... because I didn't like the alternative.

CHAPTER TWO

To: Macy Lockhart ihartmacy@mercury.net
From: Jessa Gray twinsdoitbetter@trueblue.com
Subject: Advice for the day

Stop Obsessing. Seriously- I mean it. Jenn said to tell you that if we survive, we'll stop back by your house to check on you after our yearly torture session (aka Getting dragged to the Gray Family Reunion kicking and screaming).
Love ya!
Jess (aka The hotter Gray sister)

I rolled my eyes. Jess was made of drama...everything she said or did was usually blown way out of proportion.

She and her sister, Jenn were identical- from the tips of their delicate noses to their size 6.5 feet. Very few people could tell them apart so they were definitely on an equal 'hotness' plane, although Jess always insisted that she was the beauty queen in the family. It made me laugh.

Suddenly, though, an image flashed through my mind that instantly stilled my smile. Green street signs, 34th and Elm, were being pelted with rain. My knees turned weak as I saw a black SUV barreling toward the intersection. And Jenn. She turned, her face frozen with surprise and fear. She scrambled backward, slipping in the rain and fell to the street- directly into the path of the SUV. I squeezed my eyes closed. And the vision stopped.

Oh my God. Jenn. Did I just have a premonition? What the hell was happening to me? I wasn't even touching the stupid pendant and my thoughts were being invaded by…strangeness.

Something was definitely wrong with me. And every ounce of my being told me that it had something to do with the anonymous gift left on my porch. My heart was still pounding as I started clicking my mouse and within seconds, I was faced with hundreds of web pages devoted to bloodstones.

I clicked on one.

Bloodstone makes one more knowledgeable in ways of the world.

Hmm. As in seeing strange visions of the future? I kept reading.

Bloodstone is a hero's stone and instills courage. Bloodstone enables one to see the benefits and patterns of change and to recognize the 'turmoil prior to perfection'. Ancient Middle Eastern civilizations believed that wearing bloodstone could promote wisdom, protect from evil spirits and undo what had already been done. Bloodstone can help the wearer find what is lost.

I sat back in my chair. Interesting. It was quite a piece of jewelry. Too bad it was all superstition and ancient mystical folklore. But still.

Prior to the bloodstone's entrance into my life, I had never had even one crazy vision. Now, it was like a floodgate had opened- I couldn't stop them. And I couldn't help but remember how the veins in the stone had throbbed wildly last night, glowing as if blood actually pulsed through them. It gave me shivers just thinking about it.

A bloodstone. Even the name sounded...ominous.

I glanced into the corner of my bedroom. It was still there, laying right where I had tossed it last night. It seemed perfectly harmless- there was no glowing, no throbbing veins. I sighed a long sigh and got up. There was no way I was going to be able to leave this be. I was just that compulsive.

Hunching over it, I poked it with my finger. Nothing happened. No strange visions, no throbbing stone. I chewed on my lip then took a big breath- and picked it up. Almost instantly, white-hot heat rushed into my fingertips from the stone itself, racing up my arm and spreading throughout my entire body, radiating from my shoulder. I couldn't even breathe as vivid images assailed me.

A woman crying, dark eyes, swords, soldiers, blood.... the images broke apart and swirled together. I closed my eyes as the sensations became almost too much to bear, overwhelmed with waves of emotion too great to comprehend. I almost couldn't stand it.

I forced my stiff fingers open and I dropped the bloodstone to the floor once again. It nestled quietly between my feet on the carpet as though it was a perfectly normal necklace. But it wasn't. I didn't know what exactly it was, but *normal* it was not.

My breathing came in ragged gasps and I tried to calm myself by taking cleansing breaths. Cleansing breath in, cleansing breath out. It didn't work. Panic still overwhelmed me. What the hell *was* that? Apparently, it needed to be in contact with my skin in order to... do what it did, whatever that was. So, I carefully picked it up using a pair of clean underwear and hid it in my underwear drawer next to my cotton-candy colored bra.

But I couldn't shake the dark eyes so easily. They were still haunting me from my dream. Deep and dark-almost black, they were the color of melted dark chocolate, surrounded by a fringe of thick lashes. The expression in them had been familiar, loving. I knew him. Who the heck was it? I rushed through every memory that I've ever had and came up empty.

And then a realization emerged out of nowhere, firmly planted front and center in my mind as if it was dropped there. I had dreamed about that stare before, off and on for years. The dark eyes of a stranger that I apparently knew, but couldn't remember. Intriguing. And frustrating.

My sense of wonder was rudely interrupted by a loud buzz on my dresser. I got up to find a text message waiting for me- an annoying text message from a pale, blonde cheater.

Please, Macy. Can we go have coffee? I need to explain.

Oh My God. What did he not understand? I never wanted to see him again- except for school when I absolutely had to. He had thrown away two good years for an orange colored tramp. And she definitely was a tramp- she has the stamp to prove it. I saw it on her back in gym one day when her shirt slid up. Tramp stamp, fake boobs, overly-tanned skin...that whole mess was his to own- I was so done with it. Besides, I had other things to worry about now—like a pair of dark, brooding eyes and an insane necklace.

I typed back *Leave me alone* and resisted the urge to throw my phone at the wall.

What was it about relationships that made you feel so vulnerable? Oh, right. A relationship. In any relationship, you put yourself out there. You exposed all of your sensitive nerve endings and your heart and you just had to hope that you trusted the right person. Stupid me, I didn't. But I wouldn't make that same mistake twice.

I wasn't going to dwell on that now, however, despite my own obsessive nature. I had a much bigger problem than Derek hidden in my underwear drawer. It was a mystery that wasn't going to solve itself. But before I could think about it for one second longer, I needed sustenance. My stomach was loudly reminding me that I hadn't eaten yet today.

After yanking a hairbrush through my long hair, I pulled it into a low ponytail and threw some clothes on. There was a tiny deli just a few minutes away and I could hear a toasted portabella sandwich calling my name. Grabbing my keys, I ducked out to the garage.

And froze.

A man with a shaved head and long black robes stared at me. His dark face was damp with sweat and thick black eye makeup lined his eyes. A subtle musky scent permeated the air like incense. He didn't even look startled to see me- he just stared at me calmly, as though he had been waiting for me.

"All was lost, Charmian."

His grave voice was stark, slicing through the garage with hissing precision. Just as I collected myself enough to scream, he was gone.

As in...disappeared. He didn't walk past me to get into the house and there was no way that he exited through the garage door because it was still closed. I quickly walked a circle around my car. He was just *gone.*

Holy Mary Mother of God. Had I gone crazy ? Had this whole mess with Derek stressed me out so much that I had lost my mind?

I sat down on the step with a whoosh.

Should I call the police? And tell them what? That some man wearing makeup and strange long robes was in my house and then disappeared into thin air? And if I added the fact that some strange necklace was giving me visions, they would strap me to a gurney and send me to a place where lunch consisted of small orange pills.

What to do, what to do. I picked up my phone with shaking hands and dialed... but it went straight to Jessa's voicemail. The Gray family reunion....I forgot. There was no use calling Jenn, then. She was there, too. I didn't want to call my mother- she would rush home from running errands and then promptly call one of her psychiatrist friends.

As I was debating with myself, something rustled behind me, a strange whisper-like sound and I spun around.

Nothing.

The oddly dressed man wasn't standing there, which was good...but there was also nothing else to explain the sound. And I knew, beyond any doubt, that it had been real. I scrambled up and looked behind every nook and cranny in the garage, kitchen and family room. Nothing.

It was official. I was crazy.

And about to get crazier.

I suddenly felt an inexplicable pull- the need to begin walking, as though I was being pulled by an invisible cord. I was suddenly overwhelmed with the same sensations that I had experienced when I held the bloodstone. I couldn't resist it. I felt like some sort of freakish robot as my feet began moving on their own accord, one after the other; through the kitchen, up the stairs and finally stopping in front of my closed bedroom door.

As I stared at the wood grain, I knew beyond any doubt that I hadn't left it closed. So, the burning question was...who had closed it?

My heart started pounding and I pushed the door open.

Nothing.

Not a thing was out of place. My bed was made and my room was neat, except for the shoes scattered on the floor. Most importantly, though, it was empty. I almost took a deep breath of relief.

But then the whispering began again. All around me... raspy whispering with incoherent, foreign words, getting louder and louder. The room seemed to spin and suddenly I was moving again, toward my dresser. My hand didn't even feel attached to me as it reached out, pulling open a drawer.

The bloodstone glowed wildly from among my panties, the veins pulsating. I couldn't help myself- I reached out my shaking fingers and wrapped them around the stone. It felt like I was holding a beating heart in my hand.

The whispering stopped.

"All will be lost, Charmian."

I would recognize the scary man's voice anywhere. Clutching the stone to my chest, I whirled around.

And screamed. Because that is what a normal girl does when she finds someone in her bedroom. And I'm normal. Damn it, I'm *normal*.

The man from my garage stood perched at the edge of my room, ominously out of place, like an overgrown vulture. His voluminous dark robes hung heavily around him and he stretched a gnarled, twisted hand toward me. As he moved, thick swirls of incense swirled around me and I froze.

Unbidden thoughts sprung into my head.

I was suddenly consumed with fear. Not for the obvious, sane reason- because a strange man was standing in my bedroom-but because it was rumored that high priests were actually cannibals.

Where did that come from? How the hell did I know that he was a high priest?

I wasn't even in control of my own thoughts as unbidden memories that I didn't even know I had rushed back to me, flooding my thoughts. *Testing my sanity.*

High priests were cannibals. They ate the flesh of those they considered wise, hoping that they would gain that wisdom through ingestion. I didn't know how true my sudden strange thoughts were, but the second they sprung to mind, it was all I could think of.

A cannibal stood in front of me with sunken cheeks, razor thin lips and a shaved head. I shuddered and he smiled at my reaction, his thin lips stretching even thinner across his gaunt face.

His terrifying expression was startling and my heart ricocheted wildly against my chest like a drum. The thick black kohl lining his eyes was smeared, making him seem slightly deranged as it streaked in murky rivulets down his sweaty cheeks.

"Do not fear, Charmian. I am only here to help."

Why did he keep calling me Charmian?

He reached his twisted hand out to me once again. An invitation to grasp his talon-like fingers. I took a shaky step backward. There was no way I was touching him. No. Way.

"Take it," he insisted. "You must. You are the only one who can help."

With a speed I wouldn't have thought he possessed, he snatched my hand. And I dropped to my knees in front of him with the force of the visions that passed through me.

A woman was curled into a ball, weeping. With thin fingers, she frantically clutched at her chest, scratching at the skin, drawing blood. In my vision, she turned her head and stared into my eyes. Cleopatra.

I knew it just like I knew my heart was beating.

Vivid green paint swept across her eyelids and her plump lips were stained crimson. Don't ask me how, but I knew that the stain was from henna and the green was malachite. She wore a short white shift and delicate leather sandals on her feet, the thin straps interwoven with golden strands and wrapping around her slender calves until they tied neatly behind her knees.

She rushed to me, her gleaming black hair as dark as a shadow.

"Charmian, they're coming. I can't bear it!"

She gestured through the open balcony doors to our left and then collapsed back into a heap, weeping inconsolably.

Gazing over the stone railing of the balcony wall, I stared into the harbor below us. Hundreds of ships were filling the glistening harbor. Rome. Rome had descended upon us.

How did I know that?

But I knew. Just as I knew that Rome had been closing in on Egypt for years, a suffocating, overwhelming presence that had creshendoed every day, a presence led by Gaius Julius Caesar. Otherwise called Octavian, with a bland smile and expressionless eyes. Perfectly polite and perfunctory, but seemingly inhuman and emotionless, the adopted son of Julius Caesar methodically worked to fell Cleopatra and acquire Egypt for his own. And suddenly, instead of asking myself how I knew any of this, all I could wonder was ...*How had I forgotten?*

I turned from my stance at the balcony doors and caught my own image in Cleopatra's gilded bronze mirror. I sucked in a ragged breath.

My own jade green eyes stared back at me, framed by my long, dark hair. Those things were the same, familiar. But my body was different. It was shorter, slighter, older. Exotically beautiful. Golden skin, ancient clothing. Henna tattoos delicately curled down my arms and thick ornate golden jewelry adorned my neck and wrists. My lips were plump and my skin was perfect- not a single blemish or freckle.

But it was me. I knew it as surely as I was breathing and the knowledge was dizzying.

"What is happening?" I whispered desperately.

As soon as I spoke, the visions snapped closed as though someone had slammed a book shut.

I was once again standing in front of the old priest.

Annen. His name is Annen.

"Annen," I murmured.

He seemed pleased as he stared back, his obsidian eyes glinting.

"Ah, you remember, my lady."

I gulped. He was right. I remembered. I knew him. I had known him centuries ago. Oh, Mary Mother of God. This couldn't be happening. *This is a dream. This is a dream. This is a dream.*

But it wasn't.

"Please," I whispered. "Am I going crazy? How is this happening?"

"You're not crazy," he assured me. "Give it a moment. Trust me, you've been through this hundreds of times. Focus on your bloodstone. Everything will come back to you."

He sat back patiently, his crooked fingers clasped in front of him as he waited and I clutched the cool stone in my fingers. The source of all of my recent problems somehow didn't seem separate from me- it suddenly seemed a natural part of me. And I realized that it hadn't just been given to me... it had just been *returned* to me. It had been mine all along.

Annen's ancient face swirled together as the room began to spin around me and nausea boiled in my throat. My cheeks flushed as heat washed over me. It was almost too much sensation to bear. It literally felt as though every emotion ever felt by any other human being was coursing through me right this second. The sheer force of it threw my head back.

Fragmented images of people, places, colors and even scents assailed me and I gasped to breathe. Water, ships, horses, gold, statues, children.... So many things flew in front of my eyes in just a mere matter of minutes, puzzle pieces fitting together and then ripping apart to be replaced by new ones. It was maddening, dizzying, sickening...

And then, abruptly, it was over. I slumped limply forward, still on my knees. *This couldn't be happening. But. It. Was.*

The magnitude of what I knew now was making me feel weak and shaky. But my mind was filled with knowledge.... Knowledge that hadn't been there before. Knowledge that was irrefutable.

"You have remembered who you are?" Annen probed expectantly, his black eyes missing nothing as he crossed the room to me. His claw-like fingers were suddenly gripping my arm and I flinched, not from pain but because he made me uncomfortable. High priests had always made me uncomfortable.

I raised my head and nodded.

"Yes," I whispered. "I know who I am."

I lightly fingered the bird-shaped birthmark that hovered directly over my pulse-point. Why had I not wondered about it before? It marked me for being exactly what I was. I had possessed many names over the past hundreds of years; many faces, many bodies. But my soul has always stayed the same, as well as my fate.

I belonged to the ancient Order of the Moirae. As a Keeper, my sole mission in every life has been to protect and lead my charge, my *Daedal*, through the annals of time, gently guiding her into staying on the path laid out for her by the Fates.

Because every person in life has a predetermined destiny and unfortunately, there are those who have a more difficult journey in every life. We call them the Daedal.

A Daedal…a catalyst, a complication, a change. A Daedal changes the world in some significant way even though their very significance generally causes a tragic end to their lives. They are fated to be something great-something important, in every life. Because of that, I am what I am. A Keeper, marked as such by the phoenix birthmark.

And right now, I was Charmian; handmaiden, confidante and advisor to Queen Cleopatra VII, my Daedal.

I had been raised with the queen in ancient Alexandria, running and playing with her through the ornate halls of the stone palace as we grew up. I had served her, offered her my advice and became her closest friend. And I had died with her when we were both 39 years old. I could remember every painful detail with bone-jarring clarity, just as though it was yesterday.

I stared into the all-knowing eyes of the priest. He nodded, recognizing the realization he saw reflected in my own. The gravity of who I was settled down around me like a heavy cloak and the colors in the room started to run together.

And then I fainted.

CHAPTER THREE

Scorching, smoldering eyes.

The familiarity they held mocked me as they glinted in the light, framed by lush dark lashes. A strong jaw-line led to soft lips which parted to reveal even, white teeth. And then his face was unveiled to me in its entirety, as though murky clouds in my consciousness had faded away. I gasped in recognition. He was mine.

Hasani. The man from my dreams. Bronzed skin, brilliantly white smile, shiny black hair pulled into a leather clasp at his neck. He reached for me with strong hands, his long fingers beckoning. His was the most beautiful face I'd ever seen.

"Come to me, my love. I've missed you," he murmured in a deep, husky voice and my heart stopped.

I sat up with a gasp, opening my eyes.

"Hasani," I breathed.

"Ah, you *have* returned to us, Charmian," Annen murmured smoothly. Seated across the room from me on a golden chaise, his dark robes were spread around him like a fan.

And this was not my bedroom.

I looked around quickly. Polished marble floors, elaborate silken draperies, onyx statues, glittering golden accents. Ebony balcony doors were open, allowing the lush, fragrant seabreeze to blow in, gently ruffling my hair. This was impossible. Utterly impossible. This *was* my bedroom. But not my bedroom in Pasadena. This was Charmian's bedroom. In ancient Egypt.

"We're in Alexandria," I muttered uncertainly, eyeing the priest with suspicion. "I don't understand this. This has never happened before…"

There was no way I should be here. This was the past, not the present. I had never moved through time before. Not ever. There was no need. My job was to ensure that my Daedal's plan unfolded perfectly. There was never any need to return to a life, because I was very good at what I did. But my surroundings didn't lie. I had definitely returned.

I glanced down at my body and found it to be Charmian's, not Macy's. A short filmy shift cut off mid-thigh, belted by several golden cords at my waist. Confusion clouded my thoughts.

How is this happening?

I examined my arm. The skin was perfect and golden, buffed to a soft sheen. I knew that we had used sea salt as a scrub to attain that perfection. Glistening gold bracelets adorned my wrists, with agate and jade charms dangling from them.

As strange as it seemed to be thrust back into it, I was still perfectly comfortable in this body because it had once been mine. It was a jolting notion.

"I hope you will forgive me for bringing you here, Charmian."

Annen rose from his perch and crossed to me, sitting next to my feet.

"I don't understand it," I murmured. "Why are we here? And why are *you* here, priest? Where is Ahmose?"

Ahmose was my handler, an ancient Aegis priest skilled in magic. It was he who came to me during my seventeenth year in every life to present me with my bloodstone, which triggered my cycle to begin. To my knowledge, Annen was not involved with the Order or the Aegis. I had only known him here... in Alexandria. So why had he sought me out two thousand years from where we were now standing?

As I stared at him, I knew that all of my panic and confusion was easily visible on my face. I could feel it. Annen smiled a tiny smile.

"Charmian, surely you remember that I'm not simply a priest?" Condescending and self-assured, he stared down his long, crooked nose at me.

"No, I don't remember that," I answered firmly. "My memories are coming back yet I still only remember you from the Serapis Temple. Are you part of the Aegis?"

Annen shook his head. "No, my lady. I'm not part of the Aegis. They do so tamper with your memories, Charmian. It isn't right."

Confusion clouded my thoughts and I shook my head in frustration, shaking away his words and focusing on my questions.

"Then I don't understand. Ahmose triggers my cycle. Where is he?"

"Oh, he'll be along shortly, I imagine," Annen replied mysteriously. "But I need to speak with you first. It is of utmost importance."

"Well, you've certainly got my attention," I answered, staring at him both curiously and apprehensively. This was all new. And I didn't like it. Something wasn't right here. I could feel it as the hair on the back of my neck stood up. I laid my bloodstone down on the bed and turned back to face him.

"Of course. But first, Charmian, would you like to know what happened to Hasani? I know that when you and Cleopatra barricaded yourselves in her tomb, you hadn't heard of his fate yet. You died without knowing. Would you like to know now?"

He stared at me with a kindly expression and my heart stopped. It was forbidden to know what happened to our loved ones. One of the many rules for Keepers. But I suddenly had the compulsive need to know what happened to Hasani. Regardless of the rules, regardless of the consequences for breaking them.

I nodded stiffly, despite the ever-growing heavy pit in my stomach. This was wrong, wrong, wrong. But I had to know.

"Yes," I whispered. "I would."

Annen held his wrinkled claw-like hand out to me once again and gritting my teeth, I grasped it. His long fingernails curled around until they scratched my palm. I shuddered, but didn't have time to dwell on it. Because almost immediately, the visions began.

Soldiers were marching, swords were drawn, blood was everywhere. Cleopatra was weeping, people were running. Everything was so vivid that I could smell the blood and taste the dust in the air as the people scattered. Tattered and torn warships filled the harbor and mutilated bodies lined the street. And suddenly there was Hasani, rising up in my vision like an avenging god. My heart stopped as I watched his bronzed face gleaming in the sun.

My beautiful warrior was yelling orders to his soldiers, looking this way and that as mayhem unfolded all around them. Even surrounded by the anguish and haunting sadness of war, I couldn't help but admire his abilities. He was a born leader... tall, fierce and commanding.

But suddenly, out of the chaos, the top of a Roman helmet appeared behind him- silent and stealthy. Flat brown eyes were fixated on Hasani, filled with deadly intent. Every fiber of my being screamed to shout a warning, but obviously, he couldn't hear me. My hands shook as I watched helplessly, impotent to help him.

The Roman lunged and forcefully ran his sword through Hasani's back. He yanked it out and sneered down as blood dripped from the blade. Hasani looked stunned as he crumpled to the ground, his beautiful dark eyes clouding over, his strong hands falling limply to his side as he dropped his iron shield. His head fell back and blood gurgled from his slack mouth, dripping from his chin to his metal chestplate in fat drops.

Absolute horror immobilized me and I fought to breathe as I stared at his lifeless body, the body that I knew every inch of. Tears silently streamed down my cheeks and my chest was frozen, like it was wrapped with steel bands. It wouldn't constrict or expand and I struggled to inhale.

Once I was finally able to take a ragged breath, I reacted in the only way I knew how. I screamed, yanking my hand free from the priest's. The moment my hand left his, the visions abruptly stopped. I drew my feet up onto my bed, hugging my knees to my chest.

"It's not real," I murmured shakily, trying to convince myself. "It's not real."

"But it *was* real," Annen confirmed and my heart shattered into pieces. "You can feel it. You know it was real. Just as you also know that something similar to this happens to you in every lifetime."

"But I've never seen it before," I murmured. "Knowing it in theory and actually seeing it are two different things."

"Which is why the Order prevents you from knowing these things," Annen replied, his onyx eyes glittering strangely. "There is a reason why they wipe your memories clean in every life and only let you regain specific ones- such as what you are. Knowing the other details would only make things harder for you...harder to follow through with their plans for you."

I glared at him. "Again, let me ask.. what is it to you? Why are you so interested in this...and in me?"

Annen stared at me contemplatively.

"Charmian, have you ever wondered what gives the Fates the right to control destiny?"

I stared at him blankly.

"Of course not. It is simply how things work. It has always been this way."

"But perhaps it has always been this way because we have *allowed* it to be so," Annen suggested.

"What in the world are you talking about?" I stared at him in puzzlement. "We don't *allow* anything. I don't write Fate's plan, I just carry it out. It is what it is."

"Oh, Charmian. You have more power than you know... more power than they will ever let you discover. And that, my lady, is why I am here."

I stared at him blankly again.

"And why is that?"

"Because before you continue with even one more cycle, there are things you need to know about the Fates."

At his words, I thought about the three ancient white-haired Moirae. They were frighteningly powerful. According to ancient legend whispered from generation to generation for thousands of years, the eldest sister

Clothos spun the thread of life, while Lachesis measured the length of each thread, thereby deciding how long each person would live. The youngest, Atropos, was the cutter. She determined how each person would die. I've only been face to face with them a handful of times and those few times were enough.

That was the legend. Obviously, they don't literally weave a tapestry of life with a loom full of string, but legend was shockingly close to reality. However you wanted to explain it, they controlled destiny. They literally held life and death in their hands. I turned my focus back to Annen.

"What about them?" I asked.

I glanced over my shoulder nervously, as though they might appear at any minute simply because we were talking about them. You never know. They were just that frightening.

"They aren't what you think," Annen stated calmly. "You have always believed that they are good and spiritual beings intent on keeping order in life. But they're not. They are simply drunk on power. And they have lived so long that they have grown bored. They play games with the lives that they were trusted to protect."

"What do you mean... games?" I asked hesitantly.

"I brought you here so you could see firsthand for yourself, so that you don't have to take my word for it. You and Cleopatra died tragic deaths here, along with Iras, Marc Antony and Hasani. You made sure of it because you thought it was all part of a master plan, correct?"

"Of course. That was the path meant for all of us in this life. It was my job to make it so. I don't understand what you're trying to say."

"I'm trying to explain to you that there is no such thing as true Fate. You all died horribly for no reason at all. Charmian, you have been manipulated as a tool for centuries at the whims of three old women. Period."

I sat in stunned silence for a moment, staring at him uncertainly.

"I don't believe you."

"Of course you don't. It goes against everything you've been taught. You've been groomed to believe that you have a higher purpose- that you have been acting for the good of all mankind. But you haven't. It's time for you to realize that and do something about it."

The room seemed to whirl around me as I weighed what he was saying to me. *Could it be?* But that wouldn't make any sense. The Fates, the Moirae, had always been. If they weren't meant to handle destiny, then who was?

"Charmian, as I said, I don't expect you to simply take my word for it. You know what is supposed to happen here. In one week's time, Octavian will arrive in Alexandria. Rome will crush Egypt. You, Cleopatra, Iras, Marc Antony and Hasani will all die. But I'm proposing something else. I think you should change it."

My eyes flew to his and I gasped. "Change it?"

"Yes. Change it. Change it so that you live, so that Cleopatra accomplishes what she most wanted to do... which is to keep a member of the Ptolemy family on Egypt's throne.

"You have the benefit of knowing now how things will unfold. You can anticipate Octavian's moves before he makes them. Use that ability and change everything. Then you will see that your actions don't truly matter...because there is no set destiny, Charmian, as the Fates would have you believe."

I was in a stupor. This went against everything that I had ever believed and suddenly the biblical story of the Garden of Eden sprang to mind... how Eve had been tempted by the serpent into eating from the tree of life. This must have been how she felt, because a part of me, a part that was growing larger by the moment, wanted to believe Annen, even though it felt really wrong. The Fates always placed me in horrific circumstances. If I could escape it... if I could save Hasani... nothing else mattered. I would accept the consequences.

Before I could think another rational thought, however, an enormous black shadow seemed to overtake the room, stretching from corner to corner. Giant black shadow wings appeared on the wall of my bedchamber before they quickly folded and materialized into the shape of a man standing in front of me.

Ahmose. My ancient, wise handler. I breathed a sigh of relief. He would be able to make sense of this.

"What are you doing?" he hissed to Annen. "How did you escape?"

As they stood side by side, their physical similarities were astounding. They were both ancient and wrinkled with glittering black kohl-rimmed eyes. Their heads were shaved and they both wore long black robes. They seemed to have been cast from the same mold.

"What do you think I am doing?" Annen countered calmly. "I'm explaining to Charmian a few things that she deserves to know. Did you think they could keep me imprisoned forever?"

"You know nothing!" Ahmose spit angrily. "And you should not speak of that which you do not know!" He turned to me.

"Charmian, you have known me a very long time. I would not lead you astray. Do not listen to his lies."

His tone was almost pleading and it alarmed me. He was all-knowing, always in control. Why did he feel the need to appeal to me? I was just a Keeper. He was an Aegis, an elevated priest who stood directly before the Fates on a regular basis. Before I could consider his motives further, though, Annen leaned toward me.

"Remember what I've told you, Charmian. Every word is true. We'll speak more later," he rasped, before he was suddenly gone. I spun around the room in a circle—but he had disappeared. I turned warily back to Ahmose, who was standing in place, calmly assessing me.

"I don't understand any of this," I said softly. "Was he telling the truth?"

"I'm not certain what exactly he told you, Charmian, but I can assure you that I've never lied to you."

"Not that you know of," I continued carefully. "But maybe you've been lied to, as well."

"Do not go down that path, Charmian," he cautioned. "It is true that I am not always informed of the Moirae's motives or intentions. But I do know that we have a higher purpose and it has always been just. Think about this- do you really think there is no plan to life? That things are meant to simply fall where they may? I think not. That would be utter chaos."

"But if Annen is lying, then what is his motive?" I pondered. "And who imprisoned him?"

"I do not know his motive," Ahmose admitted. "And I don't know many details of his imprisonment. All I know is that he was captured by the Moirae here in Alexandria long ago. I do not know their reason and I haven't seen him since...until now. But let us not waste any more time on it. He is clearly misguided. Come now. Take out your bloodstone- let us return you to where you belong."

Normally, I wouldn't have let the matter rest, except one important thing distracted me now. My bloodstone was no longer lying on the bed.

I whirled around, gazing at every corner of the room. It wasn't here. My panicked eyes met Ahmose's.

"What?" he demanded. "What is wrong?"

"My bloodstone," I whispered. "It's not here. Annen must have taken it with him. Which means.."

"Which means that you are trapped here," Ahmose confirmed, staring harshly at me.

"I'm sorry," I stammered. "I had no idea that he would take it…"

But Ahmose was already shaking his head.

"I cannot be angry with you for that, Charmian," he muttered. "Annen stole your bloodstone from my safe-keeping. So how could I be angry with you for the same thing?"

He turned and stared out the windows at the sparkling sea, his back rigid and ramrod straight. He stayed silent and unmoving for so long that I was getting ready to prompt him when he turned to me again.

"Charmian, whatever his motives are, he is trying to force your hand. He has trapped you here for a reason. Perhaps he wants you to change things to an outcome that better suits him. I know not. But you *must not* change anything. Do you understand the seriousness of our situation? We're treading a very treacherous line."

I nodded, even as I remembered Annen's words. He absolutely wanted me to change things. But not to suit him. The outcome was meaningless to him. Annen wanted to prove to me that my whole existence had been a lie.

"But Hasani…" I whispered painfully.

"Hasani died as he was meant to," Ahmose said firmly. "His death was not your fault."

"But I could save him now," I replied, sticking my chin out. "I don't see what saving one Egyptian soldier would hurt."

"You can't," Ahmose reiterated. "You must carry out your mission."

He stared at me with steely black eyes and I felt like crumpling to the floor in a heap.

I knew my place in the world. I had been a Keeper for centuries. What I was supposed to do was obvious. I should find Annen, retrieve my bloodstone and leave this place... letting destiny unroll as it was meant. But the attachment I felt to Hasani was absolute. I couldn't allow him to suffer a horrific fate.

Hasani was the only thing that mattered.

"Ahmose?" I whispered. "I don't think I can."

"Of course you can," he replied firmly. "You don't have a choice, Charmian. Hasani will die no matter what. Even if you intercede and stop his fate, he will die eventually. Everyone does. But if you change the fate that is meant for him, the ripple effects from that action could be devastating. You cannot."

The confusion muddling my thoughts was sickening. Was he right? Deep down, I figured he probably was. Fate was what it was. I didn't write it- I just carried it out. But that didn't make the knowledge that my own actions would lead to Hasani's death any less crippling. The very thing that I had been born to protect and uphold was now ripping my heart out.

To read more of *Every Last Kiss* by Courtney Cole,
You can find it on Amazon.